What the critics are saying...

"It is character driven books like this that keep me coming back for more. I hope that we get to visit the resort again soon." ~ *Robin Taylor, In the Library Reviews*

"To me this story spoke of a renewal, not only in body but in heart and soul as well. I truly enjoyed this book and recommend it highly." ~ *Diane T, The Romance Studio*

"Paradise Revival stands on its own as a fabulous story, this reviewer for one, would not miss the opportunity to read everything written by Jaci Burton." ~ *Gina, Love Romance*

TROPICAL HEAT

by Jaci Burton

Tropical Heat
An Ellora's Cave Publication, January 2005

Ellora's Cave Publishing, Inc.
1337 Commerce Drive
Stow, Ohio 44224

ISBN #1419950444

Paradise Revival © 2003 Jaci Burton
ISBN MS Reader (LIT) ISBN # 1-84360-684-4
Other available formats (no ISBNs are assigned):
Adobe (PDF), Rocketbook (RB), Mobipocket (PRC) & HTML

Paradise Discovery © 2003 Jaci Burton
ISBN MS Reader (LIT) ISBN #1-84360-701-8
Other available formats (no ISBNs are assigned):
Adobe (PDF), Rocketbook (RB), Mobipocket (PRC) & HTML

Edited by: *Brianna St. James*
Cover art by: *Syneca*

Warning:

The following material contains graphic sexual content meant for mature readers. *Tropical Heat* has been rated *E-rotic* by a minimum of three independent reviewers.

Ellora's Cave Publishing offers three levels of Romantica™ reading entertainment: S (S-ensuous), E (E-rotic), and X (X-treme).

S-*ensuous* love scenes are explicit and leave nothing to the imagination.

E-*rotic* love scenes are explicit, leave nothing to the imagination, and are high in volume per the overall word count. In addition, some E-rated titles might contain fantasy material that some readers find objectionable, such as bondage, submission, same sex encounters, forced seductions, etc. E-rated titles are the most graphic titles we carry; it is common, for instance, for an author to use words such as "fucking", "cock", "pussy", etc., within their work of literature.

X-*treme* titles differ from E-rated titles only in plot premise and storyline execution. Unlike E-rated titles, stories designated with the letter X tend to contain controversial subject matter not for the faint of heart.

Also by Jaci Burton:

A Storm For All Seasons 1: Summer Heat

A Storm For All Seasons 3: Winter Ice

Bite Me

Chains of Love: Bound to Trust

Devlin Dynasty 1: Running Mate

Devlin Dynasty 2: Fall Fury *also A Storm For All Seasons 2*

Devlin Dynasty 3: Mountain Moonlight

Kismet 1: Winterland Destiny

Kismet 2: Fiery Fate

League of 7 Seas: Dolphin's Playground

Lycan's Surrender

Mesmerized anthology

Passion In Paradise 1: Paradise Awakening

Passion In Paradise 2: Paradise Revival

Passion In Paradise 3: Paradise Discovery

Tangled Web *with CJ Burton*

TROPICAL HEAT

PARADISE REVIVAL
&
PARADISE DISCOVERY

By, Jaci Burton

PARADISE REVIVAL

Dedication

To Charlie, for giving me all that you have, and making it easier for me to write about that special love between two people. I can't write it if I don't feel it. I feel it because of you. I love you.

Chapter One

Morgan Brown inhaled deeply and blew out a sigh, trying to banish the queasy feeling in her stomach.

This whole idea was ridiculous. She didn't have time for it. Owning and managing Paradise Resort kept her plenty busy. Conducting a week-long interview with a freelance writer wasn't on the agenda.

Besides, he would be intrusive. Under foot all the time—watching her, studying her, asking probing, intimate questions like reporters always did. Something she had avoided like the plague ever since her divorce from David.

It wasn't good to dredge up the past. She'd successfully buried it, along with her marriage to that slimeball, and that was where it was supposed to stay.

So why had she agreed to the interview in the first place? She knew why. Much as she hated the idea of opening herself up to scrutiny, a magazine spread would be good public relations for the resort. She couldn't let her personal fears get in the way of bringing potential new clients to Paradise.

All those fears. Get a grip, Morgan. You have nothing to be afraid of. David can't get to you here. He doesn't know where you are, and even if he knew, there's no way he'd approach you. Your secrets are safe. The reporter will never find out about what happened.

Forcing thoughts of the past aside, she stepped out on the front porch of her home, welcoming the feeling of total solitude. Nestled away in the jungle-like overgrowth, it stood a good distance from the resort, completely isolated. Just the way she liked it.

The warm, Caribbean breeze blew a red curl in her face. With her usual annoyance, she quickly flipped her hair behind her ears. With a smile, she entered the gardens. The gardenias bloomed this time of year, and she couldn't resist taking a walk through the gardens to enjoy their scent. The sweet smell of the flowers reminded her of her childhood, a time when she was still innocent. Every time she surrounded herself with gardenias, she felt clean and whole again. Her idyllic little hideaway always calmed her.

She felt safe here. No one intruded, no one bothered her, and she could enjoy being alone.

It had taken her a trip through hell and back to get here, and this is where she'd stay.

Paradise was her home, her livelihood, and her reason for existence. The reason she'd started the resort was to give people a venue to live out their fantasies. No recriminations, no repercussions. It was a safe place. And when she'd finally wrenched free of David, a safe haven was what she'd craved. That, and the feeling that what she'd done hadn't been bad, that she shouldn't feel ashamed of who she was. Her desires had been normal. David's had been sick and perverted. Hence, Paradise was born. Paradise was the only place where sexual pleasures had no boundaries as long as the parties involved consented.

She might never experience that kind of freedom again, but at least others would.

A quick glance at her watch told her the reporter would be arriving soon. She'd better get ready. With a wistful sigh she left the gardens, always loath to leave her scented sanctuary. She strolled through the front door, delighting in the warm breeze the open windows provided. Her sandals clipped noisily on the hardwood floors, but didn't disturb her Persian cat, Phoebe. The ball of white fluff rolled over on its back and purred loudly, then went back to sleep.

Morgan smiled at her companion's laziness. Phoebe was her only buddy, and after three years together the cat had gotten used to Morgan talking to it as if it were human.

"What would I do without you, Phoebe?" She bent down and stroked the cat's belly. "My only friend. Now how pathetic does that make me?"

Fortunately, Phoebe didn't answer. But at least Morgan had someone to converse with, even if the conversation was one-sided.

Who else would she talk to? It wasn't like she invited people over on a regular basis. She didn't socialize with the resort staff, and she would certainly never get to know the customers on an intimate level.

Intimate. Right. No intimacy, don't get close, keep your distance, Morgan. Don't let anyone find out about you. Don't develop relationships, don't have friends. If you get friendly, something might slip and then they'd know.

In so many ways, David still controlled her. She was even afraid to make friends here at the resort. When would she be free? Would she ever be, or was she doomed to this life of solitude she'd created for herself?

She stepped into her bedroom and changed from her shorts and tank top to a long red and yellow flowered sarong. Tying it off and tucking the ends between her breasts, she stepped in front of the mirror and turned around to make sure none of the scars were visible. She wound her hair up in a twist and secured it with a clip. Satisfied, she headed to the resort to meet Anthony Marino.

* * * * *

Tony Marino surveyed the lobby of Paradise Resort. Not at all what he expected. He'd been there five minutes already and had yet to spot any whips, chains or naked people. Hell, he'd expected to find couples screwing on the front step, but this place looked just like any other tropical hotel. Women wandered around in bikinis, men in shorts and stupid flowery shirts.

They weren't all beautiful, either. All shapes, sizes and ages. The resort wasn't the typical hedonistic type of private vacation spot catering to the twenty-something crowd. This place could have easily been any hotel in any part of the world.

Except it wasn't just any hotel. It was Paradise Resort, quickly gaining in popularity as *the* place for sexual frolic. Anything you could imagine could be had here. With anyone who was game enough to have it with you.

If he wasn't on assignment, he'd consider dabbling in some of the recreation himself. Unfortunately, he was only here to observe. And gain whatever dirt he could on the owner and manager of this place, the mysterious Morgan Brown.

Despite all his research skills and resources, he hadn't been able to find anything personal about this woman. Business tidbits, information on her purchase of the resort, yeah. Personal information was nonexistent. She sure as hell hadn't dropped onto Earth three years ago. But that's how it seemed.

Which only made her more intriguing. If there was one thing Tony loved, it was a mystery. Mystery typically led to scandal, and scandal led to big money.

"Anthony Marino?"

He turned at the sound of the soft voice behind him, and his knees wobbled.

Holy shit—she was some gorgeous woman. Flaming red hair curled atop her head, a few loose pieces twining against her face. She had a cute little nose and pouty, full lips that instantly grabbed his cock's attention.

Down boy.

And where the hell had his power of speech gone? Christ, he'd just regressed fifteen years to those awkward, fumbling teenage days.

"Yeah?" was all he could manage.

She held out her hand. "I'm Morgan Brown."

Well, that figured. This was hell, and she was his personal Beelzebub. His eternity would be spent in *look but don't touch* torture.

"Ms. Brown," he finally said, shaking her petite hand.

"Call me Morgan." Her voice melted over him like butter on a hot English muffin. Smooth.

"I'm Tony."

She raised a brow and smiled. "Very well, Tony. Welcome to Paradise Resort."

If she kept looking at him that way he was going to be one painfully hard Tony in no time at all. She tilted her head to the side, studying him, then looked down at his jeans and tennis shoes and back up again at his polo shirt, concentrating on his chest.

When her gaze swept back up to meet his, she frowned.

What? This was a resort. He was a reporter. Was there a dress code no one told him about?

"When can we get started?" he asked, hoping to focus his attention on work and away from her body and face.

"I'm very busy."

"You also agreed to this interview."

She lifted her chin. "I know. However, you will have to work around my schedule."

"Fine." Morgan Brown wasn't the first reluctant interview he'd conducted. He had ways to gain her cooperation. "I have to greet the incoming arrivals tonight."

"And after that?"

"After that I go home."

"That'll work. I'll just meet you at your place."

She pursed her lips and glared, her blue eyes frosty. "I think not. My house is not within the resort grounds."

"Which means what, exactly?"

"It's a distance away."

He smirked. "The island is only so big. Can't be that far."

She sighed.

"You could stay at the hotel while I'm here," he suggested. "Make it easier on both of us."

"No."

That was definite. "Why not?"

"The rooms at the resort are for the guests. I don't stay in any of them. Besides, we're usually full."

"Well, Morgan, seems to me you have two choices here. You can make yourself more available to me during the workday, or I can do the interview at your place. As you know, you're under contract with the magazine and you agreed to give me access to you during this week."

Daggers shot out from her ocean blue eyes. "I suppose that only leaves us one choice."

"Which is?"

She studied him again for a few seconds, then said, "We'll go to my place where I don't have to worry about other people listening in."

Did she have something to hide? And if she did, why would she be telling him about it? He filed that mental note away for later. "Wherever. When can we start?"

The desk clerk handed Morgan a clipboard, which she rapidly scanned before looking up at him. "You're here not only to interview me, but observe the activities at the resort, right?"

"Yeah."

"This is welcome night for the new arrivals. You can take a seat in the bar, have an hors d'oeuvre and a drink, and when I'm finished we'll head to my place."

He followed her through the lobby and into the lounge, a large room open to the beach and ocean. Pale wood floors gleamed with a fresh wax. The tables and chairs were surrounded by potted palms and oversized hibiscus swaying gently from the ocean breeze. Stairs led down directly to the beach and swimming pool. They sure made it easy for guests to have access to all the amenities.

Morgan left to mingle with the arriving guests. After finding the bartender and ordering a double Crown and Coke, Tony settled in at the back of the room and took out his laptop to take notes.

The lounge was already packed with the new arrivals. Tony found it interesting to watch couples gravitate toward one another, strike up conversation and size each other up. The meetings either ended with the couple sitting down at a table together or separating in search of other prey. He bit back the urge to laugh out loud.

Who would be desperate enough to come to a place like this just for sex? Were these people such losers that they couldn't find compatible partners in their own neck of the woods? That couldn't possibly be the reason, since more than half of the guests in attendance were quite attractive. So what was it that drew people here?

He'd never had any trouble getting laid, wherever he was. Not that he was a stud or anything, but he did okay. More likely his success rate had to do with his job. Women, for some inexplicable reason, gravitated toward writers. Like he was some famous author or something.

He snorted. Not likely. He wasn't patient enough to sit still and write a book. That's why freelance writing worked for him. Research, write and then get the hell outta town and on to the next project. Not conducive to stability, marriage or family, but those things were for other people. Not someone like him. He enjoyed the freedom to travel way too much to ever be tied down in the traditional family way.

He made notes on questions he wanted to ask Morgan later. He'd kept one eye on her the entire time. She smiled and greeted every one of the guests, and even made a few introductions when she discovered the shy types standing alone.

Morgan stepped to the stage and asked for everyone's attention, then gave a speech about how everyone was free to do whatever they liked as long as the other participants were in agreement. She warned that if anyone forced another guest to do something against their will, the local authorities would deal with them.

Her eyes darkened in what he could only surmise was barely suppressed anger when she talked about free will and force. She took the security of her guests seriously. Not that he blamed her. All it took was one psychopath and all hell could break loose.

After she finished and spoke with a few other guests and resort staff, she headed over to him. He admired her full hips in the tropical getup she wore. It fit her snugly in all the right places, accentuating every one of her lush curves. Damn if his cock didn't begin clamoring for attention again. He liked his women to look like women, not skinny little boys.

Morgan Brown was his perfect type of woman.

Wrong. She might fit his type, but he wasn't going to have her.

"Sorry it took so long," she said as she stopped in front of him. "Part of my job."

He shrugged, mentally counting backwards from one hundred in the hopes of getting his wayward penis to behave itself. "No problem. I'm here to observe as well as interview."

She nodded. "Shall we go, then? Might as well get started tonight. I'll be busy with the guests and staff tomorrow morning."

"Shouldn't I check in first?"

"I thought you'd already done that. Come with me."

She led him to the front desk, where a harried clerk was busily working with a few of the new arrivals. Morgan went behind the desk and pulled up his reservation, then frowned.

"Something wrong?" Tony asked.

"Yeah." She looked to the clerk. "Remind me to fire our reservationist tomorrow. We're overbooked again."

The clerk glanced up, shock evident on her face. "Again?"

"Yes." She looked up at Tony. "And everyone has checked in. The resort is full."

Why did this shit always happen to him? "I don't suppose there's another place I could stay."

"Well, we do have private cabins on the other side of the island. We could—"

"Booked already," the clerk interrupted.

Morgan sighed and pushed a strand of hair behind her ear. "I'm really sorry. We've had computer problems lately, and a reservationist who will be out of a job come tomorrow. But that's not your problem, it's mine."

She skirted around the counter and motioned him toward the exit. "Grab your luggage."

He reached for his bags. "Where are we going?"

"My place. I have a spare bedroom. You'll have to stay with me."

"Stay there?" he asked. Maybe this wasn't so bad after all.

"Yes." She stopped and stared at him, impatiently tapping her foot, her irritation evident. "Unless that's a problem?"

Problem? With his cock, maybe. With him, no. Easier to watch her, talk to her, follow her around if he had access to her twenty-four hours a day. Maybe he could snoop around and find something about her. This was working out better than he thought. Although Morgan didn't seem thrilled about it. Not that he could blame her. Nothing like a nosy reporter invading her private space. "No problem. Let's go."

They exited the hotel and Morgan led him to a vehicle which looked a lot like a golf cart. He stopped and looked at her.

"It's a ways to where I live," she explained.

"I guess I expected you to live behind the hotel."

She let out a sigh as they slipped into the vehicle and took off down a well-lit path. "Hardly. I value my privacy."

The trail was bumpy and narrow. Morgan expertly navigated low hanging tree branches and palm fronds as they headed deeper into the tropical forest. The air grew thicker the further they traversed. Tony wished he'd worn shorts instead of jeans, but then again when he'd left New York it had been a helluva lot cooler than here. Sweat poured from him and he pulled his now soaked shirt away from his chest.

Morgan glanced at him and smiled. "It's a little humid here in the tropics. You need to wear fewer clothes."

Tony looked at her, searching her face. Did she want to see him with fewer clothes on? Was she hitting on him?

Yeah, right. Wishful thinking on his part. And not likely considering her cool reception. Her gaze once again focused on the road ahead of her.

For someone who ran a sex resort, she sure seemed prim and proper. Except for the lush body in the barely-covering-her-thighs dress. Her body was anything but conservative. She had curves made for a man to worship.

They finally reached a clearing, and Tony was stunned to see a nice sized ranch style house in front of them. The sandy colored siding and forest green shutters fit right in with the tropical surroundings.

Morgan pulled into a covered carport. Tony jumped out and grabbed his bags, following along behind her, watching her nicely rounded rear end sway back and forth. His cock twitched, reminding him once again how long it had been since he'd had sex.

Oh sure, women gravitated to him all right. Except during his last few assignments. Those had consisted of nothing but men. No women around. Jungle, war, politics. And no female within miles.

Now was not the time to be thinking about sex. He never fucked the subjects of his interviews. Well, not after that one time. Too messy and could lead to involvement. Or the loss of a really great story, like what had happened when he'd made the mistake of having a mattress summit with a senator's daughter. After that disaster, he swore never again to mix pleasure in with his business.

Although he could easily imagine getting horizontal with Morgan Brown, he knew that would never happen. He'd lost almost everything by getting involved with a subject once before. Never again. Fuck 'em and leave 'em, that was his motto.

For a guy whose livelihood required traipsing around the world, commitment wasn't in his vocabulary. He needed to switch his focus from Morgan Brown's backside to what secrets he could unearth during his week-long stay at this supposed erotic paradise. If he was lucky, he'd not only get the interview for the travel magazine, he'd also dig up some dirt on her that maybe the tabloids might be interested in buying.

Nobody who owned and operated a place like this had a lily-white reputation. He'd bet a million she had some major skeletons in her closet.

He followed her up the stairs, noticing the white swing suspended from the rafters of the expansive front porch. Hanging potted plants filled with purple tropical flowers danced in the breeze. Visions of Morgan sipping a cool drink while lounging on that swing in nothing but a bikini momentarily distracted him.

His attention went on full alert when he stepped through the front door. A white, fluffy *thing* pounced on his tennis shoe and immediately scurried off behind a rattan sofa.

"What the hell was that?" he asked.

"That's Phoebe, my cat," Morgan explained. "You've just been officially attack-greeted."

"For a second there I thought you had big white rat problems."

She laughed, and his heart thudded against his chest. Damn, but she had one sexy laugh. A little on the raspy side, the kind a man would want to hear in bed. And why did it seem that her laugh was a little rusty? Like maybe she didn't do it too often?

He shook his head, wondering why that thought popped into his head. Further, why he would even care whether she laughed or not.

Morgan led him down the hall and pointed to two rooms.

"Take your pick," she said. "Both have views of the pool and the one on the far left also has a view of the ocean."

He chose the one with the double view. He threw his bag down on the king-sized bed and stepped out onto a small veranda, admiring the breathtaking scenery. The rectangular in-ground pool was surrounded by palm trees and tropical flowers. Beyond the pool was a sandy beach and miles of ocean. Looked like a damn postcard picture.

No wonder Morgan liked living here. Who the hell wouldn't want paradise in their own back yard?

"Nice place," he said, sensing her behind him.

"Thank you. I like it."

He turned to her, watching as the wind blew stray strands of fiery red hair into her face. Without thinking, he reached out to brush it off her face and she backed up a step.

Whoa. The lady did not like to be touched.

"Let me show you the rest of the house," she said, seemingly calm and composed as she turned and left the veranda.

But for that brief second, Tony glimpsed fear in her eyes. When he'd reached a hand out, she'd paled and practically jumped away from him.

Why? What scared her about his movement? She certainly couldn't be afraid of him. She'd just invited him to stay at her house, which by the looks of things was smack dab in the middle of fucking nowhere.

Determined to delve deeper into Morgan's history, he followed her down the hall.

The house had a huge kitchen. Lots of windows, white tile and matching cabinets brightened the room. An island sat in the middle of the kitchen, a bowl of fresh fruit centering the countertop. It sure didn't look anything like his apartment in New York. Then again, he couldn't remember the last time he'd actually stayed in his apartment. Hotels were his home. Sometimes tents in the jungle. Anywhere there was a story.

"Something to drink?" she asked, peeking into the refrigerator.

Tony admired the view as she bent over to reach for something, her ass outlined against the silky material of her dress. Visions of him sliding the dress up her thighs and plunging his cock between those full cheeks hardened him in an instant.

When she turned, her eyes drifted over him and settled on his crotch.

Shit. He felt like a grade school kid who'd just got caught with his first boner in front of the pretty young teacher. Not like he could hide it now.

"I'd love some," he blurted, meaning the jug of iced tea she held in her hand, but knowing it had come out like he wanted some of her.

Well, dammit, that was true, too. He *did* want some of her. His penis pressed painfully against his now tight jeans, begging for release.

"Some tea, you mean?" she asked, licking her lips with a quick swipe of her tongue.

He followed the movements of her tongue and shifted, stepping behind the center island to hide his erection. "Yeah. Tea."

She turned away quickly, but not before he caught the slight smirk that lifted the corners of her lips.

This was going to be one miserably long week.

Chapter Two

Morgan tried to hide her grin behind the pitcher of tea. It wasn't like Tony was the first guy to sprout an erection in front of her. She'd seen more than most women would in a lifetime.

She'd also suffered more pain and humiliation than most of them ever would. Which was why, no matter how dark and good-looking Tony Marino was, she'd never let him get close to her. But that didn't mean she couldn't admire his tall, lean body and devastating dark eyes. And the way he filled his jeans out led her to believe he had quite a package hidden in there.

No. Don't think about his package or anything else about him. You know what happened the last time you got close to a man. No amount of pleasure is worth that kind of pain.

Not too many years ago, she'd have been dying to sample what was hidden behind that zipper. Now? She tamped down her body's base urges, knowing she'd never allow that kind of intimacy again.

Her mind knew that, her heart knew that, but her body still craved a man's touch. Especially when a man tumbled her senses all to hell like Tony did.

His skin was tanned, his hair black. With his Italian features he'd be right at home on the set of one of The Godfather movies. Sexy and brooding. And he sure frowned a lot. She could imagine that brain of his worked overtime. One didn't get to be as successful a writer as he was without doing a lot of thinking.

She'd done her research on him, even read a few of his articles. The man had exceptional talent at stringing together prose.

And scheming, she'd bet. He also wouldn't be the first reporter to try and dig up some dirt on her. But she'd buried her secrets deep. So deep no one could ever unearth them.

If only she could bury the memories as well.

Pushing the past into the far recesses of her mind, she led Tony to the backyard. The sky was clear, the stars shined brightly overhead, and the full moon reflected off the water in the pool, making it appear almost like daytime. They sat at the table on the veranda and Morgan inhaled, the smell of jasmine filling the air around them.

Then she waited for the questions.

It didn't take him very long.

"Why Paradise Resort?" he asked.

Surprisingly he had no paper or pen with him, nor had he carried his laptop outside.

"Don't you need to take notes?" she asked.

"Nah, I have a good memory. Besides, if I need to quote you on something I'll verify that's what you said before it goes to print."

She nodded. "Good to know. I'd hate to be misquoted."

It took her a few seconds of admiring the rugged beauty of his face to recall that he'd asked her a question. "I bought Paradise Resort because I felt there was a need for a place like this."

"Why?"

Typical reporter-one word question. She thought about answering *because* and leaving it at that, but that wasn't how she'd been raised. She might have thought about being a smartass once in awhile, but she'd never actually acted upon it.

"There aren't many places where people can feel free to indulge sexual fantasies to their fullest extent."

"Can't people have whatever sex they want in the privacy of their own bedrooms?"

"Some can. Some can't, or choose not to."

"You have personal experience there?" he asked, his chocolate eyes narrowing.

She smiled at him. "No comment."

He sighed and rolled his shoulders, turning his neck to the side.

"Long day?" she asked.

"Yeah. Got a crick in my neck and I'm sweating. Mind if I make use of your pool while we talk?"

Where were her manners? Tony's arrival and her obvious instant attraction to him had thrown her off kilter, making her forget the basics of detachment and cool civility.

"Of course. I'll start dinner. Go ahead and take a dip in the pool."

Morgan tried to ignore the sounds of running water and that of drawers opening and closing from the guest bedroom. She busied herself with preparing the fish and vegetables, making every attempt to block the vision of the man in the other room, and how he'd look naked. His body would be muscular, she could already tell by his biceps, broad shoulders and the well-sculpted thighs encased in denim. She'd spied a mat of dark hair peeking out the top of his polo shirt, and she imagined it would lead lower to a vee of soft, dark down, ending with curling black hair between his legs.

And in between his legs would be that magnificent penis she'd seen outlined against his jeans. Thick and long, the kind that took a woman's breath away. She licked her lips, imagining his groan of pleasure when a woman wrapped her mouth around the head and licked the moisture off the tip.

Using her forearm, she swiped at the perspiration on her forehead, and chose to ignore the dampness forming between her legs. She'd take care of her arousal tonight.

Alone. With her own hand, as she had for the past three years.

But this time, when she slid under the cool sheets of her bed and her hand found that aching spot between her legs, she wouldn't imagine a faceless stranger whose kindness and patience would somehow awaken her desire to be touched by a man again.

This time, she'd imagine Tony Marino.

* * * * *

Morgan laid the foil-enshrouded fish on the grill, then sat at the table, watching Tony swim. His face buried underwater, he used long, fluid strokes to make his way from one end to the other. Without breaking stride he dove underneath and pushed off, coming up halfway to the other side before continuing his measured stroking toward the opposite end of the pool.

She longed to jump in and join him, but she never wore her bikini when others were around. As it was, she was uncomfortable in the short sundress she'd thrown on. Typically she wandered around naked at night, loving the freedom of having her body revealed and knowing no one could see it.

But not for the next week, because she had stupidly invited Tony to stay here while he conducted his interview.

What had possessed her to invite a stranger, and a man at that, to stay in her home? She never had guests over. Other than an annual summer party for the resort staff, she lived entirely alone.

For three years she'd been satisfied with the status quo. She had enough contact with people at the resort. Typically, by the time the workday ended, she was tired of talking and craved the solitude of her private place.

So why had she invited him to stay with her? Because they'd overbooked the resort and he really had no place to stay? Or was there another reason?

"Why don't you join me?"

She shivered at his voice, that old, familiar fear resurfacing. For a moment there he'd sounded like. . .no, he wasn't David.

"No thanks," she replied.

"Why not?" He'd swum to the side and laid his chin on his forearms. His wet hair curled and with one hand he swept it back, revealing a face Michelangelo would want to paint. Rugged angles, a square jaw, deep set dark eyes with full brows, and a beautifully sculpted nose.

"I'll just watch you swim. I'm keeping an eye on the grill."

He shrugged and dove down again, and Morgan relaxed.

She hadn't thought of David in years. Why now? Simple enough. Because Tony was the first man she'd been attracted to since David. That alone shocked her, because she hadn't thought of sex for over three years. Hadn't wanted it, hadn't desired it, and other than the physical relief she gave herself, the thought of coupling with a man produced only revulsion.

So why now? Because she had one-on-one time with a very attractive man? A man who clearly desired her? Reasonable enough to assume an attraction to any man at all would dredge up the memories.

Memories weren't so bad. She shouldn't forget what happened back then. If she didn't forget, she couldn't get hurt again. If she was careful, very careful, she wouldn't make another mistake.

Mistakes had almost cost her life. Falling in love had nearly killed her and made it abundantly clear she had no clue whom to trust. Easier not to trust anyone than make a mistake again. Next time it might kill her.

The easiest way to avoid that happening was to crush the stirrings of desire she felt bubbling to life as she watched Tony. She'd already made one huge error in judgment by inviting him into her home for the week. But she was stronger than she used to be. She could withstand the temptation of a desirable man.

She had no other choice.

"Dinner will be ready shortly," she announced as he surfaced near the edge of the pool.

Despite her intent, she couldn't help but admire his body. He jumped out and grabbed for a towel on the nearby chaise. She sighed at his taut, six-pack abdomen, admired his deep tan, and enjoyed the view of his legs. Too bad his long swim trunks hid his thighs. She'd already sampled a tasty view of his fine rear end in his jeans. In the baggy shorts he wore now, most of his upper legs were covered.

"Can I help you with something?"

Oh hell, he'd caught her gawking. "Excuse me?"

He approached her, stopping a respectable distance away. But his grin reached out and touched her heart. His damp, curling hair fell across his forehead, and she pressed her fingers into her palm to keep from reaching out to push it back.

The warning bells sounded in her head. She had to remember that appearances could be deceiving. Good looking men who exuded boyish charm could also hide a heart of evil.

"With dinner. Can I help you with it?"

Oh that. She turned away. "I've got it covered. Go change. I'll have everything set out here when you get back. It's much too nice to eat inside tonight."

He tilted his head to the side, then paused as if he would speak. Instead, he shrugged and stepped into the house.

Morgan exhaled. With shaky hands she placed the fish on the table, then went inside to grab the rest of the meal.

Too close. That was just too close. She had to stop looking at him like she was starving for male companionship. He was way too sharp, she didn't need to give him any more ammunition.

She'd all but drooled all over him and had done a really lousy job of disguising her interest in him. By now, he probably thought she was some kind of nymphomaniac, out to screw every guy she could get her hands on.

She grabbed a bottle of wine. It was most definitely time for a drink.

By the time Tony changed into shorts and a tank top, Morgan had their meal set on the patio table. She busied herself with arranging the fish and vegetables onto the plates, trying her best to ignore how good he looked.

She took a long sip of wine and stared into the glass. Not that long ago she'd have been bold enough to let a man know when she was attracted to him. She'd been so ballsy back then—David had told her that was what attracted him the most. The fact she'd had guts enough to ask him out, to proposition him. How could she have known her daring nature would be her downfall?

"You seem so far away."

Morgan looked up to find Tony staring at her. "Sorry. Thinking."

"About?"

"About the resort," she lied.

He seemed satisfied with her answer and resumed eating, even complimenting her cooking skills. She beamed. How long had it been since a man had something nice to say to her?

Well, nice in the way that didn't include a sexual proposition. She expected those in her position, and easily fended off the most persistent of resort guests with a smile and a compliment so they wouldn't feel insulted.

They finished the meal in silence, then carried the dishes to the kitchen. Surprise of all surprises, Tony filled the sink and washed everything himself despite her protestations.

A man who helped in the kitchen? She could almost fall in a heap on the floor in shock. She let out a soft laugh at the thought.

"What's so funny?" Tony turned around, wiping his hands on a towel nearby.

"You did the dishes." She leaned against the center island with her arms crossed, mindful of how much wine she'd consumed so far tonight. She still had control, though. She knew her limits.

He grinned and filled their glasses with more wine. "In a big Italian family, everyone pitches in."

They stepped back outside and sat in the chairs by the pool. Morgan settled in, still a bit wary and waiting for the inquisition, but considerably more relaxed than she'd been earlier. He hadn't exactly pounced on her or propositioned her for sex. In fact, he'd all but ignored her.

"Shit!" he yelled suddenly, jumping when Phoebe leaped into his lap.

Morgan bit back the low chuckle that threatened to spill from her lips.

"Did you train this thing to pounce without warning?" he asked, leaning back in his chair as if a lion sat in his lap instead of a ten-pound cat. The cat turned around and stared at him.

"Hardly. Phoebe likes to think she's a thousand pound tiger." She leaned forward and whispered, "Don't tell her she's not, okay?"

He laughed. A deep, rich, baritone. The kind of laugh that rumbled through her body and settled between her legs. "I'll try to keep it a secret."

Once Phoebe settled in on Tony's lap and went to sleep, he shrugged and stroked his hand over her back. Morgan bit her lip and tried not to imagine his hand stroking her body in the same way.

Time to occupy her mind with something that didn't have to do with Tony's hands on her body.

"How large is your family?" she asked.

"Four brothers, two sisters and probably eight hundred cousins."

"You're joking, right?" Being an only child, she couldn't imagine that many siblings and cousins. Neither of her parents had brothers or sisters. She'd always wondered what it might have been like to have a large, extended family. As it was, her parents could hardly stand having her around, let alone anyone else. It had seemed that their universe had been the two of them, and anyone else was an interference. Like her. Morgan had always felt unwanted, as if creating her had been something her parents had felt obligated to do.

"Maybe I exaggerated a bit on the cousins. But at least thirty of them, plus their own kids. Holidays are always chaotically interesting."

From the sparkle in his eyes Morgan knew he was remembering good times. When was the last time she had a good memory? Did she even have any?

"Thinking about work again?" he asked, taking a swallow of wine.

"Yes." Eventually she'd have to come up with a better lie. Or quit zoning out on him.

"You're probably tired. I should let you get some sleep."

Morgan waved her hand in the air. "Not really. I don't sleep much." And just exactly why had she revealed that to him? She glared at her empty wine glass.

He arched a brow. "Why?"

"Always a lot on my mind, I suppose."

"Resort things, or personal things?"

Wonderful. It hadn't taken long for that line of questioning to start. "Mostly resort things, and my personal life is none of your business."

He leaned back in the chair, a smile curving his lips. "The article will focus on both you and the resort."

"I know that, I agreed to the terms. But there's personal, and then there's personal."

"And how am I supposed to distinguish between the two?"

"I'll let you know if your questions are out of bounds."

"You like being in control, don't you?"

The words echoed in her memories, calling to mind the first time David had spoken them. Of course, he'd followed up with, "That's too bad, because your days of control are over."

And after that, he'd shown her exactly what he'd meant. Repeatedly, until the thought of her controlling any aspect of her life became nothing more than a distant memory.

She shuddered. "I like my job. It requires me to manage the environment around the resort, to insure the guests are satisfied. So, yes, in that respect I like being in charge. I like knowing my guests leave with a smile on their faces."

"What about you? Are you satisfied? Personally, that is?"

"Yes."

"Quick answer."

"I know my own mind." Or at least she used to. She used to follow her desires, enjoying the journey, reveling in the destination. Before she'd made a wrong turn once and had ended up in hell. Once she'd made her escape, Paradise had seemed like heaven.

Now, looking across the table at Tony, his long legs spread out, and the clean, crisp scent of him drifting across the table, she felt an ache between her legs that she hadn't felt in a long time. Her body pulsed with the desire to feel a hard shaft ramming into her until she came, screaming.

Too bad. What her body wanted and what it was going to get were two very different things.

"What's on your mind right now?" he asked, startling her.

"Why do you ask?"

"You have a look about you."

"What look?"

He grinned. "I don't know how to describe it. Like there's something you want—something really nice. Your eyes are glassy and your cheeks are pink. If I didn't know better I'd say you were turned on."

What the hell was he—psychic? Even though he'd hit the nail right on the head, it was the last thing she'd want him to think. She steadied her gaze on him, remembering the practiced, icy stare she'd perfected over the years. "Actually, I'm thinking that we have an early day tomorrow."

"Sorry," he said, but his grin didn't completely dissipate. "We'll take this up again in the morning."

They stepped inside and Morgan followed Tony down the hall, stopping at the doorway to her room.

"Good night." She suddenly felt awkward, like she was reluctant to let him leave. How long had it been since she'd had a decent conversation with a man? Or any conversation that didn't include resort business.

Yes, this was business, but something a little bit more. And that *more* intrigued her way more than it should.

"Sleep well," he replied, heading into his room and shutting the door.

Morgan leaned against the closed door and sighed. What she wouldn't give to be a normal woman who could act on feelings of lust for a man. Damn David for what he'd done to her!

At least the anger quelled the urge to cry. She hadn't cried since the last time she'd ended up at the hospital. After that episode, she'd vowed to shed no more tears for herself. The situation with David had gone on as long as it had because she'd let it. She hadn't been strong enough to walk away the first time, or the times after that.

Instead, she'd stayed and endured his *lessons*, losing a part of herself each time until the joyous, sexual creature she'd been no longer existed. Maybe her ex had ruined her for sex in the future, but she'd gained one thing she hadn't had before she met him — strength.

If she could survive five years married to David, she could survive anything.

Including spending the week with a sexy hunk of Italian man occupying the room next to hers.

She pushed away from the door and stepped into the bathroom to prepare for bed. Water was running in the other room, and she knew Tony was in his bathroom. She smiled wistfully at the shared intimacy, even though a wall separated them.

What would a normal relationship be like? She'd missed out on those special moments between her and a man, like sharing a bathroom, waking up snuggled next to a warm body in the morning, that first kiss of the day. That sense of normalcy that she'd never had with David.

Fantasies again. Not only the regular, every day life with a man, but the intimate ones, too. She often thought of what she'd missed. Like right now, wondering if he shaved before bedtime, or even what he wore or didn't wear to bed.

Maybe she wouldn't act on her thoughts, but she still had her fantasies.

And she was damn well going to indulge that fantasy tonight. Her body rushed with heat and she hurried through her nighttime ritual, shed her clothes and slipped in between the cool sheets of her bed.

Slick satin rubbed against her heated skin, tantalizing her.

The evening breeze blew the soft scent of gardenias into the open window. She inhaled and closed her eyes, letting her imagination take over.

It didn't take long.

Her mind was already filled with thoughts of Tony. Imagining his six-foot-two frame towering over her, she conjured up the fantasy and made it real. He was all tanned muscle, his body beaded with sweat as he stood in front of her. His labored breathing caused his chest to rise and fall dramatically. She stepped toward him and boldly ran her hands over his shoulders. Threading her fingers through his hair, she pulled his mouth down toward hers and paused, not touching lips yet, just breathing each other in.

His eyes blazed midnight black. His breath brushed against her cheek. And when he wound his arms around her and pulled her firmly against him, she didn't run, she didn't panic. She welcomed his embrace. Just like she'd welcome the moment he slid his thick shaft inside her wet sheath.

First, she had to taste him. She brushed her lips against his, felt the muscles in his arms expand, which excited her all the more. There was nothing like a man with incredible power restraining himself, and letting his woman make the first move.

He could have thrown her down and fucked her easily. Her petite stature was no match for him. But he didn't. He stood motionless and let her explore his lips and slide her tongue gently into his mouth to tangle with his.

When he devoured her lips with his sensuous mouth, she moaned.

Really moaned. Out loud.

But she was too deep into the fantasy to care, too intent on visualizing how Tony would taste and feel against her heated skin, to worry about the sounds she'd just made.

The exquisite pleasure shooting through her at imagining his touch, his mouth, his body covering hers, elicited whimpers and pants of longing. Oh, how she wished this could be real.

She slid her hand over her breasts and teased her nipples until they stood upright. Her fingers snaked down to her aching, wet mound and she bit her bottom lip to control the loudest of her urgent cries.

Small whimpers and moans escaped. She couldn't help it. She'd never been quiet, even when masturbating.

Besides, Tony was probably dead to the world right now. If she made any sounds, he'd never hear them.

Chapter Three

What the hell was that sound? Tony jerked upright in bed and searched the darkness.

It sounded like a moan. A deep, throaty moan. Maybe it was Morgan's cat.

He listened, but all he heard was the wind rustling the palm trees. Warily, he settled back against the pillows, too wide awake now to go to sleep.

Sure as hell sounded like a moan. Then again, maybe he was only hearing what he wanted to hear. His body ached all over, his penis hard and waving at him under the sheet, clamoring for some attention. Hell, it had been hard since the moment he'd set eyes on the fiery redhead in the room next to his. It didn't appear to want to settle down, either. Nothing like walking around in his shorts with a hard-on, swimming with one, eating dinner with one. It's a wonder she hadn't noticed his semi-rigid state all evening. He sure as hell had.

There was that sound again.

Holy shit! It *was* Morgan! The walls must be thin. Then again, their rooms did butt against each other. He threw off the sheet and stepped naked to the open window. The gentle breeze caressed his fiery hot penis, but not enough to cool the raging inferno of lust coursing through him. As if his body wasn't heated enough, now he had to listen to her sex cries?

A long, low moan lit the night. The wind died down completely as if in answer to his unspoken prayer. Hell, now he could even hear her erratic breathing. Her window must be open.

His erection brushed the windowsill. Instinctively he grabbed his cock in his hand and squeezed. The ache was painful. He'd been fighting his arousal all night to no avail, and now that he could touch his cock, slide his fingers along the throbbing shaft, he had to stifle a groan of sheer pleasure.

Her voice was low and full of passion as she groaned and gasped in pleasure. He heard the rustle of sheets and pictured her naked body outlined in the moonlight. She'd be on her back, her hips rising and falling with her strokes.

Did she play with her clit, or did she slide her fingers into her wet pussy and pump away as if a hard cock was in there? Or both?

Sweat poured off him as he began to stroke his swollen shaft He moved his hand slowly, savoring every sound from the room next door. He visualized her movements, trying to match the sounds to what she was doing. As arousing as the images in his head were, he wanted more. What he really wanted was to see her, to time his release with hers.

This wasn't good enough. He wanted to watch her thrum her clit and fuck herself with her fingers or a vibrator or whatever she used. He wanted to come watching her do the same.

As quietly as he could, he opened the door to the veranda and stepped outside. Her moans grew in intensity as he approached her window.

Christ, he was a Peeping Tom! He couldn't believe the depths he'd sunk to. Granted, he'd do almost anything to get a story, but this was personal. He was invading her privacy—her most intimate privacy. And the worst part? His erection throbbed so hard he didn't give a shit. He wanted to watch. He was going to watch. And he was going to come in the process of doing so.

With light footsteps he eased closer to her window. He couldn't chance standing right in front of it. So he stood back, inching forward a little at a time until a vision rocked him still.

The bed faced the window. Morgan lay naked across satiny sheets, her body outlined by the soft moonlight streaming in the window. Her back was arched, her hair spread out like a fan on the pillow. Full, rounded breasts with huge dusky nipples stood rigidly erect. Her feet were planted on the bed, her knees bent. Her hand was buried in the patch of red curls between her legs, moving slowly up and down her slit until she slid two fingers inside.

Her eyes were closed, her bottom lip tucked between her teeth. And she was moaning.

Goddamn if that wasn't the most erotic vision he'd ever seen.

This was new to him, something he'd never done before. He'd never been a voyeur, never stood by and watched a woman touch herself. What a damn turn on! The only thing that could make it better would be if she knew he was watching, if she put on a show for him deliberately.

She'd already enticed him, but he wanted her participation, wanted to know she enjoyed getting off for him.

He stroked his shaft and wondered what she was thinking.

Morgan moved her fingers deep inside her pulsing core, amazed at the fluids drenching her. She hadn't been this stimulated in ages, hadn't felt the stirrings of desire and passion for a man in too many years.

Here, in her fantasy world, Tony Marino was safe. He couldn't harm her, and she could do anything she wanted with him — have him do anything he wanted with her, without fear.

Digging her heels into the mattress, she lifted her hips and mimicked the motions of fucking. Her fingers drove in deep, then slid out slowly, imagining Tony's huge cock plunging in and out of her in the same way.

He'd position himself over her, his muscled biceps straining with the effort. She'd grab his arms and hold on, lift her hips and urge him in deeper and deeper. His expression would be intense, focused on her face. They'd watch each other's reactions — so intimate, a window to the soul. Then he'd lean over and kiss her.

She moaned, imagining the magic of his mouth against hers. She licked her lips as if her tongue were his, licking and nibbling and demanding entry.

His tongue would stroke in and out of her mouth in time with the strokes of his shaft. She whimpered and circled her clit with her thumb, intensifying the near explosive pleasure. Knowing Tony was in the room next door only added to her excitement — the risky element of possibly being caught.

What would he think if he could see her like this? How would he react, knowing she was fantasizing about him?

Tony sucked in a breath and caressed his cock, his hands slick with sweat. The visual of watching Morgan masturbate was the hottest thing he'd ever seen.

Her eyes were closed tight, her mouth partly open. She panted, letting out tiny little gasps and whimpers as she fucked herself with her fingers.

Sweat poured off his chest and down his stomach. He wanted to whimper, too. His cock wanted to let loose a hard stream of come that would fly right into her window. He grasped his throbbing shaft and squeezed, then slid his hand from base to tip, feeling his knees wobble a bit at the sheer erotic joy of the sensation.

He was mesmerized watching this night vision pleasure herself, and pleasure him too. Fighting the groan that threatened to spill from his lips, he clamped his mouth shut and breathed through his nose. He didn't want her to know he was there. He desperately didn't want to stop the moment.

When she sped up her pace, so did he. As her fingers fucked faster in and out of her pussy, he jacked his cock to her rhythm. His balls tightened and through sheer force of will he held back the orgasm he knew was imminent.

He wanted to wait for her. When she came, he would, too.

Her left hand brushed her breasts and teased her nipples. She squeezed one breast, then the other, hard, and cried out softly, her lush ass rising up off the bed.

Tony increased the strokes on his cock, sensing she was close, knowing it was only a matter of time before she—

Ahhhh, yes. Cries of ecstasy spilled from her lips as she came, her body shuddering with her climax. He released the restraint on his cock and allowed his orgasm to rack his body. He bit the inside of his cheek so hard he tasted blood. What he really wanted to do was roar out her name.

Gradually, her legs relaxed and she slid them flat on the bed, her hand still gently parting and searching between the tuft of red curls. Then she stopped, sighed deeply, and seemed to fall fast asleep.

Tony crept back into his bedroom and gently closed the door.

He sat on the edge of the bed, completely drained and feeling more than a little guilty for spying on Morgan. And yet it had been the single most erotic moment of his life.

Miss Prim and Proper was one hot number. For a woman so full of passion, why did she seem so cool on the outside?

* * * * *

Morgan couldn't help it. She blushed all through breakfast.

It wasn't as if he'd known what she'd been doing last night. Still, reliving the thrilling moments and staring across the table at the subject of her erotic fantasies created a bonfire of heat in the kitchen. And it wasn't coming from the stove.

"You look well-rested this morning," Tony said.

"I do?"

"Yeah. Your face glows. Or is it just warm in here?"

"Must be warm." She was certainly heated. Whether from embarrassment at her thoughts or that knowing smile on Tony's face she wasn't certain.

Why was he looking at her that way? As if he knew her—intimately. He didn't know her at all.

She was imagining things. He couldn't have known about last night, could he?

"Did you sleep well?" she asked.

He coughed, took a quick swallow of orange juice, then looked up at her. "I slept fine. Like a baby. Took me awhile to fall asleep, though."

Morgan's hand stilled on her cup and she set it back on the saucer, afraid he'd see her hand shake. "Awhile?"

"Yeah. Kept hearing noises."

He wasn't making eye contact, instead had his head buried in the schedule of events she'd given him. But still, she caught the upturned corners of his mouth and knew he was smiling.

Oh dear God, he'd heard her getting off. That had to be it. He said he couldn't sleep right away, he'd heard noises, and he was grinning like a little kid with a secret. Her body flamed in mortification.

Which irritated her even more.

Years ago the thought of a man watching her masturbate would have excited her. Now, she was appalled. What had he heard? How could she even broach the subject this morning? What was she supposed to say—something along the lines of, "So how did you enjoy my performance last night? Did you get off, too?"

And that thought sent her libido reeling in the wrong direction. Her nipples puckered and pressed against her silk sundress. Heat pooled between her legs, making her itch to pull up her dress and shove her hand up there.

"Give any thought to what you'd like to see today?" she asked, then nearly cringed at his direct gaze. His eyes devoured her as if he were communicating that he'd like to see *her* today.

No way was that going to happen. Ever. She glared at him and he grinned.

"Oh. You mean the brochure."

He was smirking, laughing at her discomfort. *Dickhead.*

"Yes, the brochure. What activities would you like to observe?"

"What do you suggest?" he asked.

"All the activities are interesting. I'd suggest you choose something you'd like to write about, and observe that one."

He arched a brow. "Only one?"

"I'm sorry. That's all I have time for today. But you can select several and I'll escort you to them throughout the week."

Didn't that thought just make her day? Having to watch the erotic play of her guests with Tony standing next to her the entire time. Would he want to participate in the activities? Would she be forced to watch him get naked and fuck someone? More importantly, how would she feel about it? She wished she knew the answer. Although the throbbing between her legs at the visual of watching him fuck someone gave her the answer. She'd hate it, but she'd love it, too.

"Well, let's see then," he said, dropping his gaze again to the brochure. "The Roman Orgy looks interesting."

"Fine," she said, her voice more clipped than she would have liked.

"Something wrong with that one?"

"Of course not. All our guests enjoy the orgy." Before he could interject another smartass comment, she said, "Shall we go? I have a meeting this morning."

Morgan was silent on the drive to the resort. Tony was, too. Which got her to wondering what he might be thinking about. Questions to ask her, wondering about the sexual adventure she was going to show him today, or thinking about last night?

She had to admit the more she thought about him listening to her moans and whimpers as she fucked herself, the more turned on she became. It had been so long since she'd allowed a man anywhere near her, especially someone she was sexually attracted to. Besides, she was still safe. He occupied the bedroom next to hers. He couldn't touch her, so why not indulge her fantasies a bit and enjoy the thought of him listening in?

"If you don't mind, I'll tag along for a bit today," he said as they arrived at the resort. "Maybe ask you a few questions here and there when you have a free minute."

"It's your article. Do as you wish."

During the course of her day, Morgan discovered that Tony had a lot of questions.

At least they were logical, intelligent questions. And mainly about the resort. The few times he'd touched on something she felt was a bit personal, she stopped him and he backed off.

A ploy on his part? Maybe he was trying to lull her into a false sense of security, only to pounce on her later with a barrage of personal questions.

She'd been blindsided before, and had learned her lesson well. Always stay on guard.

The day flew by, and before she knew it, the scheduled orgy adventure was about to begin. Morgan found Tony in one of the empty offices, typing on his laptop.

"You ready for the Roman Orgy?" she asked.

He looked up at her and cracked a smile. "Did the Trojans like huge, wooden horses?"

She laughed. "Let's go."

Tony followed along, having no idea what to expect. From what he'd read, anything and everything could happen at one of these adventures.

Morgan led him into the expansive round theater. Some of the participants had already begun to assemble. Toga clad men and women mingled together. Wine and fruit lay around a table in the center of the recessed room. A viewing area with chairs was positioned above the *play area*, as Morgan described it. She excused herself to greet the guests.

In her strapless dress, she could have been one of the participants. Her body was draped in pale blue silk which clung to her curves, outlining the luscious breasts he'd been fortunate enough to glimpse last night.

The event hadn't even started yet and his cock was already twitching. He resisted the urge to reach down and rub it.

So far today he'd discovered that Morgan Brown was one efficient, hard-working woman. She managed the resort with a firm but fair policy, doling out reprimands with positive criticism and suggestions, and handing out praise where it was warranted.

If only more bosses were like her, there'd be a lot more happy employees.

Morgan finally returned and sat on the red velvet loveseat next to him. He inhaled her scent—a combination of vanilla and woman. He would have loved to have been close to her last night when she was masturbating. He wanted to experience the smell of sex that seemed to permeate the air whenever a woman got excited. No, that wasn't quite right. He wanted to know her scent when she was aroused. If that curious mix of vanilla and female desire filled the air. Christ, he could smell her now, knew how it would be, knew it would drive him over the edge.

And last night, Morgan had been very excited. So had he.

"Tell me what happens," he asked, as the lights in the viewing area lowered. Soft music echoed throughout the room.

Morgan leaned toward him and whispered. Tony noticed she was careful not to touch him with any part of her body.

"The women in this scenario take on the subservient role, catering to the men's every wish and desire."

"Sort of a dominant/submissive kind of thing?"

She paused before answering. "Yes."

"So, a woman has to do whatever the man wants her to do?"

"As long as she's agreeable to it, yes."

The action heated up quickly. What started out with laughter and playfulness soon turned to serious erotic business. One man pulled a woman onto his lap and peeled off her toga, slowly licking every bit of skin he exposed. Another forced a woman onto her knees and lifted his robe. The woman leaned over his swollen penis and plunged her mouth down on it, eliciting the man's loud groan.

There was so much activity Tony didn't know where to focus his gaze. One on one, two women on one man, two women doing each other—hell, there was a pleasure palace right before his eyes. Anything you wanted could be had here.

The customers seemed more than satisfied, too. Morgan Brown had discovered a gold mine.

When he turned to her, her gaze was focused on the stage. Her hands were clasped on the railing in front of their chair, her fingers gripping the iron bars so tight her knuckles were white.

Was she terrified or turned on? He couldn't tell.

"Are you all right?" he asked, following her line of vision to a woman who'd been thrown over a man's knee.

"Fine," she said tightly.

He still couldn't tell if that meant good or bad. Her gaze was riveted on that certain couple. The woman's ass cheeks were bright red, the man's handprints clearly visible on her pale skin. With every loud smack of his palm against her buttocks, the woman bucked up and squealed in delight. After a few minutes of spanking, the man pulled the woman upright and impaled her on his thick shaft.

Tony turned to Morgan again, leaning back a bit so she couldn't see he was looking at her. Not that she'd have noticed anyway. It was almost like she was in a trance. For the life of him, he had no idea whether she found the orgy erotic or frightening.

But then, as he focused his attention on her instead of the action on the stage, it became clear. Her breasts rose and fell rapidly with her panting breaths, her nipples hard and outlined against the straining silk. Oh, she was trying to hide her reaction from him, he could tell. But she couldn't hide the rapid breaths, her mouth half open as she sucked in air to fuel her excitement.

The scent of her sexual desire was so fucking arousing it made him ache.

His penis, already hard, slammed against his shorts. He wanted to take it out and stroke it in front of her. How would she react to that? She was so entranced by the glistening, sweaty bodies lustily fucking and sucking in front of her that he wasn't certain she'd even notice.

Those bodies below hadn't hardened him half as quickly as the sight of an aroused Morgan had.

And he did owe her one. After all, he'd watched her caress herself to orgasm last night. It seemed appropriate that she watch him now.

Fuck it. He was horny. The other people in the viewing area were either jacking off, sucking and licking each other, or fucking while watching the show. Besides, he needed Morgan's reaction. For some reason it mattered to him.

He quickly slipped his shorts down and his cock sprung up. His balls were already tight against his body, filling with come. He knew this one would be good.

He fit his hand around the shaft and squeezed, closing his eyes for a second as he stroked the length.

It didn't take her long. Morgan's head slowly turned in his direction, her gaze captivated by his straining cock.

She looked from his penis to his face, her eyes widening, her lips parted, her breathing scattered with short pants.

And she didn't say a word. She didn't object, didn't run out, didn't turn her gaze away. She focused on his shaft as if he were the only person in the room.

Which made him hotter than ever. He wanted to put on a show for her like she did for him last night. Even if she didn't know that she had.

Her eyes worshiped his shaft, slowly traveling the length of him. He spread his legs and lifted his hips to give her a better view. Hell, he'd give her anything she wanted if she'd touch him, suck him, fuck him.

But somehow, he knew she wouldn't. Just as he knew what he was doing gave her pleasure. So he was bound and determined to give her all the pleasure she could stand.

"Do you like to watch?"

She nodded, her voice barely above a whisper. "Yes."

"Does it excite you?"

She swallowed and nodded. Then she opened her mouth to say something more, but closed it right away. She'd wanted to say something further, but what?

"Tell me what you're thinking." He was finding it hard to think himself, or speak for that matter. Her eyes on his shaft stimulated him to the point where he knew if he stroked any harder or faster he'd shoot off like a geyser.

She shook her head but still focused on his cock. "I…I can't."

"Yes, you can," he urged in a low voice. "Tell me. I need to know what you're thinking."

Her voice seemed strained, tight, nearly breathless as she said, "You have a huge cock. It's beautiful. Long, really long, and thick."

He sucked in a breath at her words. "Are you thinking about how it would feel inside you?"

She whimpered. "Yes."

Her nipples were hard pebbles against her dress. Her breasts rose and fell quickly with her labored breaths.

"Do you want to touch yourself, Morgan?" he asked, pumping his shaft in a long, torturous stroke.

She hesitated, and her eyes met his. Desire glittered in the blue depths, so intense it made the ache between his legs throb with the need to plunge inside her.

"It's okay," he said. "No one's watching. Hell, everyone would expect you to do it."

She looked around the room as if she actually considered raising her dress and touching herself. Then she turned her gaze back at him, sucking in her lower lip. "I can't."

"Because you're the owner? You don't want people to see you?"

"I...yes, that's it."

Fuck. He wasn't going to be able to hold out much longer. She devoured him with her eyes. Her body gave every aroused signal imaginable, and those signals went straight to his penis.

"I understand. Then watch me jack my cock until I come."

Her eyes darkened like a sudden storm and she licked her lips. "Yes," she said, her body shivering. "Do it."

That's all the encouragement he needed. He leaned back and stroked harder, faster, imagining it was her hand on his aching penis. He focused on her full lips and visualized them surrounding the head — licking, sucking and drawing him into the wet warmth of her mouth. The heat inside would be near unbearable. She'd take him deep, as deep as she could until his shaft pounded the back of her throat. Then he'd hold her head while he fucked her mouth hard.

"Oh, shit, I'm gonna come," he groaned. A hot jet of come let loose so hard it made him dizzy. He continued to pump until the last drop of white fluid had fallen. Morgan's gaze remained riveted to his penis as if she were in a trance.

He fought to regain control of his breathing. She still hadn't moved, one hand holding onto the velvet cushions and the other gripping the iron railing.

He'd come. She hadn't. It showed. Arousal brightened her tanned skin with a red blush. Her nipples were still erect, her breathing shallow and labored.

"Are you okay?" he asked.

She nodded and finally moved, letting loose of the railing and turning to face the orgy below. "Fine."

Tony stood and pulled up his shorts, amused at the telltale blush on Morgan's cheeks. It perplexed him how someone that ran a sex resort could blush at anything. "Did watching me jack off like that bother you?"

She turned to him. "No, I found it quite stimulating, actually."

"Then why didn't you join in? I can tell you need to get off."

She inhaled and let it out slowly. "I will. Just not here, and not now."

"I see. Later then, when you're at home?"

Her lips curved in a slight smile. "Why, do you want to listen in again?"

Chapter Four

Tony had been rendered speechless by her comment, Morgan recalled with a smile. The entire drive from the resort he hadn't said a word. He hadn't denied that he'd listened last night, either. So, she'd been right, she'd had an audience last night.

And now, over dinner, he remained all but mute. Which unnerved her a great deal. He hadn't even asked any questions for the article—and really, wasn't that the whole point of his being here in the first place?

"You're quiet tonight," she said, watching as he peeled another shrimp and popped it into his mouth.

"I was hungry," he said with a mouthful.

"Obviously." She gazed over at the plate where more than a dozen and a half empty shrimp shells were piled. He finally leaned back in the chair and took a drink of wine.

"You were pretty silent yourself," he said.

"I was?" She hadn't realized that, but now that she thought about it, he was right. Maybe her silence was a response to his. She certainly didn't want to volunteer any information. If he wanted to know something, she figured he'd ask.

They'd both effectively skirted the issue of her comment about him listening in last night. Clearly, neither of them wanted to bring it up again. Morgan sighed, not at all sure how she felt about it. On the one hand, she was appalled at herself for her lack of awareness. There had been another person in the house when she went about screaming her bloody head off in ecstasy last night. On the other hand, the thought of him listening excited her. Really excited her. More than it should, considering what it all meant.

"Something on your mind?"

She looked up and shook her head. "No, not at all."

"I think we're both avoiding a discussion about something."

"About what?"

45

He inhaled and leaned back in the chair, giving her a delicious view of his naked chest. Great pecs, a light dusting of dark hair, broad, muscular shoulders. He was exactly the type of man she went for. Correction—used to go for.

"About last night. About what you did, what I saw and heard."

Morgan sat up straight. "Saw? You watched me?"

He grinned sheepishly. "Yeah. Couldn't help it. Those sounds you made drove me crazy. I wanted the visual to go with them, so I stepped outside and watched you through the window."

Panic slammed against her chest. What had he seen? What position had she been lying in? Then she remembered and released the breath she'd been holding. She'd been lying on her back. He hadn't seen the scars. "I see."

"How do you feel about that?" he asked, seemingly unapologetic that he'd been spying on her most private act.

How did she feel about it? She should be furious with him. She'd brought him into her home and the first night he invaded her privacy? Then again, she hadn't been quiet. But what difference should that make? It was her damn house and if she wanted to masturbate in the middle of the living room it was her right to do so. "I don't really know how I feel about it."

"Pissed off?" he offered.

"Yes."

"Violated?"

"Yes."

"Excited?"

She paused, not expecting him to be so forward. But wasn't Tony the type of man she used to like? A real man, one who took what he wanted and made no apologies for it afterward? Was she subconsciously throwing out signals to him? And how honest should she be with him? After all, the thought of him watching, though shocking, was also incredibly erotic.

"Maybe."

"Wanna know what I think?" he asked, grinning.

"Would it matter if I said no?"

"Probably not."

"Then by all means, tell me."

He poured more wine for both of them. "I think you're an incredibly sexual woman. Your body, your mannerisms, and especially your eyes, are windows into that sexuality."

"How so?"

"You have a way of carrying yourself that's sexy as hell. Dignified, but with a lazy sway to your hips that sends off 'come fuck me' signals. Your eyes travel over me as if you literally want to eat me alive, and unless I'm totally off base, I'd say you haven't had a man in awhile. A long while."

She took a quick swallow of wine to moisten her suddenly dry throat. "Why would you think I haven't had a man in awhile?"

His eyes blazed hot and dark. "You look hungry."

Morgan sucked in a breath and tried not to be thrilled at Tony's words. They didn't mean anything. He wasn't sexy, and she damn sure was not getting excited. Yeah, right.

"I'm sitting here wondering why a woman like you with so much potent sexuality is so repressed."

She lifted her brows. "Repressed?"

"Yeah. Because you sure as hell put out sexy signals, but to the casual observer you're as cold as the waters off the North Pole."

Fairly certain she'd just been insulted, she sniffed and said, "I'm running a business here, not prostituting myself for sex."

He smirked. "Obviously. Otherwise you'd be sampling the adventures right in your own backyard."

"I don't mingle with the guests."

"Seems to me you don't mingle with anyone." He stood and took his glass of wine with him, then walked around the veranda.

Morgan watched him warily.

"You have this luscious playground, but no man. You invited me here to stay the week, so obviously no boyfriend comes calling on a regular basis. Considering that there's not a huge population inhabiting this island, I'd say you keep to yourself all the time."

"What's your point?" She didn't like this turn in their conversation.

"I'm getting to it." He leaned against the arbor pillar and sipped his wine. "You're hot, but you don't have sex. I'm wondering why you're repressing your natural inclination."

"The resort is for the paying guests. The employees don't indulge, either."

"Ah, but the employees have personal lives outside their work at the resort."

"How do you know?"

The corners of his mouth lifted. "I asked a few of them. Your employees get it on regularly. Either with spouses or lovers. You don't appear to get it on at all—on or off the resort."

"I'm still waiting for your point." She couldn't believe she'd sat and listened to him for this long.

"My point is, I think you're hiding something."

"I have nothing to hide." She stood and cleared the table. He followed her inside with their glasses and bottle of wine.

"Don't you? You said your past is off limits. Most people, given the opportunity to talk about themselves, start at their birth and provide every stinking detail from then on. You don't want to talk about anything except what happened after you bought Paradise Resort. Which means every part of your life before three years ago is a complete mystery."

Morgan turned to the sink and ran water to wash the dishes, refusing to meet Tony's probing gaze. "My personal life is not the subject of this article."

"Oh, but it is. Your entire life leading up to the point you bought the resort is a subject of interest. How else will the readers know what compelled you to design and implement a place like Paradise?"

"I came into some money. I wanted to buy a resort island, and there was a lack of places where people could indulge in their sexuality so freely. It's very simple, actually."

She felt him behind her. He was so close his breath whispered against her neck when he spoke. She shivered.

"But why? Why did you buy it? Why a place like this?"

Agreeing to this interview had been a huge mistake. She hadn't thought things out properly, hadn't planned on Tony getting so personal.

"You know," she said, drying her hands on a towel and turning around, "I'm exhausted. Can we continue this conversation in the morning?"

48

He hadn't stepped back when she turned. His closeness unnerved her. She could see the warm amber flecks in his dark eyes, feel the heat of his body emanating toward her. She hadn't been this close to a man since that last night with David. Only this wasn't unpleasant. This was — too much to bear.

She made a move forward and he stepped back, giving her room to skirt around him. "I'm tired, Tony. I'm going to bed."

Without waiting for his reply she headed down the hall and quickly closed the door to her room. She flopped on the bed and tried to catch her breath, her palm instinctively resting on the frantic beating of her heart. She was damn near hyperventilating. Was it due to Tony's probing questions, or how she felt when he stood so close to her?

She already knew the answer. If she wasn't so damned afraid she'd have stepped into his arms and kissed him. Her body thrummed with desire, her pussy moist with anticipation and excitement.

Instead she'd run to her room and shut the door, putting a physical wall between them. She'd never run from a man in her life. She'd always thought herself an enlightened woman, confident in her sexuality. When she wanted a man she played no games — she went right after him.

But not now. Now she ran. She cowered. She feared.

Goddamit, she feared.

Damn David to hell for doing this to her!

* * * * *

After Morgan had made her exit, Tony contemplated taking a swim to cool off. But he figured he might as well try to get some sleep. He'd stripped and slid into bed, hoping like hell the sounds of Morgan's passionate moans and groans wouldn't permeate through the walls tonight.

And they hadn't. Okay, he admitted to himself, so he'd purposely listened for them. But fortunately or unfortunately, he hadn't heard a sound from her room. She'd probably gone right to sleep.

He wished he'd been as lucky. Rolling over again to look at the clock, he pulled a pillow over his head and cursed. Three fucking hours ago he'd gone to bed. And for three fucking hours he'd tossed and turned and rolled around and couldn't for the life of him get anywhere even near drowsy.

So now what? He supposed he could turn on the light and do some work on his laptop. He flipped it open and stared at the screen for a good five minutes, mentally damning the woman next door for screwing with his ability to think straight.

If she wasn't so damn mysterious about everything he could do his job and forget about her. But no, she had to be all secretive about her past. Which only got his journalistic juices flowing like Niagara Falls.

Right. And he wasn't attracted to her on a personal level at all.

Get over yourself, Marino. You're so hot for her you can smell her sweet scent from here.

He scrubbed his hand over his face and stared at the laptop screen. Then an idea hit.

If she wouldn't come forth with information about her past, then he'd damn well dig it up himself. He had plenty of PI contacts out there who owed him a favor. He'd put out some feelers and get the dirt on Morgan Brown himself.

He went online and shot out some e-mails, supremely satisfied with himself. That'll teach Morgan to clam up on him. He might have to resort to dirty tricks to get the goods on her past, but by God nobody pulled one over on him. If he wanted information, he'd get it.

Ignoring the niggling of guilt sledgehammering his gut, he closed the laptop and turned out the light, hoping he might be able to get some sleep. But as he walked past the window a movement caught his eye. He stopped and looked out toward the pool.

Morgan was out there, wearing a long white robe that shimmied against her body like a lapping wave. It clung to every one of her lush curves, making it easy for Tony to see she was naked underneath it.

She approached the pool and stood there for a moment, looking to her right and then her left. Then she did an about face and looked toward his room.

He ducked back quickly, not wanting to be caught spying on her yet again. Shit, he still couldn't believe he'd voluntarily told her he'd watched her masturbate last night.

What a fucking idiot. She'd have never known if he hadn't said something. And he still couldn't understand what compelled him to admit that he'd loitered outside her bedroom window while she got herself off.

Mentally counting the seconds since she'd looked his way, he took a chance and peered out the window again. She'd turned her back to him again, gingerly slipping one foot in the water, then taking it back out.

He hardened instantly, thinking about the hidden treasures under her robe. What she might look like naked, hoping against hope that she was out there to—

Yes! He pumped his fist in the air in triumph as she untied the robe and let it slowly slide down over her shoulders. His breathing quickened in anticipation of once again seeing her gorgeous body, this time from a completely different angle. He'd been dying to know if her ass looked as good in reality as it did under her clothes.

Briefly he wondered if he was turning into some kind of pervert, then cast the thought aside as lame. If she was going to parade around in the backyard buck ass naked and he just happened to be passing by his window, then she was fair game.

He'd always been good at rationalization.

The robe stopped its downward motion as it rested on the swell of her hips, then pooled at her feet after she wriggled her ass. He groaned at her movements, which certainly got his cock's attention. It was upright, wide awake and pointing toward the pool as if to say, 'Get out there and fuck her, you moron! We're horny!'

But as she stood there naked, her body silhouetted clearly in the moonlight, his heart slammed against his chest and he sucked in a breath.

On the lower half of her back were a half dozen criss-crossed scars. Not new ones because they showed white against her tanned skin. But they weren't ancient ones, either. From the looks of them, probably a few years old at the most.

Tony had done enough articles and research into the seamier side of life to know exactly how she'd gotten those scars.

She'd been beaten. Whipped. Viciously.

Son of a bitch!

Chapter Five

A red haze of anger blinded him. Tony gripped the windowsill and tried to calm the rage bubbling up inside.

He felt sick. Not because Morgan's scars were repulsive. If anything, they showed how courageous she was. To survive beatings like that must have taken incredible strength. The scars were merely physical proof of how vulnerable a woman could be.

And how sick and sadistic some fucking bastard had been to do that to her.

He caught her profile as she walked down the stairs into the pool. Despite his state of shock, Tony couldn't calm the arousal the mere sight of her caused. She was truly an amazingly beautiful woman. Smart, courageous, with a lush, curvaceous body that begged for a man's touch.

His touch. God, he wanted to touch her. Everywhere. And kiss and nibble and lick every ounce of skin—including the scars on her back.

He should give her privacy. Obviously she'd gone swimming in the middle of the night because she wanted time by herself. Not once had she joined him in the pool during the early evening hours.

She wanted to be alone. And he should let her. But he couldn't. Stupid as it was, he slid open the door and stepped outside, not bothering to hide his nudity nor the raging hard-on that wouldn't subside.

Like a water nymph, she floated on the surface of the pool, the moonlight bathing her in an almost ethereal glow. Her hair fanned out in all directions, undulating with the lapping waves.

She hadn't noticed him standing there at the edge of the pool, until she slowly opened her eyes, then widened them, shock evident on her surprised face.

Scrambling neck deep under the water she shouted at him. "You scared me half to death, goddamit!"

"Sorry."

Despite her anger she looked him over from top to bottom, her gaze lingering on his still-hard cock. Which made it stand up, even more painfully erect now that she watched him. She looked up and he smiled at her.

She wasn't smiling back. "I don't suppose I could be given a moment's privacy in my own home, could I?"

He sat on the edge of the pool and dangled his legs in the water. "Guess not."

Her face flamed. "Go away and leave me alone!"

"Why?" he asked, knowing she was trying to hide her scars. Despite the fact her breasts were visible to him through the clear water, she didn't turn her back.

"Isn't it obvious? I'm naked. I'm trying to take a swim. Alone. Do I need to spell it out for you?"

"No, I'm pretty adept at figuring out what someone's thinking." He made no move to leave. Nor was he going to. Morgan Brown needed to come out of hiding. He didn't really know why he felt like her rescuer, and frankly didn't want to delve too deeply into that thought at the moment. All he knew was the little pieces of the puzzle were starting to fit. But there was more he needed to know.

"Apparently you're not as adept as you think. Could I make it any clearer to you?"

Tony tilted his head and admired her breasts. Her nipples pebbled and he couldn't hide his smirk. "It's looking pretty damn clear to me from here, thanks."

She huffed a huge sigh, which only showed off her breasts more. His cock appreciated the view. Clearly it had no intent on deflating any time soon. He ached with the pulsing need to come. Right between the legs of the flaming siren in the pool.

"Tony, go away. Please."

"How did you get those scars, Morgan?"

She froze instantly and stared at him. He waited, then finally she asked in a near whisper. "You saw them?"

He nodded.

"Dammit, I told you to leave me alone!" She swam toward the stairs, but before she could get out he slipped in the water and blocked her exit.

"Don't run. Talk to me."

She shivered and shook her head. The water was warm, the night balmy. She was afraid, but why?

"Get out of my way!"

"No. Tell me what happened to you."

"It's none of your business."

He made a movement toward her and she quickly backed away, splashing water in her wake. She treaded water in the middle of the pool, her eyes wary.

"Morgan, I won't touch you. I promise."

She didn't answer. Somehow he knew she didn't believe him. Then again, what reason would she have to trust him in the first place? He was a stranger to her. A stranger who had already violated her privacy once.

He had to calm her down. He read the panic in her widened eyes, saw the tremors making her shiver. Her breathing was short and rapid, her body full of adrenalin. "Morgan. Relax. I'm going to sit on the stairs here, see?"

As slowly as he could he backed up and sat on the stairs, the water reaching his chest.

But still, she didn't move.

"Tell me what happened to you."

"No."

"Why not?"

"I told you. It's none of your business. My life isn't fodder for some tabloid journalist."

He held up both his hands. "Our conversation tonight is strictly off the record. Nothing we discuss will ever be printed."

She wanted to believe him, he could see it. She sucked in her lower lip and worried it with her teeth. God, the woman really needed to talk to someone.

"Come over here. Sit by me. I won't touch you unless you ask me to. You have all the control, Morgan. Please. Trust me."

Uncertainty crossed her face, then she lifted her chin and threw back her shoulders before swimming quickly toward him.

Having won some internal battle with herself, she stood in front of him, the water barely covering her voluptuous breasts. Despite the fact he itched to reach out for the succulent globes and caress them, he didn't move so much as a muscle.

"What happened to you?" he asked again.

She didn't answer.

"Morgan, I know I've given you no reason to trust me, but have you ever opened up to anyone about where you got those scars?"

"No."

"Then tell me. Take a chance and trust me. I won't print what you tell me. You need to talk to someone."

"Why?" Her eyes still held a hooded wariness that stabbed at his heart. She was like a cornered rabbit and he was filled with the desire to strangle the sonofabitch who'd hurt her.

"It'll help. You carry a fear around with you that closes you off. Do you have any friends on this island you can talk to?"

"No."

"Then talk to me." *Trust me. Please, I know I don't deserve it, but trust me.*

"I was beaten," she answered quietly. She avoided eye contact and offered a nonchalant shrug.

"Obviously. By whom?"

"My ex-husband."

Tony fought to keep his own breathing under control as a raging desire to kill the man burned within him. "Once?"

She shook her head.

"How often?"

"Frequently."

He closed his eyes for a second, unable to fathom what kind of pain she'd gone through. When he opened them again, she was looking at him.

"How long were you married?"

"Five years."

"And did he beat you from the beginning?"

Her lips curved into a cynical smile. "No, he didn't start right away. He waited until after the honeymoon."

Rotten, fucking, no good sonofabitch. Tony filed a mental note to somehow, someway, find out who her husband was and make sure he paid, one way or another.

"How did it happen? Didn't you have any signs that he was an abuser?"

"No. He was very sweet to me from the moment we met. The monster didn't show his claws until after the honeymoon."

She spoke as if she were in a trance, turning her gaze somewhere out in the distance toward the ocean. And her body no longer shivered. Instead she stood ramrod straight, her expression cold.

He wanted to wrap his arms around her and pull her against him. Then kiss her and make love to her until he melted the ice.

"Why didn't you tell someone?"

"I tried. My parents refused to believe that someone of his background could possibly hurt me. They told me I was being childish and immature, and that whatever had happened needed to stay private between me and my husband."

"You're from a prominent family?"

She nodded, but he'd already surmised that. "I met him at my debutante ball. He was the perfect catch. All the girls wanted him."

"But you got him."

She smirked. "Of course. I was young, naïve and believed in love at first sight. I was also aggressive back then, and went after what I wanted. And I wanted him."

"How old were you when you married?"

"Nineteen."

Jesus. Barely out of her childhood and thrust into the arms of Satan.

"Did he abuse you sexually?" Tony couldn't stop the questions from pouring out. Suddenly he needed—had to know everything about her. About that bastard. About what he'd done.

Now that she'd opened the floodgates, Morgan seemed to want to talk about it. But she'd started to shiver again. Before she could answer his last question, he suggested they step out of the pool and dry off.

He handed her a towel and her robe, careful not to touch her. He'd made a promise, and no matter how much he wanted to hold her in his lap and soothe away her pain, he wouldn't.

Not unless she asked.

Tony opened a bottle of wine and poured a glass for both of them. Morgan drank hers down quickly, seemingly unaware of what she'd swallowed.

She hadn't answered his question about sexual abuse, and he figured he'd let the wine calm her. And if she didn't want to talk about it, he wouldn't press her. Not tonight, anyway.

"I used to have fantasies," she said, startling him. She'd been silent for a while and he figured she didn't want to talk anymore tonight.

"What kind of fantasies?"

A hint of a smile crossed her face. "Sexual. Kinky, actually."

"Really?" Despite knowing better, he couldn't prevent the interest in his voice.

"Yeah." She finally met his gaze, her blue eyes warming, the ice melting.

"How kinky?"

"Spankings, being tied up, things like that. I told David about them, at his urging of course. He'd seemed so open, so interested in knowing how to please me, what turned me on."

Now there was the loaded-with-sexuality-Morgan he knew existed under her cool exterior. Fire and passion lurked inside her. And, dammit, he wanted to see it.

"On our honeymoon, David indulged me. Tied me up, treated me gently, but gave me my fantasies. He even spanked me."

"Did it excite you?"

"Very much. Made me wet. Made me come—hard."

Tony sucked in a deep breath, thankful he'd tossed on a pair of shorts after they'd left the pool. Not that the shorts hid his erection. But the thought of Morgan enjoying that kind of sex, the images running through his mind of her spread-eagled and tied to the bed, whet his sexual appetite like no other woman before.

"I haven't had sex since I left him."

Holy shit! "And how long ago was that?"

She shrugged. "Three, three and a half years. I bought Paradise Resort with the money from my divorce."

"Why haven't you had sex?"

"I was scared. After he'd lulled me into feeling secure, into telling him exactly what I wanted and how, he turned the tables on me. He used my fantasies against me."

"How?"

"Spankings became beatings. Being tied up became chains, collars, gags and cuffs. Sex became pain."

Fuck! How could she have survived years of that kind of torture? "I'm sorry."

She inhaled deeply. "It's over now."

Somehow, he didn't think so.

"How did it end?" Tony felt sick, wanted her to stop telling him things he could so easily visualize. He couldn't bear thinking of her being treated as she had.

"David started bringing other men over." She must have caught his horrified expression, because she held up her hand to stop him from commenting. "He let them do the same things to me. One night they beat me so badly the doctor he brought in couldn't stop the bleeding so they had to rush me to the hospital. The police arrived and questioned him. He pleaded with me not to say anything."

Somehow it didn't surprise him the guy had been a coward.

"He told me I could have anything I wanted if I didn't tell. So I made him draw up divorce papers, giving me enough money to get away from him. I changed my last name and left the States, leaving no trail behind me. Before I left, I told him if he ever came near me again I'd tell the newspapers the entire sordid story."

"That took a lot of guts."

"Guts? Hardly. If I'd had guts I'd have left him after the first time he hit me. Instead, I stayed and endured it all those years, hoping somehow he'd tire of the game, or maybe realize that he was hurting me. Anyway, by the time I ended up in the hospital I'd had enough. I wasn't going to be a whore for him. It was bad enough I'd let it go on as long as I did."

"He had a hold on you, Morgan," he said, reaching his hand out to smooth the hair away from her face. Despite his earlier vow not to touch her, he couldn't help it. She didn't even flinch. It was as if telling the story to someone had been a catharsis for her.

He let his hand linger, then slide down and caress her cheek. Her eyes met his.

"I want a normal life again."

"I know you do."

"I want to feel like a woman again, instead of an empty shell. I need to feel that life force surging through me like it did before he ripped my joy away."

So infuriated with her ex-husband he couldn't speak, Tony just nodded.

"Help me," she said, her eyes pleading.

"Anything." He'd move mountains for this woman, although he didn't know why she mattered so much to him. All he knew was he wanted her to heal. He wanted to see the real Morgan Brown. "Tell me what you need."

A glimmer of a smile traced her lips. "I need sex."

Chapter Six

If not for the pain stabbing through her, Morgan would have laughed at the shocked expression on Tony's face. But reliving every moment of that nightmare chilled her, made her feel empty, lifeless.

But it had also helped. She'd never told anyone that story. Not anyone but her family, and they hadn't believed her, hadn't come to her rescue. She had no further use for them.

But Tony, a complete stranger, had listened. Encouraged her to get it out, tell him everything, no matter how repulsive.

Only he wasn't repulsed or disgusted by her. He'd believed what she said to be true, no matter how outrageous. He was sympathetic, but didn't show signs of pity. She wouldn't have been able to handle his pity. He let her speak, let her tell the story, but didn't judge or blame her.

Somewhere deep down inside her, a tiny spark of life flickered.

She desperately needed to feel alive again—to feel whole, complete, in every way.

Especially sexually.

He swallowed. "Sex?"

"Yes. Will you help me?" It was time to put the past behind her. If she didn't, David would win. Even though he no longer physically controlled her, he continued to pull her strings as if they were still attached. Well, no more. It had to stop now.

"Hell yeah," he said, practically leaping out of the chair. That made her smile. Then his expression turned serious. "I mean, of course I'll help you. But are you sure?"

The look of concern and tenderness on his face nearly brought her to tears. But she had no more tears left to cry. She'd left them all in Boston over three years ago. "I'm sure."

She took another long sip of wine to fortify her courage. Just talking about sex again made her break out in a sweat. The thought of actually doing it, of trusting a man enough to let him touch her, might reduce her to a complete puddle of liquid.

But when she looked into Tony's dark brown eyes, she trusted him. She didn't know why—she shouldn't. And yet he'd made it so easy for her to tell the story she'd never told anyone. Maybe it was because he was a journalist and adept at getting people to reveal their secrets.

She hoped to God she hadn't been wrong about him, that she wouldn't find her story plastered all over the newspapers tomorrow morning.

"Tell me what I can do to help you," he whispered, gently stroking her cheek.

Grateful for the warmth coursing through her at his touch, she smiled. "I don't really know. I just know it won't be easy. You don't have to—"

He touched her lips with his fingertips. "I want to do this. I want to help. You need to see that not every guy is a prick like your ex."

She nodded. "We'll have to start slow."

"You call the shots. Tell me what you want."

"Touch me. Not sexually. Just touch me." She'd missed the simple pleasure of human touch, so afraid of anyone's hands on her that the simple act of shaking hands with her guests had made her shudder. But no more, she was through with being afraid.

He stood and held out his hands to her. Inhaling deeply, she slipped her hands in his and waited for the typical rush of revulsion to hit her.

It didn't. Tony's hands were warm and so much larger than hers. Instead of making her feel overpowered, she felt safe. She allowed him to pull her to her feet. Slowly he stepped toward her until his body was inches from hers, and yet not touching. Then he gently folded his arms around her back and pulled her into his chest.

A moment of panic cut off her next breath, but she fought past it. Her heart pounded when she rested her palm on his chest. His own slow, steady heartbeat comforted her, and she laid her head on his shoulder.

When he rubbed her back with light strokes, she didn't flinch.

"Is this okay?" he asked.

"Mmm hmm," she mumbled, afraid to break the spell, afraid to think too much. If she did, she might bolt and run. She didn't want to ruin the moment. She was being held and touched again, and it felt so right.

After a few moments she leaned back so she could look at him. "Kiss me."

His eyes sparkled and he graced her with a devilish smile. He dipped his head, lightly brushing his lips across hers. She felt the whimper in the back of her throat and let it out.

"Sweet," he whispered against her mouth. "Like berries."

He tasted of wine and man. Powerful and potent. Her blood roared to life and soared through her, pumping energy and desire between her legs, moistening her, readying her for him.

Not yet. Oh, God she wanted to, but not yet. Just this, Tony kissing her, his hands playing softly against her back, the silk of her robe rubbing against her aching skin, was almost unbearable in its sweetness.

"Touch me," he said as he lifted his head, his dark gaze penetrating her.

His pulsing erection pressed against her mound and she could have wept from the pleasure. Not once since he'd touched her had she pulled away or felt afraid.

She slipped her hand between them, her fingers pressing into the muscles of his chest. Rock hard. So was his stomach.

And lower. She palmed his erection over his shorts, delighting in his sharp intake of breath. He was huge. Hard and hot and ready.

"I've wanted your hand on my cock since the first moment I met you," he rasped.

A glimmer of the control she used to relish flamed to life inside her. That feeling of power when she held a man's shaft in her hand and knew that he wanted her, that he wanted to shove it into her as far as it would go.

That invincible feeling was a lifetime ago. She knew she had no control, she never had. It had all been an illusion.

She dropped her hand to the side and made to turn away, but Tony grasped her wrist. She let out a shocked gasp, adrenalin rushing through her. But he only smiled and kissed the pulse point at her wrist.

"Your touch felt good, Morgan. Don't stop."

He released her wrist and laid her arm back at her side. She realized then he really was giving her the control. If she wanted to turn and walk away, he wouldn't try to stop her.

Which only made her want to stay, to continue her exploration, to find out where it could lead.

She looked up at him, saw the restraint in his clenched jaw and rigid posture, knew what it cost him to let her play like this. And she trusted him. He wouldn't hurt her, she knew it. He wouldn't touch her unless she asked him to.

"I want to feel your cock in my hands," she said, then leaned over and pulled his shorts down. His rod sprung forward into her waiting hand.

She closed her fingers around it, felt its life force pulsing against her palm, and stroked the length of him.

He sucked in a breath and let out a low moan. He looked like a wolf, his head thrown back as if preparing to howl at the moon overhead. Then he dropped his gaze, his eyes holding her.

And she stroked again, then circled her thumb over the tip of his erection. Silken drops of pre-come spilled over her fingers. She drew her fingers to her mouth and licked the salty fluid. Tony's eyes never left her face, his gaze focused on her mouth.

"You taste good," she said, licking his essence off her fingers before grasping him again and squeezing his shaft.

Morgan leaned into him, resting her hip against his thigh as she stroked him from base to tip. The heavy feel of him in her hands was a powerful aphrodisiac. Her desire poured between her legs and down her thighs.

"You smell like sweet sex," he said, alternately watching her hand and looking at her eyes. "The fact you're turned on makes me even hotter."

"I'm wet," she admitted. Which was an understatement. She was soaked, primed and ready for his shaft.

"I know. Do you know how hard it is not to drop to my knees and lick that juice from between your legs? To hear your cries and whimpers as I love you with my tongue?"

She quickened her strokes. "Yes, I know how hard it is," she teased. But his words seared through her, making her ache for his hands, his mouth, his shaft. And she'd have them all. Soon. Very, very soon.

"I want you to come with me," he said, his hips jerking forward to propel his shaft between her hands.

But she wasn't ready for him to touch her like that. "I...I can't. Not yet."

"Yeah you can. You can come for me, and I won't touch you."

He removed her hand and led her to the chaise lounge on the deck. He lay down on his back and looked up at her.

"Sit on me," he said. "Straddle me and rub your pussy against my cock. Ride me until you come."

Her legs buckled and she felt weak, whether from fear or excitement she couldn't tell. All she knew was the invitation was too good to pass up. She throbbed, she pulsed, she was wet and near to coming already. It wouldn't take much to send her right over the cliff.

Tony gripped the sides of the chaise, letting her know that he wouldn't try to touch her. Hesitantly she dropped the robe, her heart soaring at the look of male appreciation in his hot gaze. His eyes raked over her body, settled on her breasts until her nipples hardened as if his look were a caress. Then he glanced lower, between her legs, and smiled when his gaze met hers again.

"You have a gorgeous body," he said.

She knew she had wide hips and her butt was a little bubbly. She did have nice breasts, though, and was glad he appreciated her womanly body. "It's okay," she replied.

He frowned. "You don't believe me. Baby, you've got a woman's body. All curvy and full, just the way I like it. If I wanted to fuck a woman who looked like a twelve-year-old boy I'd go search out a fashion model. I wanna fuck a real woman. I wanna fuck you."

She reveled in the sweet ache of joy at the honesty in his words, and stepped toward him. He didn't move or speak as she spread her legs. He tilted his head to the side and peered between her legs, then when he looked up at her he licked his lips.

A promise. She couldn't wait.

Leaning down, she straddled him, anticipating the moment when her wet pussy would touch his rigid penis.

She settled on him, her aching lips opening to surround him. Even though it wasn't as good as having his thick shaft buried deep inside her, sliding against him like this hit her clit in just the right way. Sparks of pleasure snaked through her and she shuddered against him.

His knuckles shone white where they gripped the chair. Slowly, she moved against him. Her pussy was slippery wet with her juices, making it easier to slide along the length of him. He groaned when her mound touched the sensitive head of his cock, and tremors quaked deep inside her.

It had been so long, so very long, since she'd been this intimate with a man. More than a lifetime ago since she'd cherished the feel of a man's cock against her.

No, even when she'd still been young and exuberantly learning about her newfound sexuality, it had never been like this. It had never been this good. Maybe it was because it had been so long. She'd tired of pleasuring herself with her fingers, her vibrator, hell even vegetables — whatever she could find that struck her fancy at the moment she needed to get off. That had to be it. She did *not* feel anything emotional toward Tony.

Other than gratitude at his patience with her.

The sensations were like fireworks, shooting off inside her every time her sensitive clit rubbed against the ridged head of his swollen penis. She quickened her pace, desperately wishing that Tony would grab her hips and force her down on his shaft. That would come soon enough. Right now, she was close, oh so close, the tension building within her.

"Come on baby," Tony encouraged, whispering to her, urging her. "Come for me. Let me see it, let me feel your come pour over me."

He lifted his hips for her, angling his penis so that she slid down over it. She grabbed onto the arms of the chair, her fingers clenching over his, and rode him faster. The first spasms tightened inside her and she felt it down to her toes. She threw her head back and screamed as her orgasm soared through her, not once stopping her sliding action against him.

The overwhelming sensations pulsed through her for the longest time, and by the time she'd relaxed and began to breathe, she could already feel the arousal build again. Amazing. She'd just come, and she wanted it again.

Then she looked down at Tony, at the tense smile on his face, and knew she had something to do first. She slipped down and sat on his thighs. With both hands she circled his now soaked shaft and stroked.

His hips rose to meet her and he thrust his cock between her hands. She turned her hands, one going clockwise and the other counterclockwise, twisting his throbbing shaft.

"Fuck, that's good!" he groaned.

She smiled at his enjoyment. He'd sunk down onto the chaise and lay flat, giving his need up to her control. She looked down at the swollen purple head, drops of come slipping out and down over her hand. She desperately wanted to suck him, to feel that thick beast between her lips and ramming against the back of her throat. With every passing moment she was beginning to think that was a distinct possibility.

Grasping his tight balls with one hand she gave them a gentle tug while swiftly stroking his shaft. The combination had the desired effect.

Tony began to thrash around on the chaise, yet not once did he release his grip on the arms of the chair. With a loud groan he shot a stream of come straight up in the air and all over her hands, lifting off the chair to drive his cock deeper into her palm.

Some day he'd thrust deep into her pussy like that.

She couldn't wait for that day.

Chapter Seven

Tony stretched and rolled over, sneering at the time on the clock. Hell, it felt like he'd just gone to bed.

He had, only a couple hours ago. His ass would be dragging today.

But last night had been worth it. One small glimpse of Morgan coming out of her shell and Tony had nearly come out of his skin. If she continued her resurrection in this way it would likely kill him before the week was up.

They'd fallen asleep in the early hours of the morning, too exhausted to play any more. But he'd wanted to. God how he'd wanted to.

Whatever was happening between them was just beginning, and he only had a few more days in this paradise. He wanted to grab all the pleasure he could get.

More importantly, he wanted to give Morgan all the pleasure she'd allow.

He turned on the shower and let the steamy spray do its job of waking him. The warm water reminded him of last night, of feeling Morgan's heated juices all over him.

Not touching her last night had almost killed him. He'd worn grooves in his palms from gripping the arms of the chaise so tightly. He'd desperately wanted to squeeze his fingers against her lush hips and drive his cock into her soaked pussy. But he knew she wasn't ready for that. When she was ready, she'd let him know.

Being forced to watch her slide her desire-swollen lips against his shaft had nearly made him come. But he held back, wanting it to be about her, not about him. And she'd certainly enjoyed it, evidenced by her juices all over him when she was done.

When she'd thrown her head back and screamed, she'd looked as beautiful as he'd ever seen her. Her face and body flushed with passion, her nipples hard and pebbled, her hips bucking against him like she was fucking him, was a sight he'd love to preserve in a picture.

And today was another work day, another day of following her along and asking lame reporter questions. Questions he was no longer interested in asking. He'd asked all the important ones last night, and was privileged that she had given him the answers.

In a way he felt like he'd been given this great gift—the chance to pleasure a woman who'd long ago given up the thought of experiencing good sex with a man.

Step by step, as patiently as he could, he'd teach her that sex with the right man could provide every pleasure she'd ever want.

And then someday, when she was ready again, she'd find the right man to give her that kind of joy every day for the rest of her life.

That man wouldn't be him. He was a vagabond, a traveler, not a beachcomber. He'd never be happy on this tiny island surrounded by nothing but miles of water. He'd go nuts.

Even if the woman of his dreams lived here.

Disgusted at his train of thought, he shook the water out of his eyes and grabbed a towel. Had to be lack of sleep making him think there was any such thing as 'the woman of his dreams'.

He didn't have dreams of women, or 'the woman'. They were for sex, laughs and fun while he occupied space in whatever part of the world he happened to be working in.

Home and family and marriage and permanence didn't fit his lifestyle. Whenever he moved on, he left no lingering feelings behind.

And he wouldn't this time, either. He felt compelled to help Morgan rediscover her sexuality. After all, she'd trusted in him enough to tell him her secrets. But once that was done, he was outta here and off on the next assignment.

With nice memories, of course.

Morgan was sitting at the kitchen table near the window, sipping coffee and reading the newspaper. As usual, her hair was piled high on her head with a few curling tendrils escaping the sides. She wore another slinky sundress that never failed to wake up at least one part of his body.

Shifting his semi-hard cock to the side of his shorts, he strolled into the kitchen. "Morning."

Morgan looked up and smiled at him. "Morning. Sleep much?"

After grabbing a cup of the streaming brew, he sat down beside her. "As much as you did."

She looked different this morning. Her cheeks were rosy, her blue eyes as bright as the glint of sun off the ocean. Life energy poured from her.

And Tony felt like he'd had some small part in that grin she wore.

"Ready for another day?" she asked.

"I'm ready for anything you throw at me."

She arched a brow. "Anything?"

"Uh huh. What's on your mind?" he asked, trying to keep his baser thoughts at bay.

"You'll see."

The smile stayed on her face the entire day. He liked that. Tony wanted to do whatever was necessary to keep it there.

Today was pretty much the same as yesterday. He followed her routine, which he found to be pretty much business oriented. He talked to a few more staff members, who all gushed with praise about their boss.

By the time the workday ended, ominous clouds had darkened the skies over the resort. It looked like they were going to be hit with a rainstorm. After listening to the weather reports, Morgan suggested they head back to her house before the road washed out.

Fat drops of rain began to fall just as she pulled into the carport. They ran inside and the skies opened up. Sheets of rain slammed down relentlessly, streams of muddy water already forming around the house.

Phoebe wound her furry self around his legs, seemingly taken with him for some unknown reason. He looked down to find the cat staring up at him, meowing, as if he was personally responsible for the lousy weather outside.

"Don't look at me, girlie. I didn't do it."

The cat sauntered off in a huff.

Tony stepped out on the front porch and watched the rain. The humidity was high and he'd already taken off his shirt. Even though he wore only shorts, he wasn't any cooler. Morgan brought him a beer and he took a long, thirsty swallow, wiping away the perspiration from his forehead. It was hot. Sticky. Humid. They were completely isolated. The only sounds were the constant tapping of heavy rain on the roof.

He was trapped in the middle of a driving rainstorm in the heated tropics, with a beautiful woman.

Damn, life was good.

"How long will it rain?" he asked her.

"It depends. Storm's pretty big. Could last a day or so."

He turned to her. "How do you get to work when it's like this?"

She smiled. "I don't. Heavy rains like this wash out the road and I can't drive the cart to the resort. I could walk it, but it would take awhile. So unless there's a major crisis going on, the staff can handle anything that comes up."

The thought of being marooned here with Morgan for two days brought a grin to his face. He could make some serious headway in her reintroduction to sex if he had access to her for forty-eight hours with no distractions.

Except the damn cat who had taken a liking to him. It had returned from its short snit and once again circled around his ankles, purring. Annoyed with the tickling furball, he bent down and scooped it up and held it in his arms. Of course, then it purred all the more.

"Phoebe likes you," Morgan said, her eyes wide.

"Seems to. Is that a problem?"

"No. It's just that she doesn't really like strangers. Just me."

Tony puffed out his chest. "Smart cat. Obviously, she's an intelligent judge of character. Not to mention charm, great looks and potent sexuality." He stroked the cat's fur, rewarded with its kneading paws and drool. Great.

Morgan laughed. "I'll take your word for it."

"Are you sure you wouldn't rather find out for yourself?"

Her blue eyes darkened like the rain-pummeled ocean. "Maybe."

She leaned against a post and held her hands behind it. Visions of her tied to that post while he did anything he wanted with her sailed across his imagination. He just had to get her back to the point where she felt comfortable, and then he knew they could have some serious fun together.

"Earlier this morning you said you had something in mind?" he asked, trying not to push things, but his cock had already sprung to life at the thought of Morgan tied up.

She nodded. "If you're up to it."

He put the cat down and ran his palm against his shaft through his shorts, slowly stroking its length. Morgan's gaze dipped and focused. Her pink tongue darted out and swept across her lips. Tony wanted to groan. He wanted her lips and tongue on the head of his cock before the night was through. "I'm up to anything, babe."

"Even a little bondage?"

Now she was talking. Had she read his mind? "Hell yeah."

The corners of her mouth lifted in a small smile. "I doubt you're thinking about the bondage I have in mind."

"Try me."

"Oh, I plan to," she said, then pushed away from the post. "I'll be right back."

After she'd stepped inside, Tony resisted the urge to jump up and down like a kid who'd just gotten his first bike. But damn he was excited about the prospect of making some sexual headway with Morgan. It was all he'd thought about today. Remembering their time together last night, her body glowing in the moonlight, the way she rode his cock until she came, had kept him semi-hard the whole day.

He shuddered and stroked himself again, anticipating what was to come.

She stepped to the doorway and crooked her finger at him. He followed behind her more than willingly, watching the sexy sway of her hips, the silk of her dress caressing her ass just like he was dying to do.

He entered her bedroom and smiled. She'd tied silk scarves to the four posts. His cock hammered against his shorts, seeking immediate escape.

"I've been thinking about this all day," she said, her arm wrapped around the post at the foot of her bed, her hip leaning gently against the footboard.

"Me too."

"I figured the only way to get past my discomfort at having a man control me is for me to be in control. At least for awhile."

It didn't take a rocket scientist to figure out where she was headed. "You want to tie me to the bed?"

She nodded. "If that's okay. I mean, if you don't want to you don't—"

"I want to." He stepped in front of her, feeling the sexual vibrations sizzling between the two of them. "I have to be honest with you, Morgan. I'm dying to touch you and kiss you and lick you all over. I can't wait to crawl on top of you and plunge into your pussy."

She licked her lips and nodded. "I want that, too."

He lifted a tendril of silken hair and let it slide through his fingertips. "But I'm also a very patient man. I can wait for it. You take this at your own pace, tell me what works and doesn't work for you. Do whatever it takes to give yourself pleasure and make you feel comfortable. You control it."

Morgan's body heated at Tony's words. She found it hard to believe that a man like him existed. Such patience, such restraint, and so full of potent sexuality.

A man like him should frighten her, but he didn't. She still didn't understand the whys of it, but for some reason she did trust him. And trusting him made her want him.

"Tell me what you want," he said, his body hovering so close his warm breath caressed her face. She inhaled the male fragrance of him, a powerful aphrodisiac. She wanted to lick the fine sheen of sweat off his neck and shoulders, then work her way down his body with her tongue.

No, not *wanted*. She *would* do these things. She could, as soon as she had him secured. "Lie down on the bed. Naked."

His dark eyes narrowed, his breathing increased. He stood in front of her and reached for the waistband of his shorts, sliding them over his hips until they fell to the floor. His huge cock sprung out at her and she ached to drop to her knees right there and suck him.

But that would put her at his mercy, and she wasn't quite ready, yet. Instead, she waited while he walked around the side of the bed and climbed in, lying down on his back and spreading his arms and legs.

And there he was, completely open and fully trusting her. Something she hadn't been able to do in years. Of course she'd never hurt him before. Then again, he hadn't hurt her, either. And that's when the door to her heart opened, letting him take a peek inside. It was all she could do right now, but it was a momentous change for her. A risk worth taking.

All men weren't like David. The logical part of her mind knew that, and yet a part of her was still afraid.

Give in. Trust him. It's time, Morgan, it's time to live again.

She'd ignored that voice inside her head long enough. Just watching him now, lying there waiting for her to tie him up, cut through the last of her fear. Her distress turned to desire and all hesitation fled.

Her legs wobbled and she stood at the foot of the bed, looking her fill of him. Everything about him was big. Shoulders, arms, legs, and especially his thick shaft and balls. She shuddered thinking of him filling her, pumping his shaft into her. By making love with her, he'd aid in making her a whole person again. A real woman again. She hurried over to each post, securely binding his arms and legs until he was completely immobile.

All the time he watched her, his eyes devouring her, making her nipples stand up and fight against the silk binding them. She ached for his mouth on her, and tonight she'd have it.

"You gonna stand there and look at me all night, or are you gonna climb on top and have your way with me?" His voice was husky with passion, his lips curled in a wicked grin.

She smiled at him. "I'm going to get naked while you watch. Then I'm going to do whatever I want with you."

He looked impatient, but not in a frightening way. No, she rather enjoyed the fact that he wanted her. His body strained against the bonds, his hips rising and falling. "Get on with it then. I want you to touch me. I want your body all over me."

Barely able to make her shaky hands work, she fumbled with the ties on her dress, finally loosening them and letting the dress fall to the floor.

"You're beautiful." His whisper echoed in the quiet room, making her aware of herself in a way she hadn't been for years. She looked down at her body, unable to believe he thought her beautiful. She'd thought herself ugly and disfigured for so long.

She shook her head, not believing him, not wanting to believe him. She wasn't beautiful, she was scarred. Inside and out. She hesitated, watching him.

"You *are* beautiful," he said again. "Those scars on your back are nothing. The only one who finds them ugly is you. Now come here and work your magic on me. I need to come, Morgan. I need you to make me come because I can't do it myself."

Jaci Burton

Hesitating no longer, she approached the bed and climbed on, starting out by sitting next to him, her hip barely touching his.

She reached a tentative hand out and stroked his bare shoulder, trailing her fingertips along his collarbone and down his chest to circle his dark nipples. They hardened under her fingertips. Her own nipples followed suit, aching for his mouth, his fingers.

Slowly, she touched him everywhere, careful to avoid his erection. She wanted to draw out the moment, having this freedom to enjoy touching a man's body again without fear. Had she ever really known what that was like? David had been an act—everything about him, even at the beginning. He'd set her up and then used her desires against her. She'd never once been in control.

Now she was. And she loved Tony's reactions to her touch. When she found a sensitive area he'd suck in his breath, his body tensing under her hands. Tony had a lot of erogenous zones. His nipples, definitely. But also the backs of his knees, his upper thighs, and under his arms. His erection seemed to grow every time she touched a particular area. Come glistened on the tip of his penis, calling to her, begging for her hand or mouth to sweep it away.

But still, she waited, wanting to prolong his pleasure, and her own.

She'd waited three years for this moment. Hell, she'd waited twenty-seven years for it.

"Do you like the way I touch you?" she asked, looking into his eyes, so dark they were almost black.

"Yes," he said, his voice tight and raspy.

"Do you want me to touch your cock, Tony?" Her hands hovered near his thighs, her nails lightly scraping against his skin.

"Yes, dammit. Touch it."

She reveled in the control he'd given her. It both humbled and thrilled her. But she'd tortured both of them long enough. Now it was time to get serious. Her body was afire with the need to lie skin to skin with him. Her thighs were soaked with her own juices, just like they'd been last night when she'd ridden his shaft until she came.

Soon she'd come again. And so would he.

"You make me hot, Tony," she admitted, wanting him to know what he'd done for her. "Hotter than I've ever been before. So hot I could come in seconds if I touched myself."

74

He panted, hard, but didn't speak.

"But I won't. You're going to make me come, and more than once. And I'm going to make you come so hard you scream."

"Do it," he said.

Thunder rumbled long and low outside, the skies almost black. The wind howled, the trees lashing against the side of the house.

Outside the storm was violent.

Inside, the maelstrom was just beginning.

She straddled him and leaned over, touching her lips lightly to his. He opened his mouth and she descended on him, her tongue eagerly entering and twining with his. It was hot, passionate and nearly overwhelming. He tasted sweet and salty and she wanted to devour every inch of him.

Trailing kisses down his neck and over his shoulder, she found a well-muscled spot and bit lightly, her body shuddering at his low growl. She sensed the barely leashed control of an animal, and loved that she brought out such passion in him.

She scooted lower, tangling her fingers in the crisp, curling hair of his chest. He gasped when her tongue circled an erect nipple and she drew it into her mouth to lightly suck on it.

"Christ!" he bit out through clenched teeth, and she looked up at him and smiled.

She moved down his body, rubbing her cheek against the fine down of fur on his lower belly. Raking her nails over his ribs and abdomen, she was thrilled by the feel of his shuddering as her mouth drew closer to his pulsing shaft.

Pausing, she met his hot gaze, licking her lips in anticipation of what was to come.

He flexed his hips, his erection stroking her cheek, and still she waited. Waited for him to lose control. It didn't take long, especially when she stroked his inner thigh with her tongue.

"Suck me, goddamit!" he commanded.

Morgan's pussy flooded with liquid heat at his words. She turned her head, keeping her eyes fixed on his, and lightly licked the salty drops of fluid from the tip of his penis.

Tony groaned and pulled at the bonds at his wrists.

"You taste salty, like your skin," she said, taking a couple more swipes of the swollen head with her tongue.

"Suck it, Morgan," he said again. "Wrap your mouth around my cock and suck. Hard."

"Your wish is my command." She took his shaft in her mouth.

Chapter Eight

Tony grit his teeth and fisted the sheets with his hands, desperately wanting to loosen the knotted scarves around his wrist. He wanted to bury his hands in Morgan's hair and move her head over his aching cock. He wanted to cup her breasts, rub his fingers over her nipples, slide his hands through the red curls between her legs and sample the wetness pouring from her.

Mostly he just wanted to touch her — everywhere.

Her mouth was made for pleasuring him. Watching the erotic play of her long tongue over the throbbing head of his shaft had him nearly losing it and coming all over her beautiful face. Through sheer force of will he held back, not wanting this erotic torture to end too soon.

If he had to watch her lips and tongue laving his penis much longer, though, he'd be shooting into her mouth in seconds.

"Morgan," he managed through rapid pants, "Let me touch you with my tongue."

She stopped and looked at him. "I'm busy here," she replied, grinning wickedly.

"Dammit, then let me lick you. Turn around here and put your pussy over my mouth."

She sat back on her heels and tilted her head to the side. Her body was flushed, her nipples distended, her mouth wet from sucking him.

"Look, I can't touch you, I'm tied up, remember?" He emphasized his point by pulling against his bonds. "Let me lick you, baby."

Morgan shuddered at his words, her body so fired up she'd gladly do whatever it took to have Tony send her over the edge.

"How?" she asked him.

"Turn around and get on your knees. Then suck me while I lick you."

Juices of arousal poured between her legs. Her mind imagined Tony's hot tongue lapping them up while his mouth surrounded her clit and drove her to ecstasy.

She nodded and quickly turned around, backing up toward his mouth.

When her face was eye level with his burgeoning shaft and she felt his breath against her opening, she knew she'd arrived at the right spot.

"You have a beautiful pussy, Morgan," she heard him say.

"And you have a thick, tasty cock," she murmured, running the tip of her tongue against the purple head. He arched his back and slid more of him into her waiting mouth. She sucked, lapping up his precome with her tongue before taking his shaft deep into her mouth, gently pressing her lips against him, wanting to prolong his pleasure.

And still, she had more of him to fit in there. She relaxed her throat and opened it wide while gliding him past her reflex.

Tony bucked off the bed and hissed a groan as she swallowed him. She stroked the head with the back of her throat.

"Christ, that's tight," he said.

She was so preoccupied with pleasuring him she'd forgotten about him being so close to her pussy. Until he took one long swipe of her with his hot tongue.

The sensation was exquisite. She gasped and held still while he applied long, soft licks around her clit, lapping up her juices and making her cry out from the pleasure. If she hadn't had a mouthful of Tony at the time she would have screamed in sheer delight. As it was she could only groan against his shaft.

Which made him groan in turn.

The tandem oral coupling was like nothing she'd ever experienced. Sex with David had been all about David, and not about her pleasures. The mere thought of pleasing her hadn't crossed his mind once. But this—this was heaven on earth. The feel of Tony's tongue and lips tenderly stroking her sensitive clit made her mouth clamp down harder around his shaft. It was, she thought wryly, tit for tat, in the best possible way.

She braced her hands on the sides of his thighs and pushed back, wanting more of his tongue on her, inside her, all over her. The only thing she didn't like about this incredibly erotic position was the fact she couldn't watch him lick and suck her. That she'd save for another time. Then again, not being able to watch let her focus on his penis, and on her own intense feelings of pleasure.

She pulled away from his shaft several times to tell him his tongue felt great, or to guide him to a particularly sensitive area. Obviously eager to please her, he complied.

The feelings were nearly unbearable—when he moved his head from side to side, she bobbed her head using the same speed and intensity, feeling like they shared a dance of sorts. A sensuous, erotic, synchronized dance. So hot, so passionate it made her legs quiver.

She leaned forward and captured one of his balls in her mouth. The skin was so soft there, and he moaned when she ran her tongue along the seam between the two sacs. She alternated licking his balls and swallowing his shaft as far as her throat would allow, all the while his tongue performed wicked magic on her throbbing pussy.

"Tony," she rasped, stroking his cock with her hands as she felt her orgasm build. "Now."

He fit his lips over her clit and sucked gently. The first wave made her tremble, then when it reached full force she screamed, arching her back and pushing her mound against his face. He licked rapidly through the spasms until she collapsed on his belly, struggling for breath.

Her hand still held his penis in a firm grip. She looked up and smiled. She'd continued to stroke him through her shattering orgasm. Then she half turned to see him, his dark gaze penetrating her, his eyes half closed as she rhythmically stroked him.

She turned and faced him, bending down between his legs so he could watch her mouth descend on his cock. He leveled such an intense look on her it made her shiver with renewed desire.

He'd given her the orgasm of a lifetime. Now it was his turn to shatter into a million pieces.

Never taking her eyes off his, she gently tugged on his balls and slid her mouth down over his shaft, snaking her tongue over the underside of his rigid member.

"You're so damn good at that," he said, lifting his hips to fit more of his cock into her mouth.

She sucked him greedily, lapping up the salty juices that spilled over her lips, knowing he was close, feeling his balls tighten against his body.

"Yeah, baby, like that. Suck it. Make me come."

She used her hands and mouth to grip him tightly and provide enough friction that soon he was groaning and thrashing, lifting his hips off the bed to pummel her mouth.

White-hot jets of liquid shot from his cock as his body stiffened in orgasm. She rode it out with him, swallowing his milky sweet come and slowing her movements until he finally relaxed underneath her.

Now what? Feeling somewhat uncertain, she didn't know whether to crawl up and snuggle beside him or sit there and wait for him to open his eyes. She didn't want to presume anything. Presumption led to trouble in her mind.

Besides, this was just sex, and nothing more. No sense in getting too comfortable with Tony. He wasn't going to be around long.

His eyes opened he smiled at her. They'd just shared something monumental. At least it seemed that way to her.

No, she wasn't reading anything emotional into what just happened between them. But it had been fantastic. She wanted her sexuality back, and Tony seemed more than willing to let her 'use' him to get it.

As she stared at the man tied up in her bed, arching a brow and grinning like a fool, she knew she'd made the right choice. He'd already given her more than she'd hoped for. And it was just the beginning.

"You gonna untie me now, or will you be having more of your way with me?" he asked.

Morgan laughed when he wagged his eyebrows at her. "I take it you'd like me to have my way with you a little bit more?"

He lifted his arms. "I'm your prisoner here. Do whatever you'd like with me."

What she'd like to do is untie him so he'd gather her in his arms and make love to her. But she wasn't ready for that. And besides, they weren't lovemaking. They weren't in love at all. She liked him, obviously desired him. Likewise with Tony, she assumed. So far they'd had great sex together. She had no reason to think that would change.

She just had to get her mind focused on sex strictly for physical pleasure. She'd never been very good at keeping emotions separated from sex. David changed that. She'd let her emotions rule with him and look what had happened.

After that, she'd spent five years disengaging herself from the sex act until she was nothing more than a lump of flesh for David to use as he pleased.

Now? Now the life poured back into her, and with it came the emotions. Try as she might, she couldn't help it.

She'd just have to try harder.

"Are you tired of being tied up? Need a break?" she asked. Surely his arms were sore stretched across the bed that way.

"If you untie me can I touch you?"

She shook her head, sad that she couldn't give him a resounding 'yes.' At least, not yet.

"Then leave me tied up. I'm fine."

She should let him go, let him stand up and relax his arms and legs. But she wasn't finished with him yet. And from the heated look he shot her, neither was he.

"You want more?" she asked.

The answer was stiffening as she spoke, but still he replied, "Hell yeah, I want more."

A sweet ache started all over again between her legs. Morgan straddled him, positioning her cunt over his thick shaft. He groaned, his erection full and promising. What would he feel like inside her? It had been so long and her last memories of intercourse with a man weren't exactly positive.

"What's wrong?" he asked.

Morgan met Tony's frown. "Nothing, why?"

"Something's bothering you. I can tell. You get this faraway look on your face sometimes, and something crosses your eyes. I can't tell if you're sad or afraid."

He knew her so well already. More than David had after five years. "Just remembering the last time I had sex—what it was like before."

"This isn't going to be like before. I'm not doing this to hurt you, Morgan. Remember, I'm still tied up here. You call all the shots—if this doesn't work for you, we stop."

Such a strong man and yet so tender with her. She'd never have guessed it of him.

"Let's do it, then," she said with renewed fervor. Every last doubt flew away with the brisk winds outside.

He sucked in a breath as she slid against him. "I want my cock inside you," he said.

The sound of his voice tripped along her nerve endings, coaxing her pleasure meter ever higher. Soft and seductive, and one thing she'd never experienced before—sincere. He *did* want her, and for all the right reasons.

"Will you fuck me now, Tony?" she asked, pressing her throbbing clit against the rigid head of his shaft.

"Yeah, baby, I'll fuck you. Wrap your hot pussy around me."

There was nothing she wanted more than that. But first, she needed to feel his mouth against hers. She leaned over, her nipples tingling when they brushed over the crisp hairs of his chest.

Hovering inches away from his mouth, she inhaled the musky scent of her own pleasure still lingering on his lips. She slid her tongue lightly over his lower lip. "You taste like me."

Her heart clenched when he responded with, "Like wild, sweet honey. I love your taste, Morgan."

Arousal built inside her, and she pressed her mouth to his, her hands traveling lower until she grasped his shaft and readied herself to take him in.

He murmured against her lips, "Do it baby," then reached for her mouth. She touched her tongue against his at the same moment she eased down onto his shaft.

Tears welled in her eyes when she felt his huge cock enter her. She was so tight she felt like a virgin being stretched open for the first time.

"Are you okay?"

She closed her eyes and forced herself to relax. "Yes. You're so big, Tony. And it's been so long."

"Just take it slow."

She did, inch by incredible inch. And oh, it was such heaven, feeling him fill her completely. Spasms contracted inside her, her juices providing ample lubrication. She began to move over him, lifting her hips and slowly dipping down again.

Tony groaned into her mouth. "Yeah, like that...just like that. Christ, Morgan, your pussy's so hot, so tight, squeezing me, milking me."

His raspy words of encouragement and praise sweetened the already near unbearable pleasure of his shaft filling her. She gasped, pushing upright so she sat fully on top of him, his shaft buried to the hilt inside her.

"You like that big cock filling your pussy, don't you?" His hungry eyes devoured her.

"Yes, "she moaned, nearly delirious with the sensation.

"Then ride it, Morgan. Fuck me."

Lifting her hips, she pulled up until only half of his long shaft remained inside her. Then she slammed down hard, shuddering with the sweet pain of his cock head hitting her womb. She braced her hands against his chest, tangling her fingers in the curling nest of hair she found, and rode him hard. She couldn't help but wish his hands were free to grab her breasts and squeeze them, or to dig his fingers into her hips and lift her up and down his magnificent shaft.

Morgan didn't want the moment to end, but her pussy was already tightening around his shaft, moisture pouring over his balls.

He lifted his hips and increased his thrusts, pounding his cock harder and faster inside her. "Come with me," he whispered, his gaze focused on her face.

She licked her lips and concentrated on Tony's movements within her. The storm lashed the windows outside with the rap of tree branches, Mother Nature's fury knowing no bounds as a maelstrom brewed around them. Morgan felt the same way—unleashed and free, able to channel her primitive energies into the storm raging deep inside.

"That's it, baby, you're almost there," he said. "Come with me. I wanna feel you come on my cock."

She couldn't hold back as the contractions overwhelmed her. Her pussy clamped strongly around Tony's shaft, wave after wave of delirious heaven squeezing every drop of pleasure out of her.

She arched her back and howled her pleasure.

With a loud groan and a final thrust, Tony pushed and held deep inside her. Morgan felt the pulsing contractions of his orgasm and squeezed him, tightening around him until he let out a string of yells as loud as the crashing thunder outside.

Exhausted, she fell onto his chest, listening to the frenetic pounding of his heart, so similar to her own raging beat.

When she could move again she reached over and untied his arms, then climbed off and sat at the bottom of the bed, watching him.

"That was amazing." Tony sat up and rubbed his wrists and flexed his fingers.

"Yes, it was." And now that it was over, Morgan didn't know what to say or do. Part of her wanted to ask him to hold her. It had been so long since a man had cradled her in his arms. The other part was either too shy or simply too afraid to let him put his arms around her. At least right now. But she trusted him so much more now than she had before, and with every passing moment she knew the next step would be to experience sex unbound—her and Tony together, with no barrier to him touching her.

She was ready for this. But when would it happen?

"So," he asked with a huge grin, "you ready for round two?"

Chapter Nine

Tony wondered what thoughts lurked inside Morgan's head. She sat at the edge of the bed chewing her lower lip, uncertainty knitting her brows. Hell, he'd only suggested another round of sex. It wasn't like he'd asked her to marry him.

"I'll be right back." She scooted off the bed and slipped on her robe, then left the room without another word.

Completely satiated, he laced his fingers behind his head and leaned against the pillows. Damn, but the woman was good in bed. He'd expected her to be reluctant, even a bit shy considering what she'd been through. But she was wild, and at that he suspected she'd held back a little.

Held back? God, if she really let loose she might kill him. He couldn't help the smirk plastered on his face at that thought. What a way to go. Fucked to death.

But now where was she? Should he get up and go after her? Was she upset? She hadn't seemed that way. Pensive, maybe, but not really upset.

And why the hell did he care? If he wasn't careful, next thing he'd be doing would be falling in love with her. His relationship with Morgan had to be all about sex, and nothing more. Emotion wouldn't, couldn't, come into play. She wasn't looking for a permanent relationship, and he wasn't either. So he had to keep reminding himself not to worry so much about how she felt about things. If she enjoyed the sex as much as he did, then great. If not, then they'd stop. No big deal.

Rain pelted the windows, the wind just as strong as it had been several hours ago. Well, if he was going to be stuck inside during a tropical rainstorm, at least he couldn't complain about the company.

Said company returned bearing a tray filled with cheese, fruits and drinks.

"Thought you might be hungry," she said.

Her hair was tousled and fell across her shoulders in red waves. Her cheeks were flushed and her smile lit up the storm-darkened room. She looked ravishing and made him hungry. But not for the goodies on the tray. He was starving for the delectable treats hidden underneath her robe.

Morgan sat on the edge of the bed, openly appraising his naked body, her eyes like a caress over him. She lifted a piece of sliced mango and slid it into his mouth. His cock sprang to life, twitching its way to a full erection in a record few seconds.

The taste was sweet, the juices running down his chin. Morgan surprised him by leaning in and licking the mango juice off his chin.

"Mmm, good," he said.

"You like mangoes?" she asked in a throaty voice that went straight to his penis.

"I like you licking me."

"I'll keep that in mind."

She followed up the mango by popping a few grapes into his mouth.

"I like this feeding thing. Makes me feel all powerful, like you're my slave."

Her blue eyes smoldered. "You like being the master, then?"

"Oh yeah. Then again, I didn't mind being tied up either. I'm pretty much an equal opportunity guy."

She laughed and it knifed through his senses, churning his insides.

"Tell me about your work," she asked.

"Nothing much to tell. I write."

"When did you decide to become a writer?" She handed him a glass of juice.

He took a long swallow, then shrugged. "I majored in journalism at NYU, convinced I was going to be the next Woodward or Bernstein."

"And you changed your mind?"

"Yeah."

"Why?"

"I didn't like reporting news. It was boring." He hadn't thought about his old job in a long time, but talking about it now reminded him how much his goals had changed since college. What if he had stayed with the newspaper? Where would he be now?

"So, you decided to go freelance?"

"Yeah. I liked the idea of travel, and I didn't care much for being told how to write my articles. I don't deal with authority that well."

A smile curved her lips. "I could see that about you."

"You could?"

"Yeah." She slid a slice of mango into her mouth, the fruit disappearing slowly between her lips.

Tony shuddered, remembering the feel of those lips sucking on his shaft. His cock ached with the need to be inside her again. "What about you? What did you want to do?"

"After I met David, my life completely changed. I never even had a chance to finish college."

"What were you going to major in?"

"International studies. I had some thoughts about law, or maybe teaching. Although I loved travel, so I figured international business would be a good place to start."

Funny how much they had in common, including the love of travel. "Why didn't you finish college after you got married?"

The smile left her face. "David didn't want me out of his sight that much. Attending college would mean I was exposed to too many people. People who might find out what he was doing to me and try to stop it."

Tony ached for what Morgan had lost. "You could finish now."

She shrugged. "What's the point? I'm doing exactly what I want to do, and I don't need a degree to do it."

"Is this really what you want to do? Run a sex resort?"

Her eyes flashed like hard sapphires. "What's wrong with what I do? I'm not ashamed of it, and I make a damn good profit. Paradise is a successful business that I built from the ground up. I'm very proud of what I've accomplished."

Boy, she was fire and brimstone when she got riled. "You're sexy as hell when you're pissed off, you know."

Her mouth hung open in surprise, and Tony resisted the urge to plant a kiss on her luscious lips.

"Excuse me?"

Nothing like being caught off guard in the middle of righteous indignation. "Your eyes sparkle, your cheeks color, and your entire body stiffens like you're ready for a brawl. It's sexy. I like a woman with a little fire in her belly."

She dipped her chin and half lowered her lashes, almost as if the compliment embarrassed her.

"What's wrong?"

"Nothing."

He reached out for her, hesitating a second before sliding his hand in hers. She looked up at him.

"Morgan, what's wrong?"

"Nothing. It's just that David used to...punish me when he thought I was out of line."

That now familiar anger at the mention of her ex-husband lit a fire of its own deep inside him. Someday, he'd find a way to make that prick pay. "I'm not David. And I like your sassy little mouth."

Her eyes widened. "You do?"

Swiping his thumb across her full lower lip, he nodded. "Hell yeah. I'm a journalist. We love a good argument, a little debate, maybe even a spot of controversy. I'd never think badly of you because you stood up for yourself. I'd be damn disappointed if you didn't."

She stared at him as if she couldn't quite fathom what he'd said. "You confuse me."

"I do? How?"

"You're not like most men."

"Thank God for that. I thrive on being unique."

A cute little snort erupted out of her mouth. "See? That's exactly what I'm talking about. You make me think, you make me laugh, and..."

He leaned up and pulled a strand of her flaming hair across his fingers. "And?"

This time she didn't drop her gaze, but held his intently. "You excite me."

And there went his penis, waving in the air, trying to garner her attention. "I hope so. Because you light the fires of hell inside me."

She blushed and tilted her head to the side, exposing her slender neck. Taking a chance, he leaned forward and pressed a light kiss against the pulse point there. Her heartbeat danced madly against his tongue. But she didn't back away, and didn't seem to be in any hurry to move, even though he wasn't restrained.

"I want to touch you," he whispered against her neck, unable to tear his lips away from her silken throat.

She hesitated for a second before answering. "Then touch me."

Breathing a sigh of relief at getting the go ahead, he pressed his tongue harder against her neck, lapping up her sweet taste, then trailed his mouth down to her collarbone and over her shoulder. She shuddered when his teeth lightly nipped the tender skin there.

"Tell me to stop at any time, and this is over." It was important that she knew he wouldn't make her go on if things got scary for her.

"I will."

He pulled away for a brief moment to set the tray on the floor beside the bed, then grasped her hands and pulled her toward him. She went willingly, even when he turned her around so her back nestled against his chest. The soft silk of her robe brushed against his chest, and her wriggles as she got comfortable placed her delectable ass right smack against his erection.

Waiting for her to balk at the intimacy of the position, she only sighed and seemed to settle in against him. Tony ignored the pulsating need to plunge his cock between the cheeks of her lush buttocks, and concentrated on taking things slowly. Making this pleasurable and non-threatening for Morgan was paramount.

And why he took so much care with her was something he refused to ponder. He'd think about that later. Much later.

Humidity hung in the air, the relentless storm sending the sweet smell of tropical rain through the shuttered windows. Darkness had long ago descended on them, but Tony really had no idea what time it was. For all he knew, it could be the next day.

He didn't care. He had Morgan to himself and planned to enjoy every moment of it.

"Let's lose this robe," he murmured against her ear. When she nodded her agreement and untied the sash holding the white silk together, he slipped it off her shoulders, following its descent down her arms with his hands.

"Your skin is so soft I can barely feel it." He took care to whisper softly, to make his movements slow, so she wouldn't skitter away in fright.

"You smell like the rain outside. Sweet and clean. I want to taste all of you." She melted under his hands, the muscles of her body completely relaxing. Her trust in him was humbling. Considering what she'd been through in her past, it was a wonder she'd even let him near her, let alone this close. No matter what it took, he'd make sure he never shattered that trust.

Discarding the robe onto the white wicker chair next to the bed, he slipped his hands along her shoulders, lightly kneading the muscles there. When little moans and gasps escaped her lips, he pressed in a little deeper.

"That feels good," she murmured.

"No, baby. Good is what follows." He shifted and turned her so she half lay in his arms, then pressed his mouth to her lips. Her breasts pressed against his chest, the contact of her nipples searing him. He pulled her against him, not once breaking their kiss.

With light pressure he kissed her, waited for her to give the signal she was ready for more. It didn't take long, he thought with some satisfaction. Soon she was fitting her mouth harder against his, her tongue frantically searching for an equal partner in a combat of erotic play. He indulged her by driving his tongue into the moist recesses of her mouth until she gasped, small whimpers escaping the back of her throat.

As he kissed her, his hand roamed freely along her back, stopping at the scars near her buttocks. She froze when he touched her, and he lifted his mouth to look into her eyes. "Does that hurt you?"

"No. It's just..."

"Just what?" He didn't move his hand away, but held it still over her scarred back.

She stared down at his chest. "It's embarrassing. I'm ashamed of them."

He tipped her chin up with his fingers. "Morgan, you didn't put them there. Don't ever be embarrassed that you were overpowered by some jerkoff who should be wallowing in prison for what he did to you. What happened to you isn't your fault."

His words must have had some effect on her, because he saw her eyes glitter with moisture before she closed them and reached for his mouth again. The ache in his heart was difficult to ignore. The pain of humiliation she suffered shouldn't go unpunished. But now was not the time. Now was the time for Morgan's pleasure.

He pulled her close again, seemingly unable to draw her as near as he'd like. When his hands slid down to cup her buttocks and press her against his shaft, she gasped and moved her hips against his hard-on. Then it was his turn to suck in a shaky breath. The feel of her nest of curls teasing the tip of his penis brought one thing and one thing only to mind — to plunge inside her moist heat.

But not yet. Even if he was raging hard and more than ready to fuck. He trailed his fingers lightly up her spine, then over her ribs, laughing when she erupted in giggles.

"Ticklish are you?" he asked, pressing a kiss against her lips.

"Don't you dare," she warned, trying for an icy glare but only succeeding in looking more hot and sultry than she did before.

"I'll put that knowledge aside for later." Then he laid her on her back and pulled away long enough to position himself over her. Her eyes widened momentarily at the submissive position he'd put her in, and he paused. Then she relaxed and spread her legs so he could kneel between them.

"That's my girl," he said, never taking his eyes of hers. "Trust me. I'm going to make you scream, but nothing like what you experienced before. This is for your pleasure, Morgan. All for you."

Her breath hitched sharply as he circled her nipples with his fingertips, then lightly rolled the dusky peaks between his thumb and forefinger. They rose and hardened against his questing hands. He gathered the mounds together and leaned over her, taking his eyes off her face so he could feast on her breasts, first with his eyes, and then with his tongue.

She arched her back and whimpered when he fit his mouth over one pointed peak, then drew the nub inside and sucked. He held her nipple in the warmth of his mouth and tweaked it with his tongue until she threaded her hands into his hair and pushed his mouth down harder. Taking that as a signal he suckled her deeply, then did the same to the other nipple until she was gasping for breath.

"Please, Tony," she said against his mouth as he took her lips in a hot kiss. "Please, now."

"Not yet, baby." The sweet, honeyed scent of her sexual desire filled the room. She was hot and ready.

But he wanted to make her more ready. He placed a pillow under her head and blazed a trail from her breasts to her belly, looking up occasionally to find her gaze following his actions. He smiled at her, then moved lower until his chin brushed the soft curls between her legs.

He settled in between her thighs. Searching her face for any sign of hesitation, he was satisfied to see her eyes glaze over with passion, her tongue swirling across her lips in anticipation. He bent down and inhaled her musky scent, which nearly drove him over the edge. His cock slid against her satiny sheets, and he imagined the feel would be similar to nestling between her legs. Soon. Very soon. But first, he had to taste her again.

This time she'd be able to watch.

He slid his fingers through the red curls on her mound. The rest of her was bare, which excited the hell out of him. Her labia was sleek, moist, the vanilla-tinged scent of her arousal driving him crazy. And she was wet. Very wet. Her juices glistened against the outer lips and he couldn't resist the urge to lean in and lap them up with his tongue. The first touch of his tongue against her skin had her moaning. The little mewling whimpers she made were sexy as hell.

Pressing a soft kiss to her silken mound, he licked her, softly, gently, until her breathing quickened with her rapid gasps. Then he covered her clit with his mouth and sucked the hardened nub inside. He held on while her hips bucked against him, taking her movements as affirmation that he was hitting her hot spots.

Her hand found its way to his head, guiding his movements as he pleasured her. She liked the action around her clit, he noticed, especially when he sucked it between his lips. Then she'd rock against him and try to push more of her hot pussy into his mouth. He licked up her juices greedily, her sweet, musky taste making him nearly delirious to plunge his shaft into such sweet flesh.

"God, Tony, I can't stand it," she said, her head thrashing from side to side as he quickened his pace. When he plunged his tongue inside her opening she bucked off the bed and groaned like a wild woman out of control.

Oh yeah. He definitely liked seeing her out of control. Her hands threaded through his hair and yanked him against her soaked pussy, guiding his movements as he took her near the brink. Then he stopped.

She looked down at him, her eyes glassy, her bottom lip clenched between her teeth. "Don't stop," she whimpered. "Please, don't stop."

"Is it good, baby?" he teased, wanting to prolong her ecstasy as long as possible, knowing the longer she waited, the better it would be.

"Yes. Yes, oh yes it's good. Please, Tony. Make me come now. Please."

Figuring he'd tormented her long enough, he slipped one finger inside her and captured her clit with his mouth, swirling his tongue around it until she ground her sweet pussy against his face.

"Yes, that's it! I'm coming!"

Arching her back, her pussy contracted tight against his finger and her juices poured out onto his hand. She screamed, a prolonged howl of pleasure that seemed to go on forever. Her body jerked with the force of her orgasm but he held on, riding out the storm with her, continuing to drink up her come as it gushed forth. Finally, she relaxed her hips to the bed and the pulses inside her subsided. Tony lapped up her juices, loath to leave the erotic spot between her legs. But there was more to come. They'd just begun. He crawled up to lay beside her.

She reached for him and cradled her hands on either side of his face, pulling him to her mouth for a heated kiss. She focused on his lips, licking all her sweet honey off him. Fuck, that was erotic as hell. Never before had a woman done that. Morgan Brown was one incredible woman.

Apparently one insatiable woman, too, since the next words out of her mouth were, "Fuck me, Tony. Now."

Chapter Ten

Morgan hoped Tony had stamina, because she had years of lost sex to make up for. Judging from the way her body reacted to him, it planned on making up all three years in less than a week.

At his wide-eyed look she smiled. "Tired?"

He arched a brow. "Are you kidding? I'm never too tired to fuck. Especially someone as hot as you."

His words kicked her sensuality level into overdrive. She simply couldn't get enough of him. He'd brought her to the brink and sent her over the edge so many times already in the past few days, she couldn't believe she still had any energy left.

"Your mouth is incredible," she said, still tasting herself on his lips as she lightly flicked her tongue over his.

He sucked in a breath. "You taste like honey. Honey that poured all over me when you came."

Her nipples tightened and budded as he brushed his thumbs over them. "I can't tell you what it feels like to have a man's hands on me again. Thank you."

She could hardly believe the tenderness she read in his eyes, but there it was.

"My pleasure. Thank you."

Cocking her head to the side, she asked, "For what?"

"For letting me be the first man to touch you again."

How could a man like him exist? So full of life, fun and potent sexuality, he was perfect for her. But also totally wrong. She didn't need or want a man again. Having been one man's prisoner for five years was enough to last her a lifetime. And then she'd spent three years in sexual solitude. Now her lonely days were over. And so were the days of being committed to one man.

She was free. Free to explore her sexuality with as many men as she chose.

Right now she chose Tony.

"So, about that sex..." she said again.

He grinned and leaped off the bed, taking her hand and dragging her with him.

"Where are we going?"

"Outside."

She dug in her heels near the front door. "Outside? It's raining."

"So? It's warm out there and I want some air."

She shook her head and followed him through the front door. He led her to the porch swing and sat down, pulling her onto his lap. The sun was beginning to rise, its light barely visible through the relentless rainstorm. But Tony was right. It was hot and humid. She inhaled the clean fragrance of Mother Nature's shower.

"Beautiful out here," he whispered against her ear, then took a nibble of her earlobe.

Morgan shivered and nodded. "Yes. Quiet, peaceful. One of the things I love most about living here. No rush, no hurry. Life is relaxed and happens at its own pace."

He brushed his hand over her tangled hair.

"I probably look a mess," she said, trying to smooth the flying tendrils back.

Tony held her wrist. "Don't. You look beautiful. Tousled, messy and sexy as hell."

She sighed and leaned back against him, letting him push the swing and glide them both. The rhythmic movements along with the warm rain lulled her into a completely relaxed state. Her eyelids felt heavy and fluttered closed. She'd just rest against his chest for a minute or two until she got her second wind. After all, they had been up all night.

The next thing she knew the sun was peeking through the last of the clouds. The rains had lessened to a light shower, and she was still curled up on Tony's lap, her head on his shoulder and his arms tightly wound around her. She looked up at him and smiled. He was asleep.

Long, curling black lashes rested against his cheeks, his hair unkempt like hers. God he was gorgeous. She took the opportunity to examine his face up close. He was sculpted like a statue with prominent cheekbones and a straight nose, full lips a woman would pay money to have and those sinfully long eyelashes.

He opened his eyes and smiled sleepily at her. "We fell asleep."

She nodded. "Yes. I don't know for how long, though."

"You snore," he said with a wink.

"I do not!" She pushed against him and stood, then stretched her sore muscles.

He laughed at her. "Yeah, you do. Little girlie snores. Kinda cute."

Instead of a response she glared at him, but he looked at her with such a goofy expression she couldn't hide her smile.

"I'm starving. How 'bout you?" he asked.

Holding her hand against her rumbling stomach, she nodded. "Let's have breakfast."

"Or lunch. Or dinner. Or whatever time it is."

They stepped inside and Morgan quickly called the resort to determine the status. As usual her assistant manager, Tara, had everything under control and told Morgan not to worry.

"Everything okay?" Tony asked when Morgan stepped into the kitchen. He had already started the bacon and eggs and she stepped beside him to make juice.

"Fine. My assistant does a great job when I'm not there. They don't need me at all."

"Good. More time for me to be alone with you, then."

He leaned over and nuzzled her neck, then slid his tongue along her collarbone. She shivered.

They stood at the counter and made breakfast. Naked. Morgan enjoyed every minute of it, especially when Tony leaned over and kissed her, or touched her, or grabbed her butt. If anyone would have told her a week ago that she'd be sharing an intimate breakfast in the nude with her lover, she'd have said they were insane.

He'd changed her so quickly. His patience, his gentleness, had brought her back to life. She'd never be able to thank him for what he'd done for her.

After breakfast they threw on a minimal amount of clothing and stepped outside to take a look at the road. Tony wanted to walk instead of driving, despite Morgan's warnings they would sink into the mud. He didn't seem to care. In fact, he held her hand as they traversed the mucky path leading into the rain forest.

Steam rose from the ground to cover them in a fine mist. Morgan was used to the lack of cool air to breathe, but she was certain Tony wasn't. Either way, he didn't complain, just kept hold of her hand and led her through the path.

"This looks too muddy to make it with the golf cart," he said, pointing to their feet sinking deeply into the mud.

"I know. But at least the rain's stopped and the sun is shining. Hopefully, by tomorrow it'll be dry enough to get through." She needed to get back to the resort. Not that she didn't trust Tara, but she felt it was her responsibility to be there for her guests.

"Yeah, me too. I'd hate to miss those sexual adventures you were going to take me to."

"Thought I was showing you a little sexual adventure right here," she teased.

He stopped and dragged her into his arms to plant a hot kiss on her lips. Her tongue twined with his, her temperature rising in a way that had nothing to do with the steamy jungle.

"I never got to sink my cock into your hot pussy again last night," he said as he dragged his lips from hers.

"No, you didn't." Her hands slid over his shoulders and cupped his face, drawing him down to hers for more of his delicious kisses. His budding erection wiggled between them.

She pulled away and smiled. "Would you like some of that right now?"

He didn't answer, just pulled her into the dense forest. She didn't speak, trusting he knew where he was going.

They came to a clearing and stepped out onto a small sandy beach. The sun glinted off the ocean, signaling the last of the storm. The sand was already dry

"Ever made love on the beach?" he asked, his eyes darkening in a way already familiar to her.

"No."

"Want to?"

"Oh, yes."

They rinsed their muddy feet in the ocean water, then Tony led her to a shady spot underneath a hanging palm frond. He yanked off his shorts and dropped them on the sand, taking her hands and easing her down on top of them. She started to pull off her sundress but he stopped her.

"Don't. I want to fuck you with your dress on."

A sweet ache pounded between her legs as moisture gathered there, readying her for him. Tony's shaft was erect and ready for her, and she hadn't even touched him yet.

He kneeled in front of her and captured her mouth in a heated kiss that left her breathless and panting. She spread her legs and he positioned himself between them, but didn't enter her.

What was he waiting for? Couldn't he see she was ready? But he left his hands on her knees and peered down between her legs, then looked at her.

"Do you know how sexy that is?"

"What?"

"Seeing your beautiful pussy under that dress. You don't wear panties, do you?"

"Not unless necessary. Actually I don't wear clothes that often at home."

"Damn," he whispered, more to himself, she thought, than her. "That's just fucking hot, babe."

He reached down and thumbed her clit, sending spirals of hot desire flooding through her. She lifted her hips and he penetrated her moist folds with his fingers, sliding one, then two, gently in and out until she was panting.

Watching him do that to her was tearing her apart. Could he feel the sweet pulses inside her?

"Tony, please."

"Please, what?" he teased, his free hand reaching out to find her nipple. It puckered and stood up against her dress.

"Fuck me."

"Now?"

"Yes." She moaned as he pressed his thumb against her clit, drawing lazy circles that made her crazy with need.

"Turn around."

He withdrew his hand and turned her over, then pulled her up onto her hands and knees. He leaned over her back and asked, "Do you like it this way?"

Morgan spoke through the shudder of excitement rumbling through her. "Yes."

"Good. Because I've been wanting to fuck you this way since the first time I saw you in your sexy little dresses." He slid the dress up over her hips, exposing her buttocks. "You have a gorgeous ass, Morgan."

Part of her wanted to reach back and pull the dress over her scars. Despite the fact she loved the position, the evidence of her beatings would be exposed to his line of vision. Knowing what he'd be looking at disturbed her.

Until he bent down and kissed them, ran his tongue over each and every one of the thin, pale scars, and brought genuine tears to her eyes that she was thankful he couldn't see. She blinked them back before they spilled onto the sand.

"You're beautiful, Morgan," he said, running his hands over her back and buttocks. "Such a perfect body, full and lush and just the way I like it."

She believed him. Whether she should or not, she didn't know. What she did know was at this moment she needed to believe his words were sincere.

His hands captured her attention and all thoughts of her scars disappeared. He touched her all over, squeezing her hips and reaching around to cup her breasts and pull the top of her dress down. He tweaked her nipples until she cried out from the pleasure. His erection pressed against her buttocks and she leaned forward so he could guide it toward her aching slit.

"You ready baby?" he asked.

"Yes." She was ready. More than ready. Ready now, dammit.

He probed between her legs, settling the head of his thick cock against her opening, then teased her by moving it back and forth over her pulsing core. When she would have shouted in protest he rubbed it gently against her clit, the rhythmic strokes of the velvety head sending a rush of pleasure through her.

"Oh, yes," she gasped, backing against him to feel more of the sensual stroking.

"I think you like that," he whispered, then pulled away.

"Stop teasing me!" she demanded, tired of being tormented with such sweet pain.

"Yes ma'am."

He chuckled, then settled against her, slowly gliding his shaft inside. He sunk inside her inch by glorious inch, stretching her, filling her until he was buried deep.

Her body instantly accommodated him, pulsing and contracting around his thick cock, moistening her cunt to provide him ample lubrication to stroke. And stroke he did, slowly at first, pushing deep until he brushed her most sensitive spot, then withdrawing. Her body clasped onto his shaft, reluctant to let him depart her depths.

It was exquisite, torture of the highest magnitude, and yet the single most pleasurable moment of her life. She fought the urge to climax all over his cock, not wanting this moment to end.

"Christ, you're tight, baby," he said, leaning over her back to pull her hair away from her neck. Dropping a kiss to the nape of her neck, he growled against her skin and she shuddered. He nipped at her shoulder, sinking his teeth lightly into her flesh, nearly sending her over the edge.

"Your pussy's squeezing me," he said against her cheek. "You wanna come on my cock, don't you?"

"Yes," she said through gritted teeth, trying to hold back the orgasm that threatened to spill. "Fuck me. Harder."

"Let it go, baby," he urged. "Come on me. You know I love it when you spread your sweet juices all over me."

She arched her back as the spasms wracked through her, then let out a loud moan of incredible pleasure, nearly unable to bear the orgasm that raged around his shaft. Pleasure pulses continued to well and peak until with surprise she yelled out again.

"Oh, God, Tony I'm coming again!"

He increased his thrusts. She shuddered beneath him, her mind awash in the sensations of the double orgasm. Barely able to breathe let alone speak, she let it flow through her, let the sensations take her along in a tidal wave of the most intense pleasure she'd ever experienced.

It took her a few moments to function again. Tony had slowed his movements, now pumping gently and slowly inside her. Her juices dripped down her legs, testifying to the intensity of her multiple orgasms.

"Mmm," he murmured, turning her chin to the side to press a kiss against her face. And still he moved inside her, relentlessly disciplined in his thrusts until she felt the tension build again.

"This time, I'm coming with you," he rasped, straightening and grabbing onto her sundress with his hand. His fingers dug into her sensitive flesh, which only served to heighten the sensation of pleasure his shaft provided.

He rode her hard, pumping his cock faster, his tight balls banging against her clit. She held back, knowing he was close, wanting to get there with him, until she felt him tense. Then she let go, allowing her orgasm to pull him more deeply inside her, her pussy milking him. He let out a wild moan as he came inside her and she bucked against him, wanting to squeeze every last drop out of him as he had done to her.

Morgan dropped to the warm sand and Tony eased on top of her, holding his

sweat-slickened body against her, but not pressing any weight upon her. Then he slid to the side and pulled her into his arms.

They lay that way for a while, both of them panting for breath in the steamy, humid air. The ocean waves crashed near the shore, the clouds parting to reveal a blistering hot sun.

"We're sticky and I'm covered with sand," she announced when she could finally manage to speak.

"Ditto. How about a little splash and play in the water?"

Her body craved the cool relief. Tony stood and hauled her up beside him, with one fluid motion pulling the sundress from her body. He grabbed her hands and ran for the waves. Morgan laughed loudly when he dove in with a belly flop.

They swam out a few yards, enjoying the refreshingly cool ocean water. Then they stepped onto the beach and grabbed their clothes.

"I suppose we need to go back to the house," he said, his voice tinged with regret.

"I guess so." Although the thought of living on the beach naked for the rest of their lives held more than a little appeal at the moment.

She turned to head back but his hand on her wrist stopped her. When she paused he pulled her into his arms and crushed her mouth with his, tangling his tongue with hers in a passion loaded kiss that spoke volumes without words.

"I know," she said, not certain if what they felt was the same thing, but knowing that they'd each experienced something monumental here on the beach. For her, it was an emotional renewal, a connection she never thought she'd feel with a man again.

For him, she wasn't certain, and was too afraid of finding out the answer to even think about asking.

Chapter Eleven

Tony paced his bedroom, knowing he'd have to go out there sooner or later. Morgan was waiting for him so they could head back to the resort.

Maybe spending all this time having sex with Morgan was scrambling his brain, but the longer he spent here, the closer he came to doing exactly what he swore he'd never do.

Get involved. Seriously, emotionally involved. How could he be so stupid? Morgan was a woman, just like any other. He'd never had any trouble fucking and forgetting one before.

No, he thought, running his hands through his hair. He was wrong. That was the problem. Morgan *wasn't* like any of the other women he'd known before. And that's why she'd wormed her way into his heart.

Shit. He didn't need this, didn't want it, and frankly, wouldn't have it. He did not want to have these *goddamn* feelings for her. Feelings led to attachment, attachment led to relationships and relationships were disastrous.

He'd simply gotten too close too fast with Morgan. He'd felt sorry for her when he'd seen her scars, and when she asked him to help he'd gotten all that juicy sex mixed up with emotion.

All she wanted from him was sex. All he could give her was sex.

Problem solved, right?

She'd never indicated she felt anything for him other than pure and simple lust.

So, what the hell was he worried about?

Ignoring the urge to hide in his room a little longer, he opened the door and searched for her, finding her outside near the pool.

She faced the ocean, the bright sunlight glinting off her red hair. She wore another one of those slinky sundresses that drove him mad with the urge to rip it right off her. Her well-shaped legs peeked out the

Jaci Burton

bottom of the dress, the wind whipping it up every now and then to show off a well-toned thigh.

Damn if just the sight of her didn't get him hard.

She turned when he stepped onto the veranda, and smiled at him.

"You ready?" she asked, sweeping the blowing hair away from her face.

Hell yeah he was ready. For more sex, not a trek to the resort. "Sure, let's go."

They hopped in the golf cart and Morgan maneuvered through the still wet trail, although the sun had mostly dried everything up. Now it was just blistering hot outside. He wore shorts and a tank top and even those felt like too many clothes. Wandering around the house naked with Morgan had spoiled him.

In more ways than just clothing.

She was quiet the entire trip. Then again, so was he. He knew what he was thinking about, but what about her?

"Something on your mind?" he finally asked.

She shook her head. "No. Just thinking about what I need to do at the resort."

"I'll try to stay out of your way."

"Nonsense." She turned to look at him, her gaze warm and inviting. "You're still here to do an article, and you've only seen one event."

Oh great, more sex events. So much for his decision to keep his distance from her. The two of them stuck together and forced to watch another erotic show wasn't going to help at all.

"What are you showing me today?" he asked, hoping it was something he found distasteful, like…like…well, hell. He really couldn't think of a single sexual act he wouldn't like.

"What do you want to see?" Her voice had gone all low and gravelly, the sound heading straight to his crotch and waking his penis from its exhausted slumber. *Shit.*

"Doesn't matter to me," he replied with a shrug, trying to appear cool and detached. Yeah right, like that was possible sitting next to a woman who smelled like sunshine and tropical flowers.

She frowned, then resumed driving without another word. When they arrived at the resort, she slipped out of the cart and headed right for her office. Tony trailed along as far as the lobby, then figured Morgan had a million things to do so he might as well look around a bit, maybe interview some of the support staff.

He found Morgan's assistant, Tara, in the lounge on a break. Wow. How had he missed seeing this woman? Mid-twenties, long raven hair streaming straight down her back, petite figure and the most gorgeous eyes he'd ever seen. A golden amber, they shimmered when she smiled. He introduced himself.

"Oh, you're the reporter that's interviewing Morgan this week?" she asked.

He nodded. "Yeah. Listen, do you have a few minutes? I'd like to ask you some questions."

She glanced down at her watch and then back at him. "I've got a few, sure. "

They sat at one of the lounge tables. "What can I help you with?" she asked.

"Are you from the islands?"

She laughed, a lilting, joyful laugh that brightened her entire face. "Hardly. I was born and raised in California, went to college at UC Berkeley and majored in marketing."

"So how did you get hooked up here?"

"I wanted travel and adventure. I started out marketing for a travel agency, which meant I got to visit vacation resorts. Since I had a few customers who were interested in more erotic vacation spots, I took the opportunity to tour several. When I came across Paradise I fell in love and never left."

"Fell in love with a guy?"

There was that laugh again. "God, no. That's the last thing I want. I'm career building. I mean I fell in love with the resort and Morgan was nice enough to hire me on as her assistant. Some day I'd love to own a place like this."

"Why?"

Her brows knit together. "Why, what?"

"Why would you want to own a place like this?"

"What's wrong with Paradise? It's open and free and I live a carefree existence far removed from the typical trappings of society. But you have to have a certain personality type to live in a place like this.

It's not for those who crave shopping malls and movie theaters and all the amenities of the big city."

"And you don't miss any of those things?"

"Nah. I've got everything I need right here."

"What about men?" Tony found it hard to believe an attractive woman in her twenties wouldn't be more into the social scene than her career.

"They're a nuisance. Use 'em and lose 'em is my motto."

Then it was his turn to laugh. Tara's motto sounded vaguely familiar.

"Oh hell, there I go shooting my mouth off again." She sighed and clasped her hands in her lap, smoothing imaginary wrinkles from her flowery sundress.

Damn, she had nice legs. Funny, though, sitting here with a beautiful woman like Tara didn't hit his sex buttons one bit. Obviously, Morgan had exhausted him.

"No problem. I just wanted to get a feel for some of the staff here, figure out what makes people want to work at a place like this."

"You mean because of all the sex?"

"Partly."

"That's easy. You have to be sexually adventurous to work at Paradise. As well as open minded." Her eyes narrowed for a few seconds before she added, "There are a lot of people with ridiculous provincial views on sexuality. One of the reasons I stay here. Anything goes."

"And do you partake of the sexual adventures here?"

A warm hand rested on his shoulder and he turned around quickly to find Morgan frowning down at him. "That's a bit of a personal question, don't you think?"

He smiled up at her. "Just doing my job."

Morgan turned her gaze to Tara. "I've gone through those contracts. They're on your desk to finalize."

Tara nodded and stood. "Nice to meet you, Tony," she said, then shook his hand with fervor before running off toward the offices.

Morgan took the seat Tara vacated. "Don't hit on my staff," she said, her displeasure clearly noted in the frown on her face.

"I wasn't hitting on your staff," he defended. "I was asking her some questions about living and working at the resort."

"Well, I don't appreciate you doing that without my knowledge. In the future, check with me first."

For some reason her irritation amused him. "Why? Are you jealous?"

Her eyes widened and she immediately shot back a retort. "Of course not! Why would I be jealous?"

"I don't know. You tell me."

She bent forward and whispered, "You and I are not involved other than sexually, and that's only for the duration of your time here."

Irritation prickled on his skin. "I see. So, in other words, what we've been doing together is purely physical, and the sooner it's over the better."

She lifted her chin. "That's not what I said."

"Hey, no problem with me." He'd been looking for a way to disentangle his emotions from Morgan. Here was his opportunity. "I think I've done more than enough to get you back to a sexual comfort zone."

Her eyes narrowed. "Fine. As far as I'm concerned, we can be finished now."

"Works for me. We're done." Now he was pissed. So much for 'thanks for helping me get through my aversion to sex'. They'd gone from intimate sharing of sexual pleasures to done-and-over-with in less than a day.

He felt used. If that thought wasn't so pathetic he'd laugh out loud. He'd never met a guy who wouldn't sell his soul to be used sexually by a beautiful woman. What an idiot he was. He looked for Morgan for a response, but she'd closed her emotions and he couldn't read her. Her lips were tight, her shoulders thrown back as she stood.

"I've got work to do," she said, her gaze not meeting his. "I'll pick you up at the front desk in an hour. Choose the adventure you'd like to tour."

After she walked away he was half tempted to *participate* in some sexual adventure. That would show her he had no feelings for her. Problem was, he wasn't the slightest bit interested in having sex with any one, or two or three for that matter, other women.

He really was pathetic. The only woman on his mind was Morgan.

* * * * *

Morgan viciously applied her signature to the documents in front of her. She could barely hold the pen because her hands were shaking.

How like other men Tony was. She should have known better. Put an attractive woman like Tara in front of him and he was hitting on her before the sheets on *her* bed were cold from their lovemaking.

Correction. It wasn't lovemaking they'd shared. It was sex. Fucking, to be more precise. After their beach sex this morning, Morgan had realized she was in trouble. Falling headlong into emotional attachment to Tony. And that couldn't be. She'd stood outside and watched the ocean after that, contemplating how to break things off between them. She couldn't—wouldn't—fall in love with him.

And now it looked like she'd made the right decision. To him, she was another notch on his keyboard, and that was all she'd ever be.

She lifted her head and smiled when Tara knocked softly on her open door. "Come on in," she said.

Tara chewed her bottom lip. "I need to talk to you about earlier."

Raising a brow, Morgan motioned Tara to sit in the chair across from her desk. "Sure. What's up?"

"I wasn't flirting with Tony Marino, honestly."

Watching Tara wring her hands together nervously, Morgan said, "I didn't think you were."

"I know, but you seemed so upset and I didn't want you to think I would ever hit on your man."

"He's not my man." Never was, never would be.

Tara tilted her head. "I thought you two…"

"You thought wrong. Really, Tara, you have nothing to worry about. I was merely trying to keep him from asking you too many personal questions."

Tara relaxed her shoulders and smiled. "You know me, Morgan. I talk too much, anyway. He wasn't asking. I was over-volunteering information."

Morgan wasn't buying it. She knew Tony was a hard-hitting journalist and would pry as much as he could get away with. Either way it didn't matter. He hadn't been given the opportunity to bug Tara for too long.

"I'm glad he didn't make you feel uncomfortable, then," she said, hoping to end the conversation by returning to her paperwork.

"He sure is good looking."

Morgan's head shot up and saw Tara's grin. "Yes, he is."

"Great body, too."

Didn't she know it. Every square inch of it, in fact. "I guess so."

Tara pursed her lips and raised a brow. "And you're not involved with him?"

"No."

"Well, why not? He's perfect for you, Morgan. Smart, handsome and funny. You really need to find someone."

Morgan set the pen down and laced her fingers together on top of the papers. "Why do you think that?"

"Because you're lonely."

This was something new. Tara had never gotten personal with her before. Friendly, always, but never pried into her personal life. "I'm not lonely."

Tara's lips crooked into a half smile. "Yeah, you are. You just don't know it. We're all lonely. Unless you have someone, we're all kind of isolated here."

"Then why don't you find someone?"

Tara turned her gaze to the window behind Morgan. "Some people aren't meant to have a someone."

Yes, Morgan thought. Some people like her.

Returning her gaze to Morgan's, Tara said, "But I think you have found someone. And if he's the right someone, don't let him go."

Morgan thought about what Tara said as she headed out of her office to meet Tony.

Had she been giving off signals? Somehow Tara had gotten the impression that Morgan had some sort of relationship with Tony.

Okay, maybe she did look at him more than she'd ever looked at another man at the resort. And maybe they had been spending a lot of time together the past several days, but that was due to his job. He was there to interview her, after all.

Right. Like there'd been any interviewing going on. No, her time and attention hadn't been spent on Tony the journalist. She'd been focusing on Tony the man.

For someone who'd always managed to keep her personal life personal, she'd been doing one damn lousy job lately.

Spying Tony loitering at the registration desk, her heart thudded against her chest. As it did each and every time she saw him. He was such a beautiful man, so tall, dark, roguishly handsome.

Hell. No wonder Tara suspected something was going on. She was all but drooling as she approached Tony.

He offered a tentative smile. "You ready?"

She nodded, distracted by the memories of his body on hers.

"If this is a bad time…"

"No, it's fine. Have you decided which event you'd like to check out?" She tried to keep her tone impersonal. They'd officially ended their intimate relationship, and Morgan was going to make damn sure they didn't pick it up again before he left.

"Yeah. How about Sensuous Spanking?"

Why did it have to be that one? "Fine. Let's go."

She turned, but Tony's hand on her arm stopped her. "Is this event going to bother you?"

When she didn't respond, he added, "You know? Personal memories and all?"

She shook her head. "Not at all. Follow me."

Bother her? Attending Sensuous Spanking would bother her all right. But not in the way he thought.

Chapter Twelve

Admittedly, Tony had purposely chosen Sensuous Spanking because he knew Morgan might be turned on by watching. Perverse, he knew, but he couldn't help himself. Men and their egos were nothing to fuck with. Since he was like most men, his ego resided in his pants. And she wasn't currently fucking with it in a fun way.

Which annoyed him. And shouldn't. It was his idea too to cool things down between them.

Then again, watching her backside sway seductively as she walked the path in front of him, he began to wonder if he'd made a huge error in ending things too quickly with Morgan. Surely he could enjoy some simple sex with her for the next couple days without getting emotionally involved, couldn't he?

She stopped in front of a small house with a thatched roof, the windows darkened with some kind of film so people walking by couldn't look in. Her hand reached for the doorknob, then hesitated.

Smiling innocently at her, he asked, "Something wrong?"

Sucking in her lower lip for a second, then letting out a sigh, she shook her head. "No, everything's fine. "

It took him a few minutes to adjust to the darkness inside. Candles seemed to provide the only illumination in the small foyer. Morgan nodded to the woman at the doorway, then took Tony through.

A long hallway led to various doors, with mirrors lining the walls. As Tony stepped past the first door he noticed the mirror was actually glass. He could see into the room. A very tall, very slim, leather clad dominatrix stood in the middle of a room equipped with paddles and whips. A naked man was bent over a stool, and the woman was lightly paddling his ass. The man sprouted a huge hard-on, so he must like it.

Whatever floats your boat, he supposed. He'd never been spanked, didn't think he'd want to be. Never spanked a woman before, either. Number one, because he didn't get off on hurting someone, and two, no woman had ever asked him to.

111

He turned toward Morgan, who inclined her head to indicate they would keep walking.

"This one looks good," she said, stopping in front of another window.

Tony peered in to find a man, this time, dressed in leather pants and no shirt. His spectacular muscles were either oiled really well to showcase them in the subdued lighting, or he had already worked up a huge sweat. A nude woman reclined over the man's lap. Instead of using a paddle, the man swatted the woman's backside with his bare hands. Imprints of his palm could be seen on the woman's very red ass.

Morgan pressed a button, which allowed them to hear the woman's moans and cries. Although she squealed when the man smacked her, she followed her squeals with moans that didn't sound like moans of pain. Her pussy was glistening with moisture, and after every few swipes of his hand on her ever-reddening ass, the man caressed the petals of her vaginal lips.

Clearly, the woman enjoyed the hell out of her spanking.

Tony chanced a look in Morgan's direction, watching the rise and fall of her breasts against the thin material of her dress. Her erect nipples poked against the silk during each rapid inhalation. Her tongue snaked out to lick across her top lip.

Watching her obvious excitement at the scene had him hard in an instant. He shifted so his erection wouldn't be so blatantly obvious. Then again, no one else was in the hallway except for one burly looking guy in a Paradise Resort t-shirt that Tony assumed was staff.

He stepped back a few inches and sidled closer to Morgan. Close enough to smell her flowery fragrance, so subtle yet invading his senses until all he thought about was her. Close enough to hear her breathing, the quick little pulses telling him the scene turned her on.

Funny, the scene itself didn't excite him nearly as much as Morgan's interest in it.

"You like what you see, don't you?" he whispered in her ear.

She hesitated for a few seconds before responding with a quiet, "Yes."

His penis raged against his shorts, demanding he take what he so desperately wanted.

Screw his stupid male pride. He wanted her. If only for another day, another hour, it didn't matter.

"Does it bother you to watch, considering what you went through with your ex?" he asked.

She shook her head. "No. It's...different, somehow. Richard knows exactly how much pressure to apply to our guest so that he doesn't truly hurt her. And she's enjoying the pain. It brings her pleasure."

"Did pain bring you pleasure, Morgan? Before David hurt you?"

"Yes."

"Do you ever think you'll be able to enjoy that pain like you used to?"

"I...I don't know. It scares me a little, thinking about it. And yet..."

"And yet you want it," he finished for her.

"Yes."

"Let me give it to you."

She turned her head and met his gaze. Her eyes were glazed with desire, and he knew he'd guessed right. She was excited.

But she also hesitated, and he knew why. The same reason he hesitated. Because they both knew something was happening with them. Something that went beyond sex and into emotional territory neither of them wanted.

He'd given up on holding back from her. And apparently she had too, because she nodded. "All right."

"Let's go. I've seen enough." He grasped her hand and led her down the hallway and outside.

"Where are we going?" she asked.

"To give you what you want" He pulled her quickly along the path.

"I can't, Tony," she said, yanking at his hand to let her go. "I'm working."

"You're done working for the day." He stopped and turned to her. "I want you, Morgan. Anyway you want it, regular or with a little kink, it doesn't matter to me. But I need to sink my hard cock into you until I can't tell where I end and you begin. And I want it right now."

Her shuddered breath told him she needed it as much as he did. "Fine. Let's go, then."

"Where? Home?"

"No. Too far. I know a place."

Then it was her turn to take the lead. He followed her along the path until they diverted into the forest. They must have walked in silence for fifteen minutes or so before he saw another path pop up. In front of them was a little building that couldn't house more than one or two rooms, at most. It stood no more than a hundred yards from the beach, and yet was completely surrounded by the forest so one couldn't see the house from the water.

"What is this place?" he said, following her determined steps to the door.

"A hideaway. "

"For guests?"

"No. For me." Without further explanation she opened the door and he stepped inside.

It was a cozy little place, with a small living area and a bed nestled in the corner of the room.

Morgan whipped around and faced him. "What's between us is purely physical, right?"

"Yeah," he answered, not really sure if that was the truth, but not wanting to delve too deeply into emotional areas he'd already worked hard to block off.

"I wanted to make that clear."

"You just did. Perfectly clear." Ignoring the stab in the vicinity of his heart, he grasped her upper arms and pulled her against his chest. "Morgan, do you trust me not to hurt you?"

This time she didn't hesitate at all. "Yes."

"Then tell me what excites you. Tell me what you need."

She wound her arms around her neck and pressed close, her thighs brushing against his, her mound meeting his erection. She moved lightly, teasing him. "I told you before there were things I liked."

"Spankings, being tied up?"

"Yes."

"Do you want me to spank you?"

"I think I do."

The hesitant look on her face concerned him. "Morgan, I don't want to hurt you, or remind you of anything bad from your past. You don't have to do this."

"Yes, I do," she replied, her gaze never leaving his. "I'll never be free of David's torment until I exorcise what he did to me. How he turned what could have been pleasure into pain. He twisted what should have been love into a nightmare of horrors."

She was right. She would never be free to truly be herself again until she experienced everything that she used to love—every sexual experience that her ex turned against her.

Including spanking.

Tony thought long and hard about it, fearful of doing anything that might hurt her or set her sexual progress back. But the way she ground her mound against his aching hard-on drove him nuts.

He looked down at her, her lovely face framed by that wild, red hair. So untamed, primal, just like the woman. He grasped her wrist and dragged her over toward a small chair in the living area.

"This is what you want," he said, "then this is what you get."

He took her mouth in a hard kiss, releasing the pent up frustrations of wanting her and not having her, of knowing that what they shared was temporary. She met his tongue willingly, tangling and mating while she wound her fingers through his hair and pulled him even closer.

He slipped his hands down over her ribs, pressing his erection against her wriggling thighs.

He sat and pulled her across his lap, trying not to flinch when her chest hit his legs and her breath rushed out with a whoosh.

"Before I start, one rule—you say 'stop', and I stop instantly. You got that?"

"Yes."

He looked at her like this for a few seconds, loving the feel of her warm belly across his legs, the way her hair swept against his thighs in this position, her long legs showcased for him.

Running his palms against her back, he took things slowly at first, feeling her muscles tense when he brushed the location of her scars, knowing she was remembering how they got there.

Slowly he lifted her dress, watching as first her thighs were revealed, followed by her rear end. That perfect, lush, ass. The one he liked to grab on to when he fucked her.

Her breasts dangled over his thigh. He ran his hands over the twin globes, squeezing them, feeling her shudder against him. He slipped the fingers of his other hand down between the cleft of her rear until he found that sweet spot between her legs. She moaned when he circled his fingers around the moist lips, then found her erect clit and flicked the hard nub with his thumb.

Morgan laid there, her body tense. He left his hand near her mound, alternately sweeping his fingers over her clit and dipping lightly into her vagina, feeling it contract around his fingers.

The other hand palmed her buttocks, gently squeezing them. Then, he lightly smacked her bottom, tensing when she gasped, waiting for her to tell him to stop.

She didn't. She raised her ass higher as if to let him know she liked it.

He brought his hand down on her ass again. She flinched, then moaned. Wetness poured from between her legs onto his hand. Red welts sprang up on her cheeks.

And Morgan whimpered, silently begging for more with every wriggle of her fine ass.

The strange thing was, he liked it, too. And that he hadn't expected.

Hearing her cries of pain and delight, knowing she enjoyed every swat to her ass, realizing how much it turned her on, excited him in ways he'd never before experienced.

He felt no sense of awesome power over her. Dominating her wasn't his idea of good sex. But how the spanking excited her — now that was damned hot. So hot his cock ached to be inside her.

Soon, very soon, it would be. As soon as he got her off. And judging from the way she moaned and squirmed against him, it wasn't going to be long.

* * * * *

Morgan could barely stand the feel of Tony's hand whacking her bottom. Not that she didn't like it. No, that wasn't it at all. She liked it so much she was ready to come all over his hand.

Gone was the fear associated with the act. Tony was so distinctly different from David that she felt no fear, none of the old memories resurfaced. It wasn't the act itself that had frightened her before, it was her partner. Tony would never hurt her, which allowed her to relax and enjoy this little bit of kink as she had before.

The stinging swipes of his hand against her ass only made her wetter, only made her insides grab on to his finger as if it were his cock, pulling it inside, squeezing, aching, needing release right—now!

With a mewling cry she let loose her orgasm, feeling it soar through her like never before. She clenched her fingers around Tony's legs and rode out the ecstasy, his fingers pumping inside her and bringing forth more pleasure than she thought she could bear.

As soon as she relaxed against him he pulled her up and cradled her in his arms, then swooped his mouth down over hers in a devastating kiss that left her breathless all over again.

She'd done it—she was free. Feeling the last remnants of hesitancy fly out the open window, she smiled at the man who had so carefully brought her back to the land of the living.

"Thank you," she said.

He smiled at her and raised a brow. "No, thank you. That was fun. And you certainly seemed to enjoy it a lot."

"Indeed I did." His erection pressed against her slightly stinging buttocks. "I see we need to provide you some relief, now."

"If you insist."

"Oh yes, I definitely insist. Only this time, I want you to tie me up and have your way with me."

The shocked expression on his face brought a grin to hers.

"Say that again?" he asked.

"Tie me to the bed over there, and do whatever you want to with me. Make me your love slave."

Seeing his eyes darken, knowing what was going through his mind, all the possibilities, aroused her all over again. She reached for her breasts and circled her nipples with her thumbs.

"Shit, Morgan, I'm about to burst right now."

"Then burst away. Only tie me up first, and do what you want to me."

He reached down and caressed his shaft, outlined clearly against his shorts. "Come here, then," he said, leading her toward the four-poster bed.

"There are some restraints in the nightstand drawer," she said, then explained when he looked at her quizzically. "I kept them to remind me of what I used to have and how easily I could be hurt. I don't really know why I did. Maybe I hoped that some day, some how I could be whole again, that I could be the sexually free person I used to be. All I know is I want you to use them on me."

He sucked in a breath and blew it out. "You drive me crazy, Morgan."

Not any more than he did to her.

"Take off that dress, " he commanded.

She reached for the straps and slowly, seductively, slid them down her arms, baring first her breasts, then her belly. Lowering it to her hips she gave him a wicked smile before dropping it to the floor.

"Get over here and lie on your back." He uttered the command in a harsh and breathless tone. His excitement thrilled her, made her wet, made her ache for his hard cock slamming in to her. She did as she was told and he grabbed the rope and tied her to the four posters.

She wriggled as she lay there spread-eagled on the bed, excitement swelling in her breasts and between her legs. Tony touched himself while he stood next to the bed watching her.

For what seemed like an eternity he stared down at her, his eyes dark and full of desire, his hand grasping his thick shaft over his shorts and squeezing it. Morgan fought against the restraints, not because she was afraid, but because she wanted him near her, on her, in her.

Now.

Tony fought for breath at the vision before him. His cock twitched, aching for release. He wanted to spill his come inside Morgan now.

And he wanted to spend a couple hours just gazing down at her naked body tied spread-eagled to the bed. He stroked his shaft. Morgan's pussy glistened in the late afternoon light, wet from her previous orgasm, her body wriggling with excitement.

"You ready?" he asked.

"Yes," she panted, lifting her hips.

"You going to do whatever I want you to?"

"Yes," she said again, clearly excited. Her nipples stood up in two points, begging for his mouth to cover them, suck on them until she begged him to fuck her.

God, he'd love to do that right now. But he wanted to please her first. And pleasing her meant taking command.

Quickly he dropped his shorts to the floor and stood beside the bed, stroking his shaft.

"Does watching me touch it turn you on?" he asked.

"You know it does." Her gaze was riveted to his penis.

"It makes me hot when you watch."

She smiled.

"It'll make me hotter to watch you suck it." He climbed onto the bed and knelt beside her head. "Suck me, baby."

Without hesitation, she opened her mouth and he slid the tip near her waiting tongue. She lapped up the drop of moisture from the head, and he shuddered at the feel of the warm wetness.

Knowing she couldn't grasp his penis and pull it toward her mouth, he straddled her, kneeling on either side of her face, and slid his shaft inside her open mouth.

Watching her take his cock in deeply, feeling the heat surrounding him, knowing she was at his mercy and it excited her, nearly set him off. But he held back, tensing up, keeping the inevitable release at bay.

"That's good, baby, suck it like that."

Her gaze focused on his face, the intensity of her look more than adding to an already intense erotic experience.

"My balls are tight, filling with come. I'm close. Tell me where you want it," he said, withdrawing to let her speak.

"Wherever you want to put it," she responded.

One last time he slid into her hot mouth and stroked it as far back as he dared. She took him all willingly and without complaint. When it was obvious he couldn't wait any longer, he pulled out, knowing exactly where he wanted to spill his seed when the time came.

He untied the restraints and lay on top of her, slipping his shaft inside her with one quick thrust. She wrapped her arms and legs around him, pulling him tighter against her.

They were eye-to-eye, nose-to-nose, and mouth-to-mouth. He kissed her delectable mouth, his tongue keeping rhythm with the thrusts of his cock. She let loose whimpers of pleasure into his mouth, and in return he gave her a groan of delight. She was so tight, felt so perfect, he knew at that moment that she was made for him.

When she tightened around him and let loose a howl as her orgasm ripped through her, he went right along with her, knowing at the moment he spilled inside her that no matter his intentions, no matter his denials, he'd fallen hopelessly in love with Morgan.

Chapter Thirteen

Morgan lay snuggled tight within Tony's arms, never having felt more content than she did at this moment. Listening to his heart thrum steadily against her ear, she sighed and scooted closer, rewarded when he grasped her tighter against him.

He'd long ago fallen asleep. After their lovemaking, after he'd held her, kissed her, made sure she hadn't suffered any ill effects from being restrained. After they'd returned to the resort so she could tie up any loose ends, and after they'd returned home and made love once again.

Ill effects? On the contrary, she'd found more pleasure in those moments with Tony than she'd experienced in her entire life. That's when the realization hit her—she was in love with him. It didn't matter that she'd told him point blank there could be no emotional involvement between them. Nor did it matter that he was leaving tomorrow.

How had it happened? How had this foray into sex turned into something deeper, so deep the thought of losing him carved a hole in her heart, making her ache with the loss already?

And more importantly, should she tell him how she felt? She could imagine the results if she did. He wouldn't be able to pack fast enough. He'd made it quite clear he wasn't interested in a long-term relationship with her, that his life, his love, was traveling the world to get the next story.

Tony's story about Morgan was over. It was time for him to move on.

And because she loved him, she was going to let him go. She didn't want him leaving with any regrets that he'd hurt her, that he'd somehow misled her into thinking he felt more than he actually did. Her feelings for him were of her own creation, and she'd deal with it on her own.

After all, she'd been on her own for years now. She'd adjust to life without him.

Yeah, right.

Now wide awake, she quietly slipped out of bed. It was very late, but she might as well do a little picking up while insomnia took hold. Maybe start some laundry.

She could sleep after he was gone.

What else would there be to do?

The house was so quiet as she tiptoed through the rooms, picking up things and gathering clothes. She stepped into Tony's room, figuring she'd wash his clothes with hers.

The beep of his personal fax machine caught her attention. A pile of papers had slipped off the machine on to the floor, and she bent to pick them up and lay them on the desk.

She hadn't meant to look, but her eyes strayed to the sender. The subject line made her shake all over.

The fax was from a Delbert Watkins, Private Investigator. The subject was entitled "Detailed Investigation on Morgan Brown."

She put the paper on the desk and stared down at the cover page, unable to believe her eyes. It was marked "Highly Confidential, for Tony Marino only." She shouldn't read it. Then again, it was about her. But what about her?

Unable to resist, she turned to the next page and read until she'd finished. By then her stomach rolled and she felt like she might be sick. Every sordid detail of her past, including David's full name, his family background, her family background, even former addresses and childhood friends was listed there.

He'd found everything about her. Everything. The man was thorough, she had to give him that. Every one of her dirty little secrets. Tony had found everything he'd come looking for, and then some.

And in the meantime, he'd skillfully gained her trust, even fucked her. Wouldn't this story look great in the tabloids?

She'd fallen in love with him, and he'd used her to gain information, to get a fucking story! How could he do this to her? He was no better than David had been. Manipulating her, bending her, twisting her inside out only to whip her raw.

Despite the humidity she shivered, completely cold inside. Remembering the times Tony had so easily taken her any way he wanted to made her want to crawl under her desk and curl up in a ball.

Her immediate thought was to run. Pull up stakes and take off where no one could find her, least of all David. Once the news leaked out he'd have access to her again. Even David had no idea where she was. Neither did her family. Soon, everyone would know.

She fought back the tears, letting the fury take over. Grabbing the fax off the desk she stormed out of his room.

She'd been screwed once, and let it happen. Never again.

* * * * *

Tony sat upright in bed, his hand immediately reaching for Morgan but finding the space next to him empty.

Where was she? He glanced at the clock. Three in the morning. Maybe she was outside. He stepped outside but didn't see her. The house was dark, no lights were turned on either in front or in back.

So where the hell was she?

He heard noises in the kitchen and found her slamming a cup and bottle of rum onto the counter, then spilling half the contents as her shaking hands poured the liquid into the glass.

"Morgan?" he asked.

She didn't answer.

"What's wrong?"

"As if you didn't know." She turned and grabbed a handful of papers from the counter and thrust them at his chest. He reared back, unprepared for the venom in her words, and scanned the papers she'd all but thrown at his face.

He felt the blood drain from his face and sat down in the nearest chair.

Watkins' report. Fuck. He'd forgotten all about sending out queries for investigating Morgan's background. He should have called the investigator, told him to cancel his search. He'd been so wrapped up in Morgan he'd forgotten all about asking Watkins to investigate her.

"I can explain this," he began.

"Don't bother. I'm pretty damn smart and I can read. I know exactly what that is."

"No, I don't think you do." He stood and stepped toward her. She stepped back.

Okay, explain first, touch her later. "Morgan, I asked for that report before I knew you, before I—" Shit. He'd almost said "Before I fell in love with you." Doubtful she'd believe that right now. He could hardly believe it himself.

"Before what? Before you manipulated me, used me, fucked me in more ways than one?"

"No, that's not what I was going to say." He had to tell her, had to make her understand that he would never hurt her.

She crossed her arms and smirked. "You know what? I don't really care what you have to say. But you can listen to me. Pack your stuff and get out of my house. Now."

No. It couldn't end this way. He wouldn't let it. He stood and reached out for her. "Morgan, let me explain."

But she backed away and folded her arms across her middle. "Don't touch me. Don't ever touch me again. Pack. Get out. Now. I'll be waiting in the cart. You can stay at the resort until the bus comes tomorrow to take you to airport."

Tony inhaled and blew out a breath, hurt and frustrated that he couldn't make her believe he hadn't meant for this to happen. As he watched her closed expression, he knew no amount of arguing would help. He left to go pack, throwing on clothes and jamming his things into his bag. He didn't have much so it didn't take long. When he came out Morgan, true to her word, was waiting in the golf cart, refusing to even look at him.

They drove to the resort in silence. When she stopped in front and waited while he retrieved his bags, she said, "I already called ahead. There's an available office for you to stay in until mid morning when the bus comes."

"Fine." He started to step out but then stopped and turned to her, ignoring the fact she wouldn't even turn her head in his direction. "I'm sorry I asked Watkins to investigate you. I want you to know that nothing in that report will ever be printed."

"Right."

"It's too bad you don't trust me enough to believe in me. I thought we were way past that point in our relationship. I guess I was wrong."

She hesitated for a second before saying, "We don't have a relationship, and no, I don't trust you. You've given me plenty of reason not to."

Nothing he could say or do would convince her. He already knew that. "I'm sorry, Morgan. I'm..." Useless, he reminded himself. He stepped out of the cart and headed up the stairs to the lobby, refusing to turn around when he heard the cart drive away.

* * * * *

Morgan fought back tears that had threatened to fall for hours, determined that she'd shed not a single one for a man who would so callously hurt her as Tony did.

She'd thought she'd loved him. Loved him! What an idiot. Would she never learn that men were not to be trusted? That there was no such thing as the man of her dreams, or true love?

How could she have been such a lousy judge of character? Why couldn't she see through people to the lies underneath? Was she so desperate for love and affection she'd been blind to Tony's true nature? It just didn't seem possible that he was that good an actor. Maybe he wasn't. Maybe she'd just seen what she wanted to see.

Either way, it was over, and once again she'd learned a very valuable lesson. She'd come to Paradise to live alone, so that men like him couldn't hurt her. For the rest of her life she'd remember there was a reason she'd chosen a life of solitude.

Glancing at the fax on the corner of her desk, she chewed her lower lip, wondering why Tony had left it on her kitchen table, and what had possessed her to snatch it up and bring it here to work? Why hadn't she given it back to him before he'd left?

Left. She glanced at the clock on the wall across from her desk. By now Tony should be back on the mainland, no doubt rushing to write his story and meet the deadline so he could dish the dirt on Morgan's past for the world to see.

He'd make a fortune publishing that story in the tabloids. David Randall was a prominent New York lawyer. The scandal would be huge. And then David would come after her, to punish her, to make her pay for breaking their bargain.

She grabbed the fax and forced herself to read it again, clutching her stomach as the pain stabbed at her. When would the story hit? Tabloids were done weekly, and with a hot topic like this one it wouldn't surprise her to see it in next week's National Inquisitor.

She'd be ruined. Paradise would go down the tubes, no one would want to come here, and worst of all, David would find her and develop some way to torture her, even though he'd promised he wouldn't.

David's promises meant nothing. She'd been lucky to live in peace for the past three years. Once he found out where she was, she knew he wouldn't be able to stay away. He owned her, he'd told her that often enough.

Dropping her head into her hands, she thought long and hard about what she could do, then an idea hit. She picked up the phone and quickly dialed the number of the investigator listed on the fax cover sheet.

A sharp voice answered, "Watkins here."

Morgan swallowed back her nervousness and said, "Delbert Watkins?"

"Yeah?"

She paused, then managed, "I need to speak with you about this fax you sent Tony Marino about me."

"Who is this?"

Cringing at his angry tone, she replied, "Morgan Brown."

Now it was his turn to pause. "I see. What can I do for you, Ms. Brown?"

"I want to know where you got the information you reported to Tony."

"I don't reveal my sources. Anyway, it doesn't—"

"I don't care whether you reveal them or not," she interrupted. "I want to know. There are facts in here that no one but my ex-husband and I know about."

"Look, Ms. Brown," he started, his voice now calmer and much more friendly, "You know I can't reveal my sources. And anyway, as I was about to explain, I already got the word from Tony."

"What word?"

"He called me in the middle of the damn night to tell me to shred the report, that he wasn't going to use it. So your follow up call isn't necessary. The data is history now."

Morgan sat stunned, unable to speak. Her limbs shook and her throat went dry. Finally, she managed, "He what?"

"I thought you knew. He said to shred the documents. It's all gone. Nothing will ever be reported about you. And you know damn well that as an investigator I can't reveal any information unless my clients want me to. So you're safe, Ms. Brown. Tony took care of that."

"I see. Thank you," she said quickly and hung up, not knowing what to make of that conversation.

She sat back in her chair and chewed her lower lip, her gaze repeatedly falling to the fax.

Tony had enough information on her and her past in that fax to write an entire book about her. Why wouldn't he use it? She didn't understand. Trying hard to recall their conversation last night, she seemed to remember he'd said he'd asked the investigator to dig into her background before he knew her, before he —

Something. But she'd cut him off and he never did finish his sentence. Before he what? Before he fell in love with her?

Ridiculous. Tony didn't love her, he couldn't. He wouldn't. He'd made it perfectly clear he wasn't interested in becoming emotionally involved with her. The idea that he'd somehow fallen in love with her was ludicrous.

As ludicrous as her falling in love with him had been? Oh God. She'd also said that love would never enter the picture, and look what had happened to her.

Did Tony love her? Correction. Had he loved her? Had he sacrificed a juicy story about her because of his feelings for her?

Her chest constricted and she fought for breath, realizing that she'd just made a huge mistake. A mistake that had cost her the man she loved.

He'd asked her to trust him, and she'd refused. He'd told her he wouldn't hurt her, and she didn't believe him. He'd done nothing to make her think he'd use that information, but her mind had been so poisoned by David that she'd refused to believe that a man could actually love her, that someone would really be honest with her.

Now what should she do? Try to find him and ask him to come back? Tell him how much she loved him and she didn't mean the things she'd said. Despite her attempts at ignoring him completely, she'd heard the pain in his voice when she refused to listen to his explanations, she knew how much she'd hurt him.

What good would it do to get in touch with him? He was a traveler, and she was destined to spend the rest of her life on this island. They had two differing lifestyles and she wouldn't ask him to give his up for her, nor would she even consider giving up this place she loved.

What a mess she'd made of things. She'd love to pass the blame to David for this, but she couldn't. This was entirely her doing. Her inability to believe in Tony had taken away her last chance at love and happiness.

For the first time in over three years, she let the tears flow freely, no longer caring to hold them back.

Chapter Fourteen

There was no point sitting in a dark house and pouting. Morgan stood and paced her bedroom, unable to even settle in and sleep, despite the fact she hadn't slept in over twenty-four hours.

She missed Tony, missed his warmth, his laughter, the way he teased her, the gentle way he'd brought her back to life again. With an unearthly amount of patience he'd allowed her to explore her sexuality, giving her the freedom to set the pace and the rules, until she'd come back fully, able to explore all the sexual positions and acts she'd enjoyed before David had taken those freedoms away.

Would she ever recover? Would she ever forgive herself for letting someone like him go? Would she ever find another man like him?

She already knew the answer to all those questions—no, no and definitely no.

With a resigned sigh she threw on her robe and stepped onto the veranda, hoping the fragrant night air would calm her as it always had before.

No such luck. Pain still coursed through her. Pain of loss, of regret, of knowing she'd let the man of her dreams slip through her fingertips as if he had never mattered to her.

Maybe a swim and a soak in the hot tub would help alleviate the tension. She walked to the pool, not even bothering to turn on the lights except for the one inside the pool wall. It was pitch black outside, not even a shining moon to light her way. How appropriate, since her light had left the island yesterday.

Shedding her robe she stepped down, the warm water lapping at her legs, then kicked off with her feet and sliced through the water, stopping in the middle of the pool to float on her back.

She stared into the utter blackness above her, feeling as void of light as the sky overhead.

"Morgan."

At the sound of a voice nearby, Morgan screamed in fright and righted herself, trying to make out the shape in the distance.

"Who…who's there?" she stammered, her heart pounding with an adrenalin rush of fear.

"I remember watching you the first time you swam in this pool. I was so mesmerized by your beauty I couldn't breathe."

Was her mind playing tricks on her? She squinted, unable to see anything except a dark form at the end of the pool.

"Are you going to throw me out, or let me talk to you?"

Her heart soared along with hope as she asked, "Tony?"

He swam toward her until his face was silhouetted by the faint light of the pool.

"Are you really here?" she asked.

"I never left the island."

"Why?"

"I couldn't."

"Why not?" She couldn't believe he was actually here, talking to her. She wanted to reach out for him, but was afraid any movement would send him vanishing into the dark night.

"Because I didn't get to explain, and it's important to me that you understand what I did, and what I didn't do."

"I have something to tell you, too," she said, swimming over toward him until their faces practically touched. She felt the warm swell of water over her belly as he treaded the water in front of her. "Follow me."

She couldn't blame him for the look of uncertainty on his face as he tentatively followed her to the shallow end, then stood in front of her. After all, she had thrown him out. Now it was up to her to make the first move, to let him know how she felt.

What if he hadn't come back to declare his love? What if he just wanted to satisfy his ego so that he could leave with a free conscience?

Oh, why did she continue to doubt? When would she stop hesitating and take a chance?

She knew when. Right now. She leapt into his arms and wrapped her legs around his waist, her arms circling his neck. Shock widened his eyes, but he twined his arms around her.

"I don't know why you came back, and I don't care. First, I want you to know something."

"Okay," he answered, his breath a warm, sweet caress against her cheek.

"I made a mistake in not trusting you, in not believing you. I should have, and I'm sorry. I'd like to blame David for making me wary, but really it was me. I couldn't believe you could care about me, that you wouldn't hurt me like David had. Tony, I'm—"

He silenced her with his finger to her lips. "I couldn't leave things between us like that. Not without you understanding why I did what I did, and what I didn't do."

His mouth hovered inches from hers. With every fiber of her being she wanted to press her lips against his, to reveal all that was in her heart. But she also sensed that he needed to speak first. "Go ahead."

"The thought of leaving the island nearly killed me. I knew as soon as I got to the airport I couldn't leave you. I can't sleep without you, I can't write without you, and I no longer want to live my life without you."

Her ears buzzed and she felt dizzy as his words penetrated.

"I love you, Morgan. So much so that the thought of ever leaving you makes me ill. I swore it wouldn't happen, but it did. And now that it did, I'll do whatever it takes to earn your trust."

She couldn't believe what she heard. "You already have earned my trust, Tony, only I was too stupid yesterday to realize it. I know you'd never hurt me. I'm one hundred percent convinced of it."

Then he did what she'd hoped he'd do. He leaned forward and kissed her, hard and with a passion she'd only dreamed existed. She tasted love on his lips, and it blended with her love for him. "I love you, Tony. With all my heart, and all my being, I love you."

He crushed her against him and buried his head in her neck, holding her that way for minutes while neither of them spoke. When he pulled back, his eyes so full of warmth and love she could barely catch her breath, she whispered, "But what about your career? You travel for a living."

He smiled. "Travel isn't as appealing anymore. Not if I have you to be with. I can write from here. Maybe even write that book my agent's been after me to write for years."

"Are you sure? Its okay if you travel on assignment. I don't want you to give up your career for me."

He reached up and caressed her cheek with his hand. "I'm not giving up anything. I'm moving in a new direction, something I've been avoiding for years. I blew off that book for a long time, thinking it would stick me in one place too long. But now, the idea of settling down has an appeal it never had before."

A blush warmed her cheeks, her heart leaping with joy at his words. "I think you could write a fabulous book."

With a grin, he said, "You know, I never thought I wanted to write a book. But my agent tells me I have talent and a lot of experiences to write about. I guess I just never thought of myself that way, but I can see the merits in giving it a try. Besides, I can still write no matter where I live. And the idea of being an island bum is suddenly very tempting."

She laughed and kissed him. "I see. A resort junkie, huh?"

He nodded. "Oh yeah. As long as I can realize my fantasies with the woman I love."

She watched his eyes darken with desire, knowing they reflected the need in hers. "You have all the control over your fantasies. Tell me what you want and your wish is granted."

He shook his head. "No, baby, you're the one with all the control here. My heart is in your hands."

For the first time in as long as she could remember, she cried in front of someone. But this time, she knew he wouldn't use her tears as a weapon. He caressed her cheek with his thumb and brought it to his lips, licking the tear off.

"I love you Tony, and I'll spend the rest of my life making you happy."

"Same here, babe. Let's start now."

Lifting her in his arms he carried her from the pool to the hot tub. The steamy water enveloped them as he held her close and kissed her, creating an internal heat that had nothing to do with the water around them.

"I've never made love in the hot tub, you know," she whispered against his neck, lightly nipping at his corded muscles.

He groaned and squeezed her hips, his penis hardening and pressing against her mound. "Your wish is my command," he said, flipping her around so that she held on to the edge of the tub.

Morgan spread her legs, welcoming his probing fingers into her heat. She moaned when he separated the folds of her vaginal lips and slid two fingers inside, pumping rhythmically until she felt dizzy with need. His other hand reached for her breasts, squeezing them and tweaking the nipples until she cried out, more than ready for him.

"Now, Tony, please," she cried, unable to bear a moment longer without him inside her.

"As you wish," he teased pressing his chest against her as he thrust his shaft inside. He bit down on her neck when he entered her, and she shuddered with the pain and pleasure.

She whimpered at the feel of his thick cock filling her, how he completed her, his repeated thrusts taking her near orgasm almost immediately.

"I'm gonna want to fuck you every day for the rest of our lives," he whispered against her neck.

"I hope so," she said, moaning when his fingers bit roughly into the tender flesh of her hips.

"Sometimes I'll spank you, tie you up, make you suck my cock until I come all over your face."

She could tell by his grunts and groans that he was as close as she was to fulfillment. "God, yes, Tony, I want that and more."

"I'll use your body to satisfy me, and then I'll satisfy you until you scream my name over and over again."

The pounding of his thrusts grew faster, harder. She felt the spasms building to a point of no return.

"I'm going to come," she cried, and he reached around to take her over the edge with his fingers, groaning as he spilled inside her simultaneously, their bodies sliding furiously and passionately together.

They collapsed against the side of the tub, Tony nuzzling her neck with soft kisses.

"Was that a quickie?" she asked when she could breathe again.

He laughed. "I think so. Sorry, but it had been an entire day since I'd had you."

She giggled. "I guess we'll have to make sure that doesn't happen too often, then. Because I like it long."

She felt his penis begin to grow inside her again.

"Long, huh?" he asked, lightly thrusting inside her.

"Mmm hmm, "she murmured, ready for him again.

He laced his fingers with hers and slowly pumped against her. "I promise to make everything last a long time for you, Morgan. Not just our lovemaking, but our marriage, if you'll have me."

She gasped, unable to believe he'd just proposed while he was inside her. But wasn't that just like Tony to do the unexpected? She smiled through tears of joy and pleasure. "Yes, Tony, I'd love to marry you."

As she and her fiancé made love a second time, this time slowly, with all their emotions and feelings poured into every touch, every caress, Morgan realized she'd truly found her paradise in the arms of the man she loved.

Epilogue
Six Months Later

Tony had a surprise for Morgan. One he'd been working on for several months.

She'd been so busy planning the wedding and attending to all those details, she hadn't even noticed the research he'd been doing, the e-mails to and from his private investigator.

But now everything was in place, the deed had been done.

And the best part was, her name wouldn't be drawn into it at all. Nothing about her would be revealed.

But David Randall? Oh yeah, he was screwed.

Tony smiled as he read the headlines in the New York Times.

"District Attorney indicted on Kidnapping and Sex Charges."

David Randall's grimacing face was spread all over the front page as he was led away in handcuffs from his office. Oh, the scandal. What would all his friends and relatives in the Hamptons think about their fair-haired boy now? Tony laughed.

It had taken some doing to get the goods on Randall. Shifty, sly, secretive bastard. But everyone had his weaknesses, especially perverts like David. And when he'd taken a woman across state lines for the purposes of holding her captive and playing his perverted sex games with her, that brought in the FBI.

When a friend in the FBI found out about what David had allegedly been doing, she went undercover. Gorgeous, voluptuous Vickie, always eager to put a slimeball away. And she reveled in this assignment, took David to the very edge with her innocent act. And then as soon as he tried to do to Vickie what he'd done to Morgan, she took him down.

Big time.

Oh yeah. Revenge was sweet.

"What are you grinning about?"

Tony looked up and smiled at Morgan, the sight of her never failing to take his breath away. For a sorry sonofabitch like himself, he'd sure gotten lucky to find a woman like her.

"I have a surprise for you."

Her dubious expression made him laugh. "Your surprises make me nervous."

"You know me too well. Now come here and sit on my lap."

She crossed the kitchen and settled on his lap, wriggling her delectable ass against his crotch.

"You're doing that on purpose to distract me."

"Uh huh." She bent and nibbled at the corner of his lip.

"Stop that."

"Nuh uh."

"I have something to tell you." He wound his arms over her silk-clad back, loving the feel of her body moving against her dress.

"Tell me."

"It's about David."

She stilled and looked at him. He waited to see the fear in her eyes, but all he saw there was wariness. "What about David?"

Tony handed her the newspaper. "Read."

She shifted off his lap and slid into the chair next to his, her eyes rapidly scanning the headlines. "Oh my God."

He didn't answer, just let her read and soak it all in. When she finished, her gaze met his. Tears pooled in her eyes. "It's over."

He nodded. "Yes, baby, it's over. That prick is going to jail for a very long time. He'll never come after you, never be able to hurt you again. And your name will never come up in this."

Her eyes widened. "You had something to do with this?"

"Maybe." He'd wondered what her reaction would be. Would she be angry at him? Probably. But he couldn't let that snake continue to hurt women like he'd hurt Morgan.

"How?"

"I have friends in high places. I really didn't do anything, just mentioned to a few people that he needed to be checked out."

"Didn't they ask how you knew?"

He grinned and reached for her fingers. They were icy cold. He rubbed them between his hands. "I'm a reporter. I don't have to divulge my sources. Besides, it didn't take long for the FBI to dig up dirt on David. He'd developed a relationship with a woman, met her, and ended up crossing state lines with her. When she went missing, they made the connection to David. They took the ball and ran with it after that. I knew it was just a matter of time before they figured it all out."

She shook her head and crawled back in his lap, wrapping her arms tight around his neck. "Thank you," she whispered.

"You needed to be free, baby. Completely free of him. Now it can be the two of us looking forward. You never have to look back again."

"I don't know what I did to deserve you," she said, pressing a light kiss on his lips.

He shuddered, his body warming, readying for her. "You loved me. That was all it took."

Tony lifted Morgan in his arms and carried her off to the bedroom. "You're going to be late for work today."

"I hope so," she answered, kissing his neck. "I hope I'm very, very late to work."

PARADISE DISCOVERY

DEDICATION

To my editor, Briana St. James, for encouraging me to put onto paper the strange worlds that live in my head.

To Mel, for always being around to listen and to brainstorm my wild ideas. You know I couldn't do this without you.

To my Paradise group. You make me smile every day. Thank you for spending your time with me.

To Tracey, and you know why. May your life always be a paradise.

And to Charlie, whose love makes all my fantasies come true. I will always follow you to the ends of the earth and beyond.

Chapter One

The balmy breeze lifted her hair and blew it across Isabelle's cheek. She smiled and looked out over the turquoise water, happy to be in the Caribbean again.

How long had it been since she'd stood with her toes buried in the warm sand, her gaze searching far into the horizon? Years, it seemed. The waters off Texas weren't the same as the sandy beaches of the Caribbean. The ocean not nearly as compelling or jewel-like.

She inhaled the salty air and squinted, her eyes focusing on an object in the distance. Something bobbed in the water, but Isabelle couldn't tell what it was. Scenes from her childhood on the beach in Puerto Rico flashed before her. She must have been thirteen or fourteen years old at the time. Back then she'd seen something too. Only it hadn't been some*thing*, it had been some*one*.

A very special someone. A man. She'd smiled at him, and he'd smiled back. He'd been the most beautiful man she'd ever seen, and she could have sworn she'd just seen him again.

Of course, that was impossible.

She lifted her hand to shield the setting sun from her eyes, but all she could make out was a glint of something on the ocean surface.

As a marine biologist, she should know everything that lurked in the warm waters of the Caribbean. Whatever it was, it wasn't a man.

It also wasn't a fish, that was for certain. Although she could swear it looked like a man's head. But that couldn't be since there were no boats nearby and it was too far out to be a swimmer.

She rubbed her hand against her lower stomach, a twinge of pain on the right side annoying her again. For the past day she'd felt little stabs of pain in the lower right of her stomach, but cast it aside as indigestion from the new foods she'd been eating at Paradise Resort.

It was nice of Morgan Marino, the owner, to let her occupy one of the bungalows on the far side of the island, considering she wasn't the least bit interested in the hedonistic activities that took place at the resort. She was here to do research, but certainly not the sexual kind.

Shaking her head at the various activities outlined in the brochure she'd seen earlier in the day, she dismissed the thoughts of sex running rampant on the other side of the island right now, and concentrated instead on the object in the distance.

It seemed to be watching her, but that was ridiculous. More likely it was a discarded piece of trash, maybe someone's beach ball or something, and in her weird mind she'd conjured up a man's head.

She hadn't thought about that episode in Puerto Rico for years, although she'd never forgotten the way the man had smiled at her. Every now and then the memories crept into her thoughts, especially when she stood at the water's edge and looked out over the white-capped sea.

Too bad she hadn't been close enough to really make out his face and features. She'd just known it was a man from the shape of the upper half of his body.

"Ouch!" She reached for her abdomen and caressed the pain that had grown sharper by the hour. She should know better than to eat rich food.

She pushed the discomfort aside as the object appeared again. The sun was now a bright orange glow, melting into the horizon and obstructing her vision of the mysterious object in the water.

Too small for a dolphin or whale, but about the right size for a sea turtle.

If she stepped into the bungalow to grab her dive gear she'd lose sight of it. She had to go into the water now and check it out. At least get closer so she could identify it.

It had to be a turtle. It couldn't be *him*. He didn't exist except in her childhood imaginings.

Shedding her wrap skirt, she walked into the water, thankful she practically lived in her swimsuit. The eighty-degree water soothed her aching muscles. That's what she got for lugging around suitcases filled with dive gear and instruments as well as her laptop. Good thing she didn't have much of a wardrobe.

She sliced through the ocean in quick strokes, keeping her eyes on the object that hadn't seemed to change locations. It almost seemed like it wanted to stay put so she could find it.

Ridiculous. Sea life wasn't that welcoming to humans. Even if it was a dolphin or a sea turtle, they'd swim in the other direction once they saw her coming, or at least change course.

Another fifty yards and she'd be there. It still hadn't moved, appearing and disappearing with the roll of the waves. She could almost make out its shape now as she drew closer. How strange. If she didn't know better she could swear it was a—

"Ow! Dammit to hell!" An unbelievable pain knifed through her side. Nausea bubbled up into her throat and she fought back the piercing stab that threatened to double her over.

Not now. Not in the water. She stopped and treaded, circling around to search for the shore. Damn, what an idiot she was. The pain pierced her and she could barely stay afloat. Despite the body-cooling water, she broke out into a full body sweat and began to pant.

Don't panic. Stay focused. She had to reach shore, had to get help. The pain seared hot and knife-like. She cried out, but no one heard her. No one *could* hear her. She was completely alone.

Making her way back to shore wasn't going to be nearly as quick as her swim outward. In fact, she could no longer stretch her arms over her head to make the strokes. Her feet wouldn't work.

Oh, God, all she wanted to do was curl up in a little ball and hold onto her side.

Someone please help. She wasn't ready to die. Not like this. Even though the ocean was her love, she didn't want to be buried here.

But she was already losing the fight, the agony too much for her conscious mind to bear. She slipped under the water, sucking in a quick breath and fighting her way back to the surface. It wouldn't do any good. Between the pain and the lightheadedness she was doomed.

Too dizzy to even think clearly, she prayed for forgiveness for the sins she'd committed during her life and hoped that drowning was as pleasant an experience as she'd read about. She inhaled deeply and held her breath as she lost control and spiraled downward into the abyss.

She wouldn't be able to hold her breath long. Her lungs expanded as she desperately tried to hang on, but failure was imminent. Her chest burned from the need to breathe. Opening her eyes, she took one last look at the rainbow of coral rising up to greet her. She sank into the depths and opened her mouth to inhale the water.

Her eyes fluttered closed and it was almost the slow fade of falling asleep, that brief moment between consciousness and unconsciousness. Between life and death.

Then, a sudden rush of water swirled around her. Instead of sucking in the salty ocean, a warm, full mouth covered hers and strong hands slipped under her arms, cradling her against a rock solid body. A man's body.

Was that a kiss searing her lips? It was. A kiss that sent life-giving oxygen sliding down her throat. She gulped in as much of it as she could take.

Maybe drowning really wasn't unpleasant. Maybe it was just like breathing. At least her mind registered that she was breathing air. The sensation of lips covering hers certainly wasn't unpleasant. It wasn't sexual, more of a soft, gentle layering of mouth over mouth. She'd never felt so protected, so cared for in her life. A strange, almost languorous feeling swept through her, as if everything was as it should be.

Everything but the pain that still cut through her side. Funny how that hadn't left her body yet. Wasn't death pain free? It still hurt, bad. Why wouldn't the hurt go away? She'd give anything for that.

A voice whispered in her mind. "Relax. I'll take the pain away."

Who spoke to her? The body holding her? She couldn't open her eyes no matter how hard she tried. It was all she could do to linger on the fringes of consciousness.

A hand palmed her lower stomach and a burning heat spread through her. She jerked upright, then relaxed immediately as the pain began to dissipate.

She was dying, the pain was going away and she was finally, blissfully dying. Her world slipped away and faded to nothing.

* * * * *

"You can't have her."

"I know," Dax replied to the voice of Ronan, the guardian of all the sea people. Dax didn't turn around—Ronan wasn't there. But his consciousness found Dax, as always.

"Then, why the interference?" Ronan asked. "You could have interfered in her destiny."

Dax glanced down at the dark-haired beauty resting in his arms, instinctively wanting to pull her closer, to protect her. "It wasn't her destiny. She swam out because she saw me. If I hadn't been watching her, she'd have sought help for her pain instead of swimming toward me."

Ronan laughed, a deep rumble that spread throughout the oceans. "You see only what you want to see. You are like so many of the other guardians. Why is it you're all so stubborn?"

"Maybe because we take after you?"

No response to that one. But Ronan was right. Dax shouldn't have watched her, shouldn't have lingered long enough for her to see him. But he'd known she was coming to the island, had felt her presence the moment she stepped foot on the sand. For someone who rarely approached land humans, this was a first for him. Despite the fact he knew he shouldn't get close, knew he shouldn't make his presence known, he couldn't stop himself.

Because of him, she'd nearly died out here.

What was he hoping would happen when she swam out to him? Was he even going to linger long enough to see her face to face?

He was such an idiot.

Once he realized she was in trouble, he'd made the swim in seconds, giving her the oxygen she'd so desperately needed. Then he felt her pain and removed it.

Now she slept, nestled tight against him, and he wanted to hold her there, never let her go.

But he couldn't do that. She was land and he was the sea.

He stepped out of the water, cradling the woman's unconscious form close to his chest. He didn't even pause at the gritty sand clinging to the bottom of his feet despite the fact he rarely ventured onto land.

The woman's even breathing and relaxed state led him to believe she'd recover from her ailment. Thankfully, he'd reached her the moment she took her first breath of ocean water.

Laying his hands between her breasts, he felt the clear exchange of oxygen through her lungs. No water inside.

"She'll be fine, Dax. Let her go. Walk away before she wakes and finds you."

Sometimes, having Ronan in his head was more than a little annoying. He laid the woman down on the beach. "I should take her inside the bungalow."

"No need for you to stay on land longer than necessary. Someone might see you."

Dax was reluctant to leave. "There's no one for miles out here. All the activity takes place on the other side of the island."

"You know too much about this place already. Your curiosity is not good. It takes away from your duties."

Dax turned and glared at the moonlit sea. "I've never failed in my duties."

"That's true, you haven't. But I worry about you. This attachment to a land human goes against everything we try to accomplish. You know there must be no contact."

"This woman lives for our oceans, Ronan, and you know that as well as I do. The sea is her life's breath, her love. She could be of use to us."

"We don't need land humans to help us. There are already too many that know of our existence. Don't make the mistake of thinking with your cock instead of your head, Dax. You desire the woman for yourself, for physical pleasure only. No wonder, considering how little contact you've had with the sea women here."

Right. Like he wanted to talk about his sex life with Ronan. Sometimes he hated big brothers, and he had way too many of them. "I have plenty of contact."

"Sex isn't enough contact, Dax, and you know very well what I'm talking about. You've lived nearly a century and still you don't have a life mate."

"You're one to talk. You're the oldest, our leader. I don't see a woman at your side, either."

Ronan paused before saying, "We're not talking about me today. We're talking about you."

"I've been kind of busy." He threaded his hands through his hair and blew out a sigh, tired of having this same conversation.

"It's time, Dax."

"I'm not going to choose the first sea woman I run into and you know that."

"I think the lure of the land humans blinds you to choosing a sea mate."

"I am not lured to the land humans. I just haven't found the right sea woman, yet. Give me time."

Ronan sighed, his thoughts disconnecting from Dax.

Finally.

Dax turned to the woman sleeping peacefully on the sand. Something about her called to him, compelled him to reach out to her even though he knew he shouldn't.

Like he had time for a dalliance with any woman, let alone a land female. But this human was different. He'd seen this one before on one of the other islands, many years ago when she was just a child.

The island they called Puerto Rico, he was certain he remembered right. She'd been no more a child of twelve or so Earth years, and he'd found her standing knee deep in the water, her mother watching behind her from the beach.

She'd seen him then, and smiled, her eyes a golden amber sparkling in the sunlight, her sable hair flying behind her in the breeze. Her beauty and innocence had struck him immediately, as had her instant psychic connection with him.

Then her mother had called her out of the ocean and she'd run off, but waved at him as she went.

That had been over fourteen years ago, and he had never stopped thinking about the girl who had found him despite his camouflage. And tonight she'd seen him again.

She'd grown into a beautiful woman. Her hair still shone like mink in the sunlight, and her eyes had widened like saucers when she'd spotted him. Had she felt it too? That connection like the sudden shock of an eel's charge?

Dreaming. He was dreaming about things that couldn't be. He was sea and this woman was land, and he had no more business standing in her world than she had swimming in his.

Besides, he had a job to do and he'd better get it done before Ronan jumped all over his ass.

With a resigned sigh, Dax stepped into the water and disappeared into the surf.

Jaci Burton

Chapter Two

Isabelle was floating. Weightless, water surrounding her, warm hands caressing her body to a fevered pitch.

She moaned and arched her breasts against greedy fingers that tweaked her nipples, making them rise and beg for a heated mouth to cover them. When lips closed over one distended bud she gasped, slipping her hand between her legs to massage the ache that grew in intensity by the second.

Desperately, she tried to open her eyes and see who touched her, who licked her, but she couldn't. It didn't matter, anyway. Abandoning her struggle to open her eyes, she immersed herself in the sensations of strong hands. A soft tongue licked at her breasts and slowly moved upwards toward her neck.

"I've waited a lifetime for you, Isabelle," the strange masculine voice whispered in her ear, taking the lobe between his teeth and nibbling lightly. She shivered and groaned.

Her pussy dampened, desperately needing release. She slipped her fingers between the moist folds and found the bud hidden there, lightly caressing it. Sparks of intense pleasure shot to her core. Spreading her legs, she slipped two fingers inside her pussy and thrust in and out, the delicious sensations making her shiver despite the heat surrounding her.

Oh, why wasn't he fucking her? She needed his cock to fill her. Where was he?

"I'm here, Isabelle," he murmured, his voice still no more than a faint whisper. His tongue bathed her nipples to hard peaks. "Touch yourself for me. I want to watch you come apart for me."

Unable to stop herself, she picked up her movements and pressed her breasts against his mouth as she plunged her fingers deeper inside, her thumb frantically rubbing against her swollen clit.

But still, she wanted more. Craved his cock inside her.

"Soon, Isabelle, but not yet. Now make yourself come for me."

At his command, she let go and moaned out her orgasm. A rush of juices soaked her fingers and she pumped repeatedly through her climax. When it was over, he kissed her lips softly, his tongue lightly teasing hers.

Isabelle struggled to open her eyes, shielding them from the bright sun with her hand. She was lying on the beach. Her swimsuit had been pulled to the side, her fingers still buried inside her pussy. Remnants of her orgasm still pulsed against her fingers.

Holy shit, she'd just made herself come in broad daylight!

She withdrew her fingers and sat up, guiltily scanning the area around her. Thankfully, she was alone on the beach.

A dream. She had dreamed the man with the husky voice coaxing her to touch herself. But she hadn't dreamed the orgasm she'd just had.

Reality mixed with fantasy in her fogged brain. She couldn't remember. What the hell had happened last night?

She looked out toward the calm turquoise sea.

The last thing she remembered was swimming out there, looking for something. Then the sharp pain in her side and slipping under the water. How had she ended up here?

She touched the spot on her side that had hurt so badly she couldn't stay afloat last night. A bit tender, but the pain was gone. How odd.

After a quick shower back at her bungalow, she trekked over to the hotel to pick up some supplies. Morgan had equipped her with a golf cart to ride back and forth from one side of the island to the other. Although the path was bumpy, the ride didn't take much time at all. Besides, it gave her an opportunity to think about the night before.

Had she dreamed the warm mouth kissing oxygen into her lungs? The strong hands supporting her and taking her pain away? And why had it all seemed so familiar, so comforting, as if she'd finally found home?

Stupid dream. She hated the ones that lingered in her memories well into the next day.

And this one went from underwater lifesaving to rip-roaring on the beach masturbation. Maybe she was tense. Although the orgasm she'd awakened to certainly should ease some of her stress.

The hotel was busy this morning. Isabelle shook her head at couples sharing intimate kisses and touches right in front of everyone else.

"I hope all this doesn't bother you."

Isabelle turned at the sound of Morgan Marino's soft voice and smiled. The gorgeous redhead looked perfectly outfitted in her snug tropical dress complete with hibiscus in her hair. "Not at all. I'm just not used to it."

Jealous was more like it. Had she ever had a man who wanted her so much he didn't care where or when he touched and kissed her?

Easy answer. No.

A very attractive, dark-haired man peered over Morgan's shoulder and said, "You'll get used to it, trust me. Eventually you won't notice anyone around here or what they're doing."

Morgan smiled and caressed the man's cheek. "Dr. Isabelle King, this is my husband, Tony Marino."

Isabelle shook Tony's hand and smiled. "I hear you and Morgan just returned from your honeymoon. Congratulations."

"Thanks." Tony kissed his wife's cheek. "We had a great time but Morgan doesn't like to leave the resort for too long, so we had to hustle back."

Isabelle looked over at the woman. "It's tough when work gets in the way of your personal life, isn't it?" Not that she would know about that, since she had no personal life.

"It's okay. We've been on a constant honeymoon for the past six months, anyway."

"Yeah, and I had to drag her off the island just to get her to marry me. She made me wait forever before she made an honest man of me."

Isabelle laughed.

Morgan blushed and kissed her husband goodbye. "You go write. I'll see to Isabelle."

After Tony left, they walked toward the small grocery store. Morgan asked, "Is everything okay out there?"

"It's lovely. And very quiet. Perfect for my research. And thank you again for letting me stay there even though I'm not participating in…in the events here."

"Don't be ridiculous. No one has to participate unless they want to. However, if you do change your mind and decide to check out some of the activities, you're more than welcome."

Participate in the activities? Not a chance. She nodded and smiled at Morgan anyway. "Sure thing. Thanks. By the way, is anyone else staying on the other side of the island? I noticed there was a bungalow next to mine."

Morgan shook her head. "No, it's empty. Why?"

Isabelle took out her list and grabbed a basket. "I thought I saw someone in the water last night, and was just wondering if there was another guest staying on that side of the island."

"The other bungalow wasn't booked this week. Would you like me to send someone to check it out?"

"No, don't do that. I think it was a sea turtle anyway. I wasn't feeling well last night and shouldn't have gone in the water, but I just thought I'd seen someone. I was probably just delirious from the fever."

Morgan stopped and turned to Isabelle. "Are you ill? We have a doctor on staff here, even a small hospital."

"I'm fine. Just a sharp pain on my right side and a little fever. It's gone now."

Morgan pressed her palm against Isabelle's forehead. "You don't feel warm, but I'd still like our doctor to check you out."

"No, really, I —"

"I insist."

From Morgan's serious look, Isabelle knew she wouldn't be able to work in peace until she allayed the woman's fears. "Fine."

An hour later she was sitting in Dr. Shalay's office. About sixty-years-old with white hair and a long beard, the doctor frowned.

"Based on your symptoms I'd say you had an acute appendicitis attack. But that can't be."

She hadn't thought of that. Dear God, she had no business swimming out that far last night. She could have died. "Does it need to come out?"

"Does what need to come out?"

"My appendix."

"What a silly question. The ultrasound showed you have no appendix, which you obviously already knew. But you also have no scar."

"Of course I don't have a scar, since I've never had surgery." Then, his words registered. "What do you mean I have no appendix?"

The doctor regarded her over his glasses as if she were a simpleton. "Would you like to see the ultrasound pictures? There's no appendix there, dear. Perhaps you never had one."

"I have to have an appendix."

"No. Yours has been removed or was never there."

After the confusing talk with Dr. Shalay, Isabelle made her way back to her bungalow. Last night was the worst pain she'd ever endured, and this morning she had no appendix.

She stripped off her clothes and stood in front of the bedroom closet. Sure enough, there was a red mark on her lower right side. How could she not have noticed it earlier? Inspecting it closer now, she could have sworn it looked like a palm print.

Ridiculous. Odd things had been happening since the moment she'd stepped onto Paradise yesterday. First that strange feeling of being watched, that sense of someone she knew waiting for her, then the whole episode last night and the bizarre dream.

She hadn't been sleeping well lately. Maybe the lack of rest was affecting her ability to think rationally. That was the only logical explanation she could come up with for her state of mind lately.

She put on her swimsuit and went outside with her dive gear and camera, figuring it was past time that she started on her work. She had sea turtles to find and catalog and coral reef to photograph.

After checking the gauges, she put on her tank and mask, then fastened her camera and notebook around her.

The dive down was lovely, the water clear and calm. The beauty of the sea never failed to take her breath away. She'd catalogued marine life from many locations around the world, but the Caribbean had always been the place she loved the best. From her earliest childhood memories, she recalled snorkeling in the waters and looking down into the depths, wondering what secrets the sea held. Now she had the chance to do it as a professional.

Visibility was at a maximum today, at least one-hundred-twenty feet. Thankful for the warm waters, at least she didn't have to wear a wet suit, which would have added even more weight to her already full load.

Clusters of coral stretched as far as she could see. Vibrant colors of the rainbow painted the homeland of the exquisite sea creatures. She looked up to see the sunlight sparkling like diamonds off the surface. Tourists snorkeling peered down from the top of the water, their fins undulating lazily as they gazed at the beauty she was fortunate to see close up. She must have traveled far enough out to end up on the other side of the island where they offered snorkeling excursions to the guests. She quickly moved off beyond the prying eyes of the floaters above.

There were definite advantages to her work. One of the main reasons she'd decided to become a marine biologist was to get closer to the sea. She'd been drawn to it her entire life. Something about being submerged in the depths and surrounded by all this beauty made her feel complete.

And it never bothered her to dive alone, in fact she preferred it, unlike her colleagues who always insisted they have a companion diver. Not her. When she did a dive by herself, the ocean was hers to explore as she wished.

Be careful.

Isabelle stopped and glanced around at the sound of a familiar whisper, then shook her head. Right. Now she was hearing voices and actually turned to see if someone was talking to her. Underwater.

She had to start getting more sleep at night.

Isabelle, hold still. Don't move.

Okay, now that wasn't funny. She really *had* heard a voice. A man's voice, almost like a flutter in her ear. Her first thought was to shake it off and move on, but some instinct told her to heed the warning.

She stilled. Seconds later, a shark swam past her, its fin brushing against her skin as it wound its way through the water.

Holy shit! How had she missed that? Gawking at the coral no doubt, her mind occupied with anything but what she should be thinking about—namely staying alert and keeping an eye on her surroundings.

The adrenalin rush sent her heart pounding against her chest. She watched the shark disappear ahead and tried to normalize her breathing. Over-inhaling the tank's oxygen would be the last thing she needed right now.

But she *had* heard a voice. A man's voice. Twice. And last night too, the same whisper she'd heard in her dream. She wasn't hallucinating this time and she was fully awake so she couldn't be dreaming. Someone watched her down here, she was certain of it.

But who? And more importantly, how? She searched the clear depths but could find no sign of bubbles from another tank, nor were there any boats parked above her.

She really needed to get a grip. Who was she looking for, anyway? Even if the floor had been populated with divers, no one down there could speak to her.

You're beautiful, Isabelle.

Not funny. She knew damn well that someone watched her. She could feel his presence. Or its presence. Or something. And she wasn't the type of person to hear voices in her head.

Her attention shot, she surfaced, swam to shore and pulled off her gear, storming into her bungalow and pacing.

Someone had been down there with her, and that someone had spoken to her. She didn't know how they'd done it, but she was sure that she hadn't lost her mind. She'd been diving for too many years and knew enough about the ocean to know that the military had advanced sonar capabilities. That had to be the explanation.

But how did he know her name? And why did his voice seem so familiar?

She was startled when a knock sounded at her door. No one was supposed to be on this side of the island.

It was probably housekeeping, and she was worrying for nothing.

She took a breath to calm her rattled nerves and opened the door.

It wasn't housekeeping. Not unless Paradise Resort had hired male centerfolds as maids these days. This guy looked more like a surfer.

"Can I help you?" she asked.

His smile showed white, even teeth made brighter by a tanned, chiseled face. He appeared kissed by the sun. His light brown hair was tipped with blond highlights and golden flecks danced in his green eyes.

Wow.

"Hi," he said, holding out his hand. "I'm Dax."

Warily, she shook his hand. "Isabelle King. Again, can I help you with something?"

That half-smile he gave her was sexy as all get out. "I just wanted to introduce myself. I'm staying in the bungalow next to yours and thought since we were gonna be neighbors, I'd be neighborly."

Isabelle swallowed, wishing she had a handy glass of water to quench her suddenly dry throat. "I was told I'd be alone on this side of the island."

He shrugged and crossed his arms, leaning against her doorway. "I just checked in a few minutes ago. Kind of an impromptu visit. I won't bother you. You working here or something?"

"How would you know that?" Suspicion crept into her thoughts.

Inclining his head toward her discarded dive gear, he grinned. "Looks like official stuff there. Besides, it says Oceanic Institute on your bag. Figure you're a marine biologist or something along those lines."

"Oh. Yes, that's right." He didn't seem to be in any hurry to leave. Her telephone rang and she excused herself to run and answer it, determined to dial up the hotel immediately and confirm this stranger's appearance.

She didn't have to, since it was Morgan on the phone, telling her she'd had an unscheduled guest show up not more than a half hour ago, and he'd be occupying the bungalow next to hers.

At least she now knew he wasn't some escaped psychopath. She hung up the phone and went back to the door. He still leaned against her doorway with his arms crossed, his emerald eyes watching her.

Despite wanting to shut the door in his face and not deal with him, she hadn't been brought up to be rude. She motioned him inside and shut the door.

"You have a last name, Dax?"

He paused for a second, then grinned and said, "Seagrove."

The name didn't ring a bell, but somehow he seemed familiar to her. Maybe everything about her stay on the island here was some kind of weird déjà vu experience. "I was about to have some iced tea. Would you like a glass?"

"Sure, thanks."

She poured him a glass and they stepped out back onto a covered porch.

"What brings you to the island?" she asked, hoping he wasn't there to indulge in some wild orgies. Not that she'd object to him having them, of course. It was simply the thought of all that noise bothering her when she was trying to work.

"I'm here on a hunt." He stretched his long legs out and Isabelle admired the view. He was tall, probably more than six feet. He didn't have an overly muscular body. Rather, he was lean and in good shape. Nice muscles. Six pack abs.

He also sported a very interesting tattoo of a symbol and a dolphin on his left bicep. "That's the Greek symbol for Delta on your arm."

"Yeah, it is."

"Curious. Why that symbol for a tattoo?"

He shrugged. "I studied ancient Greek. Learned the letters. I liked this one."

"I see."

He crossed his arms and his biceps bulged nicely. Not overly large like those sweaty guys at her gym who grunted and groaned trying to build huge muscles. Just nice and strong with defined muscles that made her mouth water. Damn he was good looking.

Then what he'd said earlier finally registered. "A hunt? What kind of hunt?"

"Well, typically I do wreck diving. You never know what kind of buried treasure you're going to find at the bottom of the ocean," he replied with a wink.

Wreck diving? Buried treasure?

Oh, hell. Dax was a treasure hunter.

Chapter Three

"You're a scavenger." Isabelle didn't even try to keep the irritation out of her voice.

"I'm a businessman." Dax didn't seem offended in the least. In fact, he grinned.

"You're a thief. Removing things from the sea which should be left untouched. You're no better than a grave robber."

Was that admiration she saw in his eyes? Couldn't be, since she'd just insulted him.

"I didn't say I was going to remove anything. I'm just looking."

"For?"

"Sea turtles."

Now she didn't care if she insulted him outright or not. "Hunting sea turtles for profit is forbidden. They're endangered and protected by the laws here."

He held up his hands and laughed. "Calm down, Isabelle. I'm not out to harvest any. I've been hired to search for one of the more elusive species. My employer figured since I'd hunted down shipwrecks I should be able to find a sea turtle."

"What species?"

"It's special. Unique. Never been seen before, actually."

She sucked in a breath. Surely she and Dax couldn't be after the same thing. "You're talking about something that's nothing more than a myth."

He nodded. "The Pegasus Turtle."

"It doesn't exist."

"Are you sure?"

"Yes. There's no documented evidence of a turtle like that in existence. It's nothing more than myth and folklore." But she'd still searched for it. Every time she entered the water it was foremost on her mind.

"Many things exist but remain hidden from humans," Dax said.

Isabelle stood and stepped into the sand beyond the veranda, digging her toes into the hot granules. She turned to Dax, who smiled enigmatically at her. "You sound like you have some experience in that area."

"I might."

"You've seen one." She wasn't buying it.

"I might have."

"Where?"

"Not too far from here. Offshore a bit. It's been a couple years ago, though. Want me to help you locate it?"

"No."

"Why not?"

"I work alone."

"That's no fun. Let me help you. Two sets of eyes out in the water are better than one any day."

Suspicious by nature, Isabelle wondered if Dax had some ulterior motive in wanting to work with her. She crossed her arms and leaned against the porch wall. "Who's paying you to do this? Please tell me it isn't one of those millionaires who wants a one-of-a-kind trophy."

"Nah. Just an interested party. He wants pictures…proof. That's all."

She searched his face, but couldn't tell from his expression whether he was lying or not. Then again, there were habitual liars in the world who were expert at hiding their secrets. "I see."

"Good. So, do you want help with your search?" he asked again.

She had a feeling this would cost her. If he was even telling the truth. "And what do I have to pay you for *helping* me?"

"Nothing."

"Right. How much?"

"I told you," he said again, laughing, "nothing."

"What's in it for you?" Because no one did anything for free. There was always an angle, an ulterior motive. And Dax didn't look like a boy scout.

Dax shrugged. "A diving companion."

She threw him a dubious glare. "Really. Why am I having trouble believing all you want out of this is someone to dive alongside you? Is this a come on? If so, I'll give you credit for being original, but I'm not in the market for a man."

He arched a brow. "You don't like men?"

"Of course I do. I'm just not interested in having one right now."

He smirked and said, "I don't believe my offer included you *having* me. But we can negotiate on that part."

Isabelle's face heated uncomfortably at Dax's gaze scanning her body. "That's not what I meant. I meant if you want to dive with me then you need to know it's going to be strictly business between us."

"If that's what you want."

"It's what I want." Despite the fact his eyes burned through her, as if he could see into the deep recesses of her heart. Something about Dax Seagrove was familiar, and it nagged at her. Certainly he was gorgeous and charming in a boyish way. She'd seen a face like his on countless fashion magazines and in hunk-of-the-week movies. But there was something else about him that she couldn't put her finger on. A sense of déjà vu, as if she'd met him before.

"Would you like to get started or did you want to stare at me awhile longer?"

Would the embarrassment never end? Gawking like a teenager. Hell, she hadn't gawked at a guy when she *was* a teenager. So, why now, and why him? "Yes, let's get started. There's plenty of daylight left and I have to catalogue some coral anyway."

"Great. I'll help you."

She grabbed her gear and they headed outside, but she stopped him before they reached the water. "You know how to catalogue coral?"

"Yes."

"How? You're not a marine biologist."

"I'm familiar with coral."

"Tell me what you know about the coral indigenous to this area, then," she asked, determined to expose him as the fraud she knew he was.

"I'm assuming you don't want a running list of every species in this area, so I'll limit the number of descriptions. Fire coral is orange-yellow in color and appears to not have any pores which is a typical coral characteristic. Mountainous star coral has no specific coloring but is considered to be an important reef-former in this area. It does have one distinguishing characteristic in that its cups rise above the coral surface. Now the pillar coral is fuzzy and looks like giant fingers. Or there's the—"

"That's enough." So he did know his coral. Didn't mean he wasn't a fraud in other areas.

"Did I pass the test?" he asked with a wink.

"For now. Okay, Mr. Expert, let's go." She'd see if he really knew one end of the ocean from the other. Then she'd decide if she'd let him come along on any further dives.

She threw on her gear and grabbed her camera and notepad, then waited for Dax to fetch his tank and fins from his bungalow.

But he didn't. He just stood there.

"Don't you need to get your stuff?"

He frowned. "What stuff?"

"Your dive gear." And he was an expert? Who the hell was this guy, anyway? She began to doubt her instincts. For all she knew he could be a drifter.

"I don't use dive gear."

She looked at him, hands on her hips. "No dive gear. You dive without an oxygen tank?"

His grin irritated the hell out of her. "Yeah. I can handle it. Trust me. You ready to go?"

"Fine, but if you drown don't expect me to save you." She trudged into the water, her fins slapping at the waves. Refusing to look back at Dax, she dove under, fully expecting to do this dive alone.

He was completely full of shit and she'd called his bluff. Treasure hunter, Pegasus, diver her ass.

Determined to ignore the irritating Dax Seagrove, she dismissed him from her thoughts and concentrated instead on the coral samples she was to catalogue. Her blood pressure leveled off as soon as she nestled among the beautiful creatures under the sea.

It had always seemed kind of strange to her, but she *felt* the life force of these creatures. All the sea creatures. They weren't mindless objects that swam aimlessly or clung to the sea floor. They were intelligent beings and they called to her in a way that even she couldn't understand.

Which was why she spent most of her time alone. Mentioning her feelings about sea life to any of her colleagues would make her the laughingstock of the Institute. So she kept her opinions and her feelings to herself and went about her business.

Alone. Just the way she liked it.

She quickly turned when something brushed against her shoulder. Her heart pounded a staccato beat at the thought of the shark she'd encountered earlier. But this time, it wasn't a shark.

It was Dax. Sure enough, no dive gear. She shook her head and motioned with her thumb upward, hoping he'd hightail it to the surface before he ran out of air. No such luck. He merely shook his head and smiled.

What a fucking lunatic! He was going to drown. She tried again to signal him to surface, but he waved her off and pointed to the coral.

Damn difficult trying to communicate under the ocean.

No, it's not. Just listen, Isabelle. Can you hear me speaking to you?

What the hell? There was that whispering voice again, the one she'd heard earlier, the one she was convinced didn't exist. She turned to Dax to see if he showed any reaction. He hung suspended in the water, that goofy smile plastered to his face.

Moron. She hoped he'd drown soon.

And she was *not* hallucinating! She'd heard someone talking to her, almost in answer to her silent musings about the lack of communication under water.

She gave up. She was slowly losing her mind. There was no way in hell that someone could be speaking to her underwater. People didn't talk underwater.

People didn't. Humans didn't. But what about something else? Some other kind of being? Maybe she'd discover more than just a Pegasus Turtle on this expedition. Maybe, there was intelligent life in the sea that could communicate with humans.

Then again, maybe she just needed a nap.

She immersed herself in the coral review, throwing the other odd thoughts out of her head. She'd completely lost track of time until Dax tapped on her wrist and pointed to an unusual species of blue coral.

By then she was way more interested in him than she was the coral. Dax had been holding his breath and hovering next to her for more than five minutes. By rights he should have lost consciousness and drowned by now.

He wasn't dead and he was still smiling. Why wasn't he dead? What the hell, or *who* the hell was fucking with her?

Dax. He was the one screwing with her head. Everything in her neat and orderly world had fallen apart from the moment she met him. True, maybe even before she'd met him, but how did she know it hadn't been him before?

Are you gonna finish that job or just hang out here and wax existential the rest of the day?

There it was again. Thoughts. Not words spoken aloud, but thoughts. Someone else's thoughts, yet she heard them as if they'd been spoken. Goosebumps broke out on her skin and she flushed hot at the same time.

She looked at Dax, and made the connection.

Dax?

Yeah.

You're speaking to me. Or thinking to me.

I know.

Under water.

Yes.

It's really you? Despite the fact this could not be happening, she already knew the answer. It was the same whispering voice she'd heard in her dreams last night, the same one that had warned her about the shark this morning. Not like his regular speaking voice at all, this one was soft, like a caress near her ear.

How are you speaking to me? How are you breathing under water? What the hell is going on here?

It's a long story.

I've got time. I'm the one with the oxygen tank.

Later. Finish your work and we'll talk topside.

Before she could utter another word...or thought, he swam away so lightning quick her eyes barely registered his departure. Other than a wake of bubbles, there was no sign of him.

Stunned didn't even begin to explain her mindset right now. Unbelievable, unfathomable, couldn't possibly happen.

She'd just dreamed this whole episode. Dax had never even dived with her. She was hallucinating and needed some kind of psychiatric help.

That, at least, would be easier to accept than the fact that Dax could breathe underwater and think his thoughts to her. But the bottom line was, she was a scientist and as a scientist sometimes the unbelievable had to be taken at face value.

Cataloguing coral no more than a distant memory, she quickly made the trek toward the water's surface, her thoughts filled with Dax and the wondrous magic he'd just revealed to her.

What was he? Who was he? Why was he here and how could he be communicating telepathically with her?

The questions raced through her, too numerous to list. But the one question first and foremost on her mind had already been answered.

No way in hell was Dax Seagrove human.

Chapter Four

By the time Isabelle surfaced from the water, Dax was nowhere to be found.

Dammit! Curiosity ran rampant through her, forcing all other thoughts aside. Who the hell was he? She had to know.

She walked over to his bungalow and rapped on the door.

No answer.

A quick turn toward the ocean showed no sign of him.

He had to have surfaced. He told her, or rather he sent his thoughts to her that they'd talk after she surfaced.

Well, she *had* surfaced, dammit! Where was he?

After hanging outside for several minutes, she gave up, figuring this whole episode was just another case of bad indigestion or some kind of screw-with-her-brain plant life she'd rubbed up against in the forest. The way she'd imagined the weird things happening to her lately, Dax probably hadn't even been down there with her. She'd just hallucinated the entire episode.

After all, humans did not breathe and talk under water. None of that had happened.

Disgusted with her tenuous grip on reality, she grabbed her gear and went into her bungalow to shower. Then she threw on a sundress and decided to check for Dax at the hotel.

But thoughts of the mystery man who dove without an oxygen tank remained prominent in her mind. Despite knowing it couldn't have really happened, she couldn't shake the memories of what she'd seen and heard.

She'd find Dax and get at the truth. Either he was some kind of non-human species who could breathe and talk underwater, or she was having a really bad hallucinatory episode and needed therapy. Either way, she'd get some answers from Dax.

It was dinner time and the guests were mingling about in the lounge and dining area. Isabelle searched both rooms for Dax, but didn't find him.

Tired of standing around wringing her hands, she stepped up to the bar and ordered a cocktail to settle her nerves. Then she took a seat at one of the tables and observed the couples occupying the lounge.

Human behavior had always fascinated her, especially the biological aspects of sexuality. Granted, this venue went beyond the ordinary, but she still enjoyed watching the interplay between the sexes.

There was plenty of interplay going on. Couples whispering, holding hands, kissing and even the not-so-accidental touching of asses and breasts. She was no voyeur, but watching the intimate foreplay occur right out in the open had her breasts tingling with excitement. Her nipples hardened and she immediately wished she'd taken the time to put on a bra. She shifted in her chair as the ache between her legs became more prominent.

Not that anyone would notice. Couples were paired off in twos like the animals on Noah's ark. There were even groups of four or six...orgy gatherings, maybe? And there she sat, all alone at her little table. She couldn't help but feel like a wallflower. Which was ridiculous considering she wasn't on this island to partake of the sexual adventures, anyway.

Still, it was difficult not to think about sex when it permeated the entire room.

How long had it been since she'd had sex? Too long to remember, that much was certain. And at that she hadn't had great sex in...well, never.

The earth had never moved for her in bed. She knew the basic biology, knew how to get herself off, and yet when coupled with a guy the results had been disappointing. Then again maybe she'd have to actually feel something for a man before she could get that great sex she'd always read about.

She'd had sex, that was for sure. But she'd never been in love.

Maybe that's what was missing in her life. Her soul mate, if such a person even existed. Her career had always come first. That, and the fear that she'd end up like her mother some day. Both were reason enough to shy away from any deep emotional entanglement with a man.

When the gentle, swaying lilt of an island beat started up from the band in the lounge, Isabelle wished she had someone to dance with. She'd loved dancing as a child. Her mother would always have music playing and grab her to swirl her around the kitchen. She'd even taken several years of dancing lessons and had become rather adept at it.

Too bad she'd been so immersed in books in high school that she'd never had the chance to show off her dancing prowess to a boy. Not that any of them would have noticed her anyway. Always more interested in books and research than in the social activities at school, the kids had nicknamed her Isabore.

She'd missed so much. And not once in all those years had she thought about what she hadn't experienced.

Until now. Right now she wanted to get up on that dance floor more than she wanted anything.

"Would you like to dance?"

She looked up at the sound of Dax's voice. Her heart slammed against her ribs at the sight of his tall, lean body dressed in swim shorts and a tank top like one of those surfer boys in a catalog. With his dark tan and sea green eyes he stood out as the most handsome man in the room. But what really got to her was his smile. Wickedly sexy, a little lopsided, but full of sensual promise. She sensed some talent in those full lips, and her body went on alert as images of what he could do to her with his mouth flooded her mind.

In an instant she was drenched between her legs, her cotton panties clinging to her damp pussy. How could the mere sight of him excite her that way?

"Where have you been?" she asked. "When I surfaced I couldn't find you and then you said you'd meet me topside but you weren't anywhere around."

He smiled and took her hand, casually sliding his thumb along the inside of her wrist as he pulled her to the dance floor. Idly she wondered if he could feel her thumping pulse. She shivered when he pulled her body close to his, her breasts brushing his hard chest. If he noticed her distended nipples poking his chest he didn't say anything.

They fit well together. If she lay her head against him it would rest nicely against his collarbone. He splayed his palm against her bare back and she bit her lip, fighting back the urge to grab him by the hair and kiss him.

He hadn't acknowledged her comment about talking to him underwater. Did that mean it had actually happened and he didn't want to talk about it yet, or did it mean he had no earthly idea what she was talking about?

Where was the calm and cool Dr. Isabelle King? Why hadn't she dragged him out of there and barraged him with question after question on his origin and how he managed to breathe without an oxygen tank and talk to her underwater? Where had the scientist in her gone?

She must have left that part of her personality back at her bungalow because for the life of her she couldn't come up with a single non-sexual thought. Her body tuned into him and nothing else could interfere.

Since it didn't appear he was going anywhere any time soon, she relaxed. When she did, he pulled her tighter against him and she decided to go for it. She rested her head against his shoulder, inhaling the crisp, clean scent of him. His skin was soft and yet muscular and the way his hand constantly moved against her back drove her crazy.

He could dance, too, his body moving in perfect time with the slow, sexy island beat. His pelvis brushed against hers and she lifted her head, her gaze shooting to his. He was hard. Long and hard and rubbing against her mound in a way that made her hot and wet.

Reacting like this wasn't in her nature. Sex wasn't first and foremost on her mind...ever. Yet Dax clearly had a physical reaction to their close proximity and she couldn't deny her own response.

"You have the most beautiful hair," he murmured, tucking her head against his shoulder and petting her hair, following the trail of tresses down her back with his hand.

She shivered and inhaled his scent, her hands instinctively clutching him closer as she wound her arm around his neck. "Thank you."

"And you smell like summer. Like peaches. I love peaches, did you know that?"

Swallowing past the huge lump in her throat, she said, "No."

"They're soft, pliant, juicy and ripe with flavor that bursts into your mouth and makes you desperate for another taste. Are you ripe with flavor, Isabelle?"

Oh God. She couldn't answer. What would she say, anyway? Her mind flooded with visions of Dax's tongue swiping over her clit and pussy. She desperately wanted to grind her mound against his hard cock and beg him to fuck her right here.

No. That wasn't her. She didn't act that way. Forcing her thoughts to the myriad of questions she had about this mysterious man, she said, "We have a lot to talk about."

"Mmm hmm." He slowly stroked her back from shoulder blade almost to her rear, pressing in at her lower back. When he rocked his hard-on against her, her body quivered.

"This isn't the place or the time for sex," she managed to blurt out.

He leaned back and arched a brow. "We're not having sex. We're dancing."

Why couldn't she think? "There's a lot more than dancing going on here."

"So I noticed. You'd think some of these couples were going to drop to the floor and do it right here, wouldn't you?"

Other couples? What other couples? She'd been so focused on Dax she'd forgotten there were other people around. As she glanced around she noticed a half dozen or so other couples on the dance floor, kissing and touching in an intimate fashion. Way more intimate than Dax had touched her. "I...I hadn't noticed."

"Mind occupied elsewhere?"

Flames of embarrassment licked at her neck. "Yes, I have a lot on my mind."

"Am I one of the things on your mind?" He brushed his knuckles against her cheek.

Did he have to touch her like that? How could she think when the mere swipe of his skin against hers sent her reeling? "Yes, you're first and foremost, but not for the reasons you think."

"Is that right?"

"Yes. I have so many questions, Dax. Who are you, what are you, where are you from? How can you—"

He pressed a finger to her lips. "There's plenty of time for answering questions later. Right now I just want to hold you, touch you and do the one thing I've been dying to do since I first saw you standing on the beach."

Anticipation and dread mixed within her. She was almost too afraid to ask the question, yet too curious not to. "What's that?"

"Kiss you."

Her breath caught as he leaned in and covered her lips. A strange heat soared through her body, both calm and feverish at the same time. His mouth teasing hers felt so right, so perfect, so incredible.

His tongue dipped between her lips and tangled with hers, stealing what was left of her ability to think. He licked inside her mouth gently at first, then harder as she let him know without words that she accepted him. How could she not? Despite the fact this wild-woman behavior wasn't at all like her, she couldn't help the roaring attraction she felt to Dax. His touch, his kiss, his body pressed so intimately against her was like coming home, as if she stood exactly in the place she was meant to be.

Part of her wanted to object, to push him away. She needed some distance, time to clear her head. Too much had happened and she couldn't think straight right now.

The other part of her wanted to live in this fantasy for as long as she could. She didn't understand her reaction to Dax, but she couldn't deny that at least that part was real. She wanted him and if she knew anything at all about biology, he wanted her, too.

The fact she didn't really know a damn thing about him should have given her reason enough to put a skidding halt to his deep kiss, but for the life of her she couldn't dredge up enough strength to stop his tender assault on her body.

"Let's go," he said, pulling away from her only long enough to grab her hand and lead her out the door of the hotel.

"Where are we going?" The humid night surrounded her, the scent of gardenias tingeing the air with the sultry, tropical sense she loved so much.

"I don't know. I don't care. Somewhere away from other people."

"I have a little golf cart we can drive back to the bungalow in."

He didn't answer, just dragged her along. She really should object, but she couldn't help the excited thrill at the thought of heading into the dark rainforest alone with Dax.

Good thing he had hold of her hand because they weaved back and forth, in and out of the lighted path. She'd have been lost without his lead. It seemed as if he knew where he was going. She'd already given up trying to guess at who or what he was. She'd given up trying to figure out why someone who'd always had her head screwed on straight had suddenly popped one of those screws loose. She was heading into a dark forest with a complete stranger.

Too many questions, too many emotions and physical sensations running through her body. She threw out the logical and focused on the thrilling adventure before her. As far as questioning Dax about who he was, there was plenty of time for that later.

They'd traveled deep into the dense rainforest. No lights shone on the path he took.

"Trust me?" he asked over his shoulder, his voice tight with what she could only assume was tension.

Trust him? That was a helluva question to ask since he'd just taken her into the jungle where no one could see or hear them. Did she?

Without hesitation, she knew the answer. Yes. She did trust him. She didn't know why, but she instinctively knew she'd come to no harm as long as she was with Dax. And that feeling she refused to analyze right now. She just went with her instincts and said, "Yes, I trust you."

"Good." He stopped abruptly in a clearing. The moonlit night shone overhead in the space between the dense palm fronds, shining on a small grassy area clear of bushes and trees.

Before she had a chance to ask why he'd stopped, he swung around and grabbed her roughly around the waist, pushing her back against one of the thick tree trunks.

The look of intense desire in his eyes froze her to the spot. His gaze was so heated it was almost tangible, as if she could reach out and touch his passion. Her breathing quickened, knowing what was on his mind. She wondered if she was ready for this. Her attraction to Dax had been instantaneous, almost combustible. Could she do this and survive it with her heart intact?

Dax's warm breath caressed her face and she inhaled his fresh, ocean-like scent as if she couldn't breathe without it. He rested his hands on either side of her, palming the trunk of the tree and trapping her between his arms.

Vibrations of energy surrounded them, heightening her awareness of her surroundings and the barely coiled tension inside the man who held her trapped between his outstretched arms.

"Tell me to stop and I will," he said, his voice dark and dangerous and thrilling as hell. "Tell me you don't want this and I'll walk away."

Did she want this? Confusion reigned supreme. She still didn't have the answers she sought. Did it matter?

If there was one thing Isabelle did, it was think before she did something. Acting on impulse wasn't in her nature.

If she said the word, he'd stop. Which was exactly what she should do, and right now before things got out of hand. She should tell him to stop, she should tell him they had to talk about who he was and where he came from. He could be the biological find of a lifetime...she'd want to study him, write papers. The impact of his presence would make news around the world.

That's what she should be concentrating on. Not his rigid body, not the moisture of desperate desire between her legs, not the realization that if he didn't put his hands on her in the next thirty seconds she might just self-combust. She shouldn't think about any of that.

But she did. And that was all she thought about.

"I don't want you to stop," she admitted.

He nodded, leaned in and took her mouth in a kiss that seared her senses.

Chapter Five

It had been so long since he'd touched a woman. Dax gathered Isabelle in his arms and pulled her against him. Their bodies molded together and his cock rose, pressing insistently against his shorts.

Damn clothes, anyway. If they were both naked he'd be inside her by now. Her tongue slipped feverishly inside his mouth and he sucked it in, tasting her sweet flavor in a way that made him eager to sample her juices elsewhere.

Somewhere in the back of his mind he knew what he was doing was wrong, that he shouldn't have revealed himself to her, shouldn't touch her, shouldn't do what he knew they were going to do...hoped they were going to do. But he couldn't help himself. It was if he'd known her for years, since that first time she'd waved at him from the beach. He'd waited for her to grow up, hoping he'd some day catch a glimpse of her again.

And now that she'd reappeared in his life, he took it as a sign of destiny. Foolish, he knew, because they were not destined to be mated. He could have her, but he couldn't keep her. She didn't belong in his world, and he couldn't live in hers.

But right now, she was his for the taking. And he was damn well going to take her.

Dax pulled away from the embrace and held her at arms length, devouring her with his gaze. A light breeze blew her hair away from her face. She stood still like a siren with her dark hair flowing behind her, her amber eyes glowing like a jungle beast in the darkness of night. Her breasts rose and fell with every panting breath.

He reached for her, trailing his fingers along the soft skin of her shoulder and collarbone. He circled the swell of one breast visible from the top of her dress. His cock jumped at the sound of her indrawn breath.

Go slower. You have time. Don't rush this. Yeah right. It was like trying to slow down a tsunami after an underwater earthquake. He closed his eyes for a second and inhaled deeply, forcing restraint when all he really wanted to do was step between her legs and drive his shaft deep inside her.

"I've wanted this for a long time," he said, pulling her against him.

He shouldn't have said it, but he couldn't stop the revelations any more than he could stop his need for her. Before she could respond, he dipped his head and captured her mouth in a deep kiss that left them both breathless and shaking.

Never before had it been like this with a woman, any woman — neither from the sea nor on land. His dalliances had been quick fucks to release the tension and nothing more. The women he'd been with had been after the same thing as he — a sexual release with no entanglements. There had never been emotion in his sex life.

Until now. Now one woman, one promise of pleasure with sable hair and eyes the color of gold, took his breath away.

"That dress touches you where I want to touch you," he whispered, reaching for the thin straps on her shoulders and slipping his fingers underneath them. While he slowly slid them down her arms, her gaze remained fixed on his face. She licked her lips and inhaled deeply, her breasts straining against the barely-there material of her flowery red dress.

Dax paused midway down, waiting for her reaction.

"Please," she murmured, her husky, desire-laden voice tightening his balls painfully. Going slow was going to kill him, he was certain of it.

Was she begging him to hurry, or begging for him to stop? He waited and counted to ten, hoping he wouldn't hear the words that would put an end to their dance. The words didn't come.

Breathing a sigh of relief, he pulled the dress down to her waist, revealing full, high breasts with thrusting nipples that puckered and hardened. No longer content with just looking, he slipped his hands underneath her breasts, lifting them. When his thumbs grazed the tightened peaks, she gasped.

"You're so beautiful in the moonlight. Your body shines like a golden angel." And he wanted more.

But before he could pull her dress off, she stopped him and reached for his shirt, smiling seductively at him. "It's only fair," she said, then pulled the shirt over his head. She threaded her fingers through the fine hairs of his chest and sought out his nipples, mimicking his earlier movements on hers. When she caressed the flat nubs with her thumbs, he sucked in a breath and his erection lengthened, drawing his balls up tight until he ached with the need for release.

Isabelle glanced down at his shorts and then back up at him, offering a half-smile. "We need to undress, Dax, and quickly."

And he thought she'd want it slow and easy. After all, to her they were strangers and he didn't want to frighten her. Still amazed that she'd even want to be anywhere near him after everything he'd revealed earlier, he nodded. "I couldn't agree more."

He sat on the grassy hill and pulled Isabelle down next to him, laying her gently on the soft ground. Her flat stomach quivered under his touch when he splayed his hand over her bare flesh. Leaning in a little, he moved his mouth over one hardened nipple and blew gently, watching it stand up further as if begging for more.

Tasting her was heaven. He'd waited an eternity to see her again, to touch her. And now that she lay before him, her bronzed body open to his touch, he knew he'd never be able to get enough of her.

When his lips covered one bud, she whimpered and threaded her fingers into his hair, pulling him closer. He moved his other hand over her hip, loving the feel of her curved woman's body, her skin like the silky water of the ocean.

He closed his eyes and sailed through the water, her skin the glistening ocean in the daylight, her sighs the mournful cries of the sirens. His senses tuned in to every breath, every rasping moan. Each of her reactions mirrored the need he had to groan out loud with the joy of discovering her.

This woman is mine. Always has been, always will be.

That smell of peaches assailed him and he licked ravenously at her nipple. First one, then the other, until she gasped and writhed against him, lifting her hips against his aching hard-on.

Slow down. But he couldn't make his body listen to his mind. He'd waited so long for this moment, and the fact she was eager and ready for him only made the wait that much more difficult.

Her scent drove him crazy, calling to him, demanding he taste her arousal. He shifted, pulling her dress over her hips and over her legs as he made his descent down her body. Her colorful panties gleamed bright in the moonlight. She bit her lower lip but didn't say a word as he knelt between her legs and grasped her panties, dragging them off.

The image of her spread out on the grass would stay with him forever. Naked and gloriously bronzed, her knees bent and her gorgeous pussy lay open to his perusal. Her mound was covered in a tiny thatch of dark hair, but her outer lips were bare, glistening with moisture.

He threaded his fingers over her stomach, watching her tensed reaction as he trailed slowly over the dark curls and lower. Tiny pants and moans escaped her throat and her pupils darkened as his fingers slid against her swollen pussy lips. He dipped one finger over the moisture gathered there and licked her juices off.

"Oh God," she whispered, shifting to sit up, her arms reaching out to him.

"Not yet," he said, gently nudging her back down and spreading her legs further apart. He flipped over onto his stomach and nestled between her legs. Inhaling her sweet scent, he licked and nibbled his way up her thighs. She clutched the grass around her, her body tight in anticipation of his next move.

What he'd wanted for hours was within his reach. He licked her outer lips, shuddering at the sweet taste of her nectar and drinking in her cries of delight. He slipped a finger inside her cavern and moved rhythmically in and out. With every sexy movement she made, his body responded with painful throbbing. Isabelle was amazingly responsive to his tongue and fingers. Her desire spurred him on, her sweet flavor making his entire body tighten with a painful need. His balls filled to the point of bursting.

He searched and found the hard nub of her clit, covering the hood with his mouth and gently sucking it in his mouth. She cried out as her orgasm hit, her cunt clenching tightly around his finger. A rush of juices poured onto his hand.

Damn! She thrashed around having the longest orgasm he'd ever watched. Her slick fluids drenched his fingers as he continued to pump inside her core, taking her up the long hill again until she bucked her hips against him and he bent down to lick her quickly.

"Oh, Dax, oh, I'm coming again!" This time she did scream. Loud and long as another intense climax tore through her.

He'd never seen anything like it. He pulled her close and held her shuddering body, gently pushing her sweat dampened hair away from her face, ignoring the intense pounding between his legs.

This was her moment, her release, and he wanted to experience every second of it with her.

He held her like that until her breathing became regular again, until the little whimpers in the back of her throat subsided. Those sounds she made, knowing he'd given her pleasure, pleased him more than he thought possible. In fact, he wouldn't mind hearing them again. And again. And then again. Because he wanted to pleasure her. Over and over and over until she screamed his name into the night.

"You haven't come in awhile, have you?" he asked, stroking her breasts with his fingertips, enjoying the way her nipples tightened at his slightest touch.

She didn't respond for a few seconds, finally answering with a soft whisper. "Was it that obvious?"

Drawing her against his side, he pressed a soft kiss to her lips. "I'll say it was. You came like a flash flood."

She went quiet.

"Hey," he said, wondering if he'd somehow hurt her feelings. Land humans were difficult to interpret sometimes, and Isabelle was a woman, which doubled his confusion factor.

"Yeah?"

"Are you all right?"

"Yeah."

"Something bothering you?"

"I'm a little embarrassed."

Dax sat and pulled Isabelle up with him, then turned to face her. "About what?"

"I was loud."

He grinned. "I know."

"I screamed."

"Hell yeah you did." Just the thought of her cries of pleasure made his shaft throb again.

Her eyes widened, amber pools of liquid warmth that mesmerized him. "That's not a bad thing?"

"No, not at all. It means you enjoyed what I was doing to you. I take it as a compliment."

She exhaled in a rush, as if she'd been holding her breath waiting for his approval. "Trust me, it was. No one has made me come like that before. I haven't even made myself come like that."

Now she was stepping into territory that got him hotter than a week without the ocean. Mental visuals of Isabelle lying spread-eagled on her bed flashed before him. Would she thrum her clit and fuck herself with her fingers or would she use a toy? Thoughts like that had his erection firing up hot and ready to go. And he knew just where he wanted it to go.

"How often do you make yourself come?" he asked.

"Not nearly often enough, obviously."

He laughed and pulled her up, brushing the grass off her body. "Let's go."

Isabelle stared at him when he handed her dress over. "Where?"

"I need to get back in the water."

"Oh. Of course." She put on her dress and followed him through the forest.

Dax led her back to the beach in front of the bungalows.

"I guess this is goodnight, then?" she asked.

"Huh? No, it's not goodnight. Come with me."

"Into the water?"

"Yeah."

She stood there indecisively for a few seconds, then shrugged and pulled her dress over her head. He sucked in a breath at her magnificent body, tanned golden-brown and glowing with an ethereal light under the full moon. "You take my breath away, Isabelle."

In that same moonlight, he saw her blush.

He quickly took off his shorts and stood before her, pleased when her gaze roamed over his body. Her eyes widened when it settled on his erection, which had now decided to remain damned painfully hard.

"And you take *my* breath away, Dax."

He planned to do just that. And then some. But not tonight. Not yet. Tonight was for making love with the bronzed beauty before him. There'd be time later to…

To what? To take her to his world, tell her everything about him? Not likely. Ronan would have his head, or more, if another land human found out about them.

Pushing those thoughts aside, he held out his hand, intent on taking a dip to refresh his body, and that was it. Tonight he'd forget about the complexities of their situation, and focus on enjoying the woman he'd wanted for what seemed like a lifetime.

*   *   *   *   *

Isabelle let Dax lead her into the waves, the cool water lapping against her skin and refreshing her overheated body.

He'd been amazing, licking and stroking her nonstop. It had seemed as if he hadn't even stopped to breathe.

She made a mental note to ask him about that.

Later, not now. Now they had unfinished business.

Her body still thrummed with desire for him. He hadn't had release yet, and she was determined to give back some of what he'd given her.

Astounded by her wild response to him, she shook her head. Guilt panged in her stomach, but she pushed it away. Yes, she was a biologist. Yes, she should be hitting him with a thousand questions about who he was. But the woman in her had taken over, and there was no going back now.

They swam out for a while, then Dax stopped and pulled her toward him.

She pushed him away, knowing they couldn't tread water while they were so close. "We'll sink."

He gathered her in his arms again. "Trust me, we won't sink."

Their bodies entwined together like a pretzel, their legs caressing each other. She wasn't treading, and neither was he. Surprisingly, they weren't sinking, either. "How do you do that?"

"Later. I'll explain it later." He reached up and slid his palm into her hair, wrapping his hand around the back of her neck. Then he bent his head to hers and fit his mouth over her lips.

She sighed, her body quaking with a rush of desire. His tongue tangled with hers, a slow, seductive rhythm that sent shots of intense pleasure between her legs. Instinctively she pressed her aching mound against his erection and wrapped her legs around his hips.

How he held them both in the water was beyond her comprehension, but she felt no struggle to stay afloat. They bobbed in and out of the waves, weightless.

The tip of his shaft probed between the throbbing lips of her pussy. With a little maneuvering, he'd be inside her. God, she had no idea until just this minute how much she wanted that.

"Let me," she whispered against his ear, licking the side of his neck. He rewarded her with a groan of pleasure as his cock surged against her. She reached between them and grasped his long shaft, palming it, stroking it, watching his pupils darken, the gold flecks nearly obliterated by the stormy sea green. "You do want to fuck me, don't you?"

He sucked in a breath and blew it out forcefully, moving his hips and thrusting his shaft against her hand. "What do you think? Put my cock inside you, Isabelle. Now."

She shivered at his forceful tone, knowing he was on the brink, loving the fact he wanted her that much. She teased him, rubbing the head of his shaft against her clit. Sparks of intense rapture shot straight to her core and she let loose a loud moan.

"Now, Isabelle. I want to feel your pussy around my cock."

Unable to wait any longer, she positioned his shaft against her and slid down over his cock. Her pussy grabbed it immediately, pulling it in. God, he was thick, stretching her. She gasped at the sensation of being so thoroughly filled and rocked against him.

"Oh yeah, that's good," he groaned, tightening his hold on her.

He pushed her back until she lay just on top of the water, as if she were lying on a bed. Dax ran his hands over her breasts, pulling at her nipples until she cried out in ecstasy.

Waves of delight rolled over her, rhythmically stroking against her body like the white-tipped waves of a crashing ocean. She tightened her legs around Dax's waist, drawing him against her. He thrust slowly at first, pulling out and then inching his way back in. Isabelle whimpered at the sensation. The tension built and she knew she couldn't hold off much longer.

Dax pulled her up and smothered her lips in a scorching kiss, plunging his tongue inside her mouth with hard, deep strokes, using the same tempo to drive his shaft inside her pussy.

Her gaze met his, the tight, drawn look of his features sending her to the edge. He strained against her, holding back his own orgasm so she could find hers. She felt it. Close, drawing closer, like a flame drawing her ever nearer. She wanted to reach that crashing wave with him. Then it hit.

"I'm going to come," she whimpered, panting rapidly.

"Come for me, Isabelle," he urged. "Come all over my cock."

She pushed her hips against him and rode his shaft fiercely, clutching his shoulders and digging her nails into his skin. The sensations pummeled her, his shaft pulling away and plunging back inside her until she couldn't take it any longer.

"Now, Dax, now!" she whimpered, and he quickened his pace, stroking faster and harder until she screamed. Her climax washed over her like a stormy wave.

"Come on, Isabelle, come for me!" Dax was relentless, driving harder and faster against her as her orgasm spiraled out of control. She cried out and held on tight to his back as he crushed her against him, taking her mouth in a devastating kiss.

She drank in his groans when he stiffened and came inside her, his body shuddering with the force of his climax. It went on for as long as hers did. He pumped repeatedly inside her, filling her with his hot come.

She'd never felt more connected with someone like she had with Dax. What they had together went way beyond the physical and into the frighteningly emotional territory she'd always tried to avoid. And, God help her, she couldn't stop herself.

Their lips stayed connected as they both slowed the pace, his tongue lazily tracing swirls over hers. Her body quivered with the aftereffects of her orgasm and Dax caressed her, holding on to her, murmuring against her ear.

And still, they floated on top of the water, weightless, like flying.

It was an out-of-this-world experience. She'd never felt like this before — so tied to someone, so connected.

When he pulled back and searched her face, she nearly turned away. His searching gaze hit her like a lightning bolt. He could see inside her, she was certain of it. He knew what he'd done to her, he realized the connection.

And it scared her to death.

Chapter Six

"I think we need to get out of the water now," Isabelle said, gently extricating herself from Dax's embrace.

He quirked a brow. "Are you cold?"

Cold? Hell, no. He just had her in a blazing meltdown and already her body was more than willing to stoke the fire again. And more than just her body was involved, which meant she needed to back off, and fast. "No, I'm fine. It's just late and I need to get some sleep. It's been a long day."

Without waiting for his response, she swam to shore and gathered up her dress, quickly slipping it over her wet body. She heard Dax behind her, but she needed to get her emotions under control before she faced him again.

Visions of what she'd done with him raced through her mind, both exciting and appalling her. She wasn't here on vacation, dammit, she was being paid to do a job. And her job did not consist of fucking a man, correction, a whatever-the-hell-he-was.

Which reminded her that despite the fact she'd become intimately familiar with Dax, she still didn't know a single thing about him.

And frankly, she didn't want to remain close enough to him to find out.

"I'll see you in the morning, then." She turned to leave but Dax grabbed her arm.

"Why are you running away?"

She met his gaze, already hating herself for what she was about to do. Funny how self-preservation seemed like a good excuse to hurt someone. "I'm not running away. I'm tired."

"Afraid you've just made a mistake?"

She didn't like the glint of anger she saw in his narrowed eyes. Immediately on the defensive, she said, "Look. The sex was great. You're a wonderful lover. I came like gangbusters. I'm just tired and I need to get some sleep."

"I see." His reply was short and clipped, his anger more than evident in the biting words. "Well, I'm glad I managed to get you off. I would have worried, otherwise. You know all we guys think about is our technique. Sweet dreams, Isabelle," he finished and walked swiftly away.

Waves of guilt crashed over her as she watched his departing form. She tucked herself inside the safety of her bungalow and bolted the door, as if the act of doing so could protect her from her own thoughts.

Not a chance. Her mind, her entire body, was filled with Dax. She ached in places that had never before been touched. At least not how he had touched her. The delicious remnants of their lovemaking were still apparent in her throbbing body.

Instead of satisfying her completely, he'd left her wanting more. How easy it would be to invite him inside to spend the night, make love over and over again and curl up together as they rested in between bouts of fantastic sex.

And then what? She still didn't have answers about him, and even if she did, she'd already vowed that her chosen career as a marine biologist meant traversing the world's oceans, not staying put and having babies with some man who'd just end up leaving her when he got bored. Just like her father had left her mother.

Long ago she swore she'd never end up like her mother, broken-hearted and pining away for a man who'd forgotten all about his wife and daughter the minute he'd walked out of their lives. No, Isabelle's work gave her all the fulfillment she needed. She wasn't going to base her happiness on a man.

Her mother never loved again, never lived again, after Isabelle's father left. She swore every time the tears of loss rolled down her mother's face that she'd never let a man do that to her.

Not ever.

The first thing she did was connect her laptop and get online, sending out some emails to the Oceanic Institute. She wanted to know who the experts were on humans diving without oxygen tanks, and what the known record was for holding one's breath while in a dive.

She'd read about it before, but never researched it and had certainly never seen it firsthand as she had with Dax. He had to have been down there at least ten minutes today, much longer than any human should be able to survive without oxygen.

And yet he hadn't seemed the least bit uncomfortable, not even when she'd heard his words in her mind. Even when he had swum away, it hadn't been in an upwardly direction.

She'd get some damn answers about him. There was something fishy going on around here, and she wasn't referring to the fish in the ocean.

After she'd sent out her queries, she closed the laptop and put it away, then readied herself for bed.

The waves crashed against the shore, the salt-tinged air streaming in through her open window. Night creatures walked the beaches and swam in the oceans, their calls and cries filling her ears with thoughts of Dax. No matter how hard she tried, the ocean she loved so much was now irretrievably connected to a man she'd known intimately, and yet didn't know at all.

Despite the fact she was still wide awake, she slipped under the covers and turned out the light, determined to put Dax and whatever feelings he'd stirred out of her mind. First thing tomorrow, she'd get some answers to the questions about who he was. Next time, she wouldn't let sex distract her.

* * * * *

The ocean called to him. Tired of trying to sleep in the bungalow on the beach, Dax paced back and forth. His mind and body stayed connected to Isabelle. Isabelle and his home in the sea.

But mainly, Isabelle. He felt her tension, her wariness and her desire. Her thoughts filled his head. Her uncertainties registered like a shout in his mind. She doubted both him and herself, and he wanted to go to her and offer comfort.

Exactly the last thing he should do, and he damn well knew it. The best thing would be to get as far away from her and her thoughts as possible.

He slipped out of the bungalow, glancing over at hers and noticing the lights were out. Maybe she'd gone to bed, but she wasn't asleep. Her mind was filled with images of their lovemaking. His was, too. In that, their connection remained. Dax's cock hardened at her visions, her wishes, her unspoken desires so similar to his own.

It was time to get away, and fast. Before he did something really stupid like walk through her door and grant all her secret wishes.

He ran down the beach and dove into the water, its salty chill somewhat relieving the ache between his legs. The dolphins came to greet him, chirping their hellos and filling him in on their day. He spoke in their language, laughing at their jokes and descriptions of the tourists of the day.

After he bid them farewell, he headed to the depths of the ocean, going deep for miles, way beyond the level where land humans could survive.

He swam through the doorway to his sanctuary. The glass enclosure was his haven, and his place to work. The large screens within the lab played a constantly running silent picture of his assigned area. Surveying the action on the monitor, he breathed a sigh of relief. The seas were calm. At least nothing major went on while he was topside fooling around with Isabelle.

Something he knew damn well he shouldn't be doing. But he couldn't help himself. The situation presented itself, she was warm, smelled good, alluring as hell silhouetted in the moonlight, and he'd taken advantage of her.

Not that she'd seemed to mind one bit. His cock twitched as visions of the two of them entwined in the water came to mind. Her scent, her sweet taste, the feel of her body merged with his all combined into one irresistible combination.

And then she'd dropped him faster than a tuna running for its life from a hungry shark.

But why? What had he said or done to upset her? It seemed as if she couldn't get away from him fast enough, almost as if she were afraid of him. At least the wide-eyed look on her face and nearly dead run toward her bungalow gave him that impression.

Then again, maybe she was afraid of herself, of how she reacted to him.

Yeah, right. Like he was some kind of super lover.

He dragged his hand through his hair, his gaze fixed on the clear wall in front of him. The world's oceans had been peaceful today, thankfully. Of course, if they hadn't been he'd have already heard about it. He'd have known, or one of his brothers would have let him know.

Someone was always in his damn head, anyway.

"Pisses you off, doesn't it?"

He wasn't surprised in the least to hear his brother Triton's voice. He felt the concern of his brothers, of Ronan, of the entire League. He knew it was inevitable that Ronan would send someone to talk some sense into him.

"Does what piss me off?"

"Having us in each other's heads."

Dax turned and grinned at his older brother. Triton's dark blue eyes sparkled with mirth despite his brotherly frown.

"I can tune you all out when necessary," Dax replied.

"You mean during those times you're fucking a hot little land lubber named Isabelle King?"

Dax shot a glare at Triton. "Mind your own goddamn business, Triton. I don't need you interfering in mine."

Triton raised a dark brow. "I see."

"See what?"

"This land human means something to you."

He didn't want to get into this discussion, knowing a lecture would follow about how he was taking chances he shouldn't be taking. Tell him something he didn't already know. "Tell Ronan I have a handle on things and I know exactly what I'm doing."

Triton snorted. "Famous last words. Ones I've spoken myself before. And I was dead wrong, if you'll recall."

His anger forgotten, Dax walked over to Triton and placed his hand on Triton's bicep, over the dolphin tattoo that matched his own. "Your situation was different. It's not the same thing at all."

Triton's eyes darkened with the pain and anger he clearly still harbored for all land humans. Dax knew his brother's pain stemmed from one woman who'd broken his heart.

"I'm sorry, Triton. I didn't mean for this to bring up the past."

"She didn't break my heart," Triton said, replying to Dax's thoughts. "Best damn thing that could have happened was her decision to leave the oceans. I don't need or want a life mate who doesn't want to live with me in the sea."

Shit. He hadn't meant to dredge up Triton's pain. They all knew how much Leelia had hurt him despite his efforts to show an uncaring front. "You cared about her. She hurt you. In doing so, she hurt us all."

Triton shrugged it off, then narrowed his eyes. "This isn't about me. I'm here to talk about you."

Dax sighed and focused on the scanners, comforted by the soft whirr of oceanic images playing across the screens. "There's something special about her, Triton."

When Triton didn't respond, Dax looked up. The hard glint in his brother's eyes had softened and he said, "I know. I felt it. Hell, Dax, you know how it is. We all felt it. Whenever one of us connects to someone like that we all know about it."

He wondered what privacy would feel like. Just for one damn day, to keep his emotions to himself. But that wasn't their way and it had never bothered him before. Until he met Isabelle. "There's nothing going on between me and Isabelle. She doesn't want there to be. It's just...I don't know. Sex."

"Uh huh. Just sex."

"Exactly. I'm not tied to her in any way. This will play out and then she'll be on her way and so will I."

"You don't operate like that, Dax. You never have, although I've tried my damndest to get you out for some fun. I just worry about you getting too close with this woman. Fun is fun, but you know every time we let a land human into our world, that's one more person who knows about us."

"That's not going to happen. We're not heading in that direction. Hell, right now I don't even think she likes me." Although she sure as hell enjoyed the fucking tonight. And she writhed and panted and screamed to the heavens when he licked her pussy.

"You know," Triton said, a gleam forming in his eyes, "there are a helluva lot of water sprites more than eager to fulfill every one of your fantasies. And they don't mind sharing you with each other, either. They give the best damn orgies under the sea."

Dax laughed. "I'm not looking for a fuck, Triton."

"Then what are you looking for? A life mate? A woman who'll live under water with you, raise some babies? And will this woman give up her life topside to do that? It's a very rare land female who'll sacrifice all she knows to be with one of us."

He massaged the ache at his temples. The one that had been growing to near pounding size by the minute. "Don't you have work to do, Triton? Surely Ronan has some task more important for you to do besides watching over me."

"Nothing more important than you, Dax. I don't want to see you hurt like…"

Dax's gaze met the pained eyes of his brother, and he nodded, knowing Triton's intent was to spare him the same pain he, himself had gone through. "Thanks. Duly noted. Now go watch your corner of the world."

They grasped arms and Triton said, "Think about what I said."

As he watched Triton swim away, Dax realized grimly that it was all he'd been thinking about since the moment he'd spotted Isabelle on the beach.

Chapter Seven

Early the next morning, Isabelle rapped on Dax's door, fully intending to question him about his origins.

Of course, he wasn't there. She turned and scanned the beach and water, looking for signs of him. The sun had barely risen, its cheery rays highlighting the glassy surface of the turquoise ocean.

No one was out there. No boats, and certainly no people diving.

And no Dax. Which didn't surprise her in the least. She'd bet a million he was hiding out somewhere, hoping to avoid answering questions about himself.

Irritated, she stalked to her bungalow, grabbed her bag and set off for the hotel. He was probably mingling around with the masses on the other side of the island. What normal male wouldn't? All those sexual games? Would be difficult for a guy to resist.

Either that or he was diving somewhere. And the ocean was way too expansive to even attempt to find him.

But find him she would. And when she did, she'd get answers to her questions.

The resort was busy this morning, couples scurrying off to various sexual activities, no doubt. Her thoughts drifted to the sexy fun and games she'd enjoyed with Dax last night. Her body thrummed to life, heating up at the images of his warm mouth covering her nipples, the way he licked her pussy until she screamed into the night, the feel of his cock stroking rhythmically inside her.

She fought the emotions that had grabbed onto her mind, forcing her to think about Dax in a way that was anything but clinical. This connection she'd felt last night had been nothing more than a fleeting aftereffect of some really great sex. She was a biologist—she knew how chemistry affected one's emotions. And that's all it had been with Dax. Just great sexual chemistry and nothing more.

The fact her body wanted more of it was just too damn bad. They'd had fun, she'd gotten the sexual release that she'd obviously needed, and that was the end of it.

Blowing out a sigh of frustration, she forced her thoughts away from the sexual and concentrated instead on looking for the source of her anxiety.

"You look lost."

Isabelle turned and smiled at Morgan Marino, then nodded. "Some days it seems that way to me, too."

"Are you looking for someone? Can I help you?"

How was she going to explain she was searching for her bungalow neighbor who'd fucked her brains out the night before and now she needed to ask him some questions to find out if he was even human. "You know that guy who checked in next door to me?"

"Dax Seagrove? Yes." Morgan frowned. "Is there a problem?"

"No, not at all. He was supposed to dive with me today and I can't find him."

Morgan pursed her lips. "You know, I think I saw him early this morning, following a group heading towards one of the activities."

Isabelle's heart fell to her feet. Activities? Like, sex activities? "Uhh, do you know which one?" And did she really want to know?

"Let me think a minute. Oh, now I remember. *Water Fun*. They'll be down at the beach. You should go join them. Have a little fun yourself while you're down there!"

Isabelle smiled politely at Morgan, thanked her and then headed down the path toward the private beach. A mix of emotions swirled through her. Dax hadn't seemed the type to engage in the sexual play at the resort, and had specifically told her he was only there to do some diving. So why did he suddenly decide to take part in the activities?

Had he been lying to her? Tricking her into thinking he was someone else, only to get her to spread her legs for him? Not that she hadn't been more than eager to do that, she thought with some disgust.

And now he was probably in the water with some strange woman, fucking someone else the same way he'd fucked Isabelle last night. Fury roiled within her and she stopped dead in her tracks.

What right did she have to be angry? Dax wasn't hers exclusively. In fact, she'd run like hell from him last night as soon as they'd finished having sex. He was free to fuck whomever he chose.

But still, it hurt that he'd no sooner pulled his cock out of her before he'd stuck it in another woman. And to think that last night she'd been worried about them getting emotionally involved.

Ha! Not likely considering his current whereabouts.

And yet she still marched down to the beach, intending to do what? Pull him away by the ear like a wayward husband? Give him a stern talking to?

Get real Isabelle. Turn around and go back to the other side of the island, and do your damn job! And they say it's only men who think with the brain between their legs? Ha!

Her feet ignored her wishes and kept walking. The end of the path opened up onto the sand beach. Isabelle's eyes widened and she skidded to a halt.

She gasped. Couples engaged in varying sexual activities were spread out all over the place. Many lay on blankets in the sand, the already steamy sun baking their naked, sweat-soaked bodies. Her gaze was riveted to the carnal pleasures they enjoyed. Oral sex, fucking, touching, any type of intimacy imaginable.

Others played in the water either on floating rafts for two or lying at the ocean's edge, the waves crashing over them.

Everywhere she turned there was sex going on! Didn't these people believe in privacy? She was no prude, but really!

"Shocking, isn't it?"

She jumped and turned at the sound of Dax's voice behind her, her momentary delight at seeing him immediately replaced by irritation. Maybe she'd been wrong about him. Maybe he did want to join in the intimate fun and games on the beach. "What I'm shocked about is the fact you aren't out there joining in."

He raised a brow and smiled. "Why would I join in?"

"Isn't that why you're here?" She hated the accusing sound of her own voice, but couldn't help herself. The mere fact she'd found him here confirmed her suspicions that she'd been royally used last night by an expert con man.

"Nah. Just studying human nature. Fascinating isn't it?"

She turned to follow his gaze. A couple kneeled on a blanket spread over the shimmering sand, naked and entwined. The woman was on her hands and knees, the man situated behind her, his cock plunging slowly in and out of her pussy. The woman had a death grip on the blanket spread underneath her, her eyes shut tight and howls of pleasure escaping between her open lips. As Isabelle watched, another man dropped to his knees in front of the woman, grabbed her hair and thrust her head back, then plunged his thick cock all the way down her throat.

It was savage, brutal, the woman immersed in the throes of pleasure. Despite Isabelle's annoyed state, her body responded to the hot sex on the beach. Her nipples tingled and hardened beneath her thin tank top and she instantly wished she'd worn a bra. But in this oppressive heat it had been the last thing on her mind. Looking down, she saw twin peaks poking against the nearly transparent white cotton and fought the urge to cross her arms to hide her arousal.

She shifted uncomfortably, trying to ignore the moisture seeping between her legs. Dax's position behind her wasn't helping. She'd clipped her hair up this morning and his breath caressed the wispy curls at the nape of her neck.

"Does watching other couples have sex turn you on, Isabelle?" he asked, his voice no more than a husky whisper.

"Not really. It's just biology," she lied. She'd never thought herself a voyeur, but her gaze was fixed on the threesome rocking and writhing together.

"I think you like that three-way over there." Dax lightly rested his fingers on her shoulders, caressing her enough to elicit goosebumps all over her skin. And yet her body burned at his touch.

"Do you ever think about having sex with more than one man?"

She should move away, should throw off his hands. She didn't want him to touch her. And yet her body melted at his light touch. Damn him! "No, I never think about things like that."

"Really." When his lips brushed the back of her neck, his teeth lightly grating across her sensitive flesh, she shivered, her nipples tightening into hard nubs. "I think you're lying to me. I think you do fantasize about all kinds of naughty things. Care to share?"

"I will if you will," she blurted, then closed her eyes and sighed, wishing she'd never come down here.

"Okay, let me tell you about my fantasies."

Oh, God. Did she really want to hear about them? "That's okay, I don't need to—"

But he started telling her, anyway. "They take place on a private island, a very small island with sand, trees, fresh water and plenty of fish and fruit. I'm marooned, shipwrecked maybe, washed ashore unconscious. When I wake, I realize I'm the only survivor."

Her imagination put him on the island. Weak, clothing tattered, and alone.

"I build a shelter and find food, but I'm desperately lonely. Days, weeks, possibly months pass by and I'm going crazy, talking to myself, desperate for companionship. Until one morning when I'm fishing on the beach, I see two women swimming out in the ocean. I can't believe it, either. They're beautiful...and naked. They dive under the water and I see fins. They're mermaids."

"Of course they are," she said, not bothering to keep the sarcasm from her voice. Every man's fantasy come to life. The only thing missing from Dax's description was a television and ESPN.

"I watch, transfixed for awhile, unable to believe my eyes. Then suddenly they step out of the water, their fins replaced by long, sexy legs."

Between Dax's story and the beach sex in front of her, Isabelle was sweating, beads of perspiration settling between her breasts and across her brow. She longed to strip off her clothes and head straight for the water, but for some reason she couldn't move.

"They approach me. They're dripping wet, gloriously naked, their soaked bodies glittering like diamonds in the harsh sun. One's a blonde, with long, curling hair all the way down her back. The other has raven hair, straight and long. Both have beautiful breasts...full, not overly large, with dusky nipples."

Dax moved his hands over her shoulders and down her arms, the straps of her tank top slipping down with his movements. Isabelle stilled, realizing she wore only her tank top and shorts. If she allowed him to continue, she'd be standing there bare-breasted in front of the other people on the beach.

The other people on the beach currently fucking each other to the point where Godzilla could step foot on the island and they wouldn't notice.

"Tell me what happens next in your fantasy," she said, the sun heating her breasts as he pulled her tank top down to her waist.

"The mermaids approach me, smiling, their arms held out as if they were there for the express purpose of pleasing me. They take turns kissing me, their lips soft and tangy like the ocean."

Right. And then they suck him and fuck him and he gets off and they go back to their watery lives while he lies there eating papaya with a shit-eating grin on his face. Gawd, how many times had she read this scenario about a man's fantasy?

"So, I lay them both down on the palm fronds I've used to make a bed, shading them from the sunlight. They look so beautiful lying side by side like that, one light and the other dark."

Isabelle resisted the urge to snort. Next he'd watch the two women go at it. Another top ten on the male wish list.

"I kneel down between them, running my hands over their feet and ankles. Their skin is like the softest silk. I feel their calves, their thighs, watching as their breathing begins to labor the closer I get to the treasure between their legs."

Isabelle's breathing was doing a little bit of its own laboring, imagining Dax inching his hands up her body slowly, knowing he was going to touch her *there*, but not yet.

He moved his hands over her arms, his knuckles brushing the sides of her breasts every time he passed them. She sucked in a breath and shuddered at the contact, her body crying out for his hands to cover her breasts, tweak her nipples, turn her around and kiss her so hard she couldn't think straight.

Not that she was thinking straight right now. Her mind was befuddled with mixed thoughts of needing to ask him about his origins and begging him to fuck her right there on the sand.

"The women reach for me, but I just smile down at them," he continued, his hands stopping at her waist to knead her flesh. He gripped her hips and said, "Instead, I lean over and slide my hands over their breasts, watching their nipples stand up in their excitement."

He demonstrated by cupping her breasts, his hands blazing a scorching trail as he swept his palms over the round globes. Her nipples stood painfully erect and begging for his touch. As he rolled the sensitive buds between his thumb and forefinger, shocks of pleasure pulses sailed straight to her pussy.

"The women lick their lips in anticipation, knowing I'm so close to giving them what they crave, and yet I want to hold off, make them nearly beg for it, make it good for them."

She let loose a whimper when he moved closer, his hard cock pressing against the cleft in her ass. Hell, she needed more than shorts to keep his touch from firing her up. She needed damn body armor. Steel-plated.

He flexed his fingers against her hip and slowly slid the zipper down on the side of her shorts. Resting his chin on her shoulder, he whispered so softly his breath fluttered against her cheek. "Each woman watches me touch the other, knowing that whatever the other feels they soon will too. I kiss them both, our tongues hot and wet and sizzling together in a slow mating dance. While I kiss one I fondle the other, pinching her nipples until she gasps in pleasure."

With one quick movement her shorts puddled at her feet. Dax reached around and palmed her lower stomach. It jumped and quivered against his hand. His fingertips rested on the top half of the curls covering her mound. Maybe if she stood on her toes his fingers would dip down and relieve the throbbing torture he'd begun.

"Finally, they're begging me to help them, to release them from their torment. I lie down on the palm fronds and pull the dark-haired girl over my hips, watching as she impales her pussy on my straining cock. The other, the blonde, knows what to do and she straddles my face, positioning her dripping pussy over my eager mouth."

Isabelle whimpered as Dax's fingers began a slow march down her mound, nearly reaching her aching clit only to slide back up and out of reach of the intense pressure building between her legs. With his other hand he cupped her breast, beginning a relentless petting of her nipple until she nearly cried out. She bit down on her bottom lip to keep from begging.

"Both the mermaids are hot. Very hot. The raven-haired beauty rides my cock like a forty-foot wave, gliding back and forth and grinding her pussy against my pelvic bone. The blonde moves her hips rapidly over my face, her sweet nectar pouring over my tongue and chin. I'm licking her lips and clit as fast as I can."

"Dax, please." Isabelle couldn't help it. The couples on the beach had reached a near frenzied state. Some of the other couples had already come. Others were near the edge, the crescendo of moans and cries of ecstasy building like an orchestra finale.

He moved against her, the fabric of his shorts sliding down and rustling against her legs. Then he was naked behind her. She backed against his cock, his scorching shaft nestling between the cheeks of her rear. He rocked against her and she knew that he wanted this as much as she did.

And yet he still hadn't slid his cock deep inside her, still hadn't made that first move to release them both from this torment.

"Now it's getting intense," he continued, his voice tight with desire. "They're close to coming and so am I. The dark-haired woman digs her nails into my chest as she raises her hips and plunges down hard onto my cock. The blonde is shrieking as her orgasm approaches, grinding her pussy into my face."

The threesome she'd been watching reached the pinnacle together, the one in front pulling out to spray his come all over the woman's eager tongue. The other gripped the woman's hips and drove hard inside her, his body shuddering with his release. Finally the woman screamed with her climax, throwing her head back and howling like a wild animal.

"And then I'm coming along with them, shooting hot jets deep into the dark-haired girl's pussy. She's whimpering uncontrollably, the blonde has come all over my face and I'm lapping up her juices, and then the three of us cuddle up for a nice, long nap afterward, knowing this is just the beginning of some seriously hot and heavy sex."

"Dax, fuck me. Now, please." She hated begging, hated to be the one to ask him to do it when she knew damn well he was primed and ready for her, but she couldn't wait any longer. Her fingers slipped between her legs in search of her clit, but Dax grabbed her wrist and yanked her hand away, then turned her around. Her breasts pressed against him, her nipples hardening as they brushed the firm planes of his chest.

He took her mouth in a kiss that seared her senses. She held on tight, not wanting to let go of the spiraling need that flamed at the touch of his lips to hers.

Keeping his hands on her body, he dropped to the ground, then pulled her down on top of him. She dug her fingers in the sand and straddled him, his cock probing the entrance to her drenched pussy.

"Is this what you want?" he asked, his tone harsh and guttural. "My hand on your clit like this? He searched between the folds of her pussy until he found her aching nub, then slowly massaged it with his thumb. Pleasure burst like a rocket between her legs.

"Yes," she moaned, lifting her hips and positioning herself against his burning shaft.

"And this, is this what you want, too? My cock buried deep inside that hot pussy, so deep it makes you scream?" At that moment he plunged inside her with one quick thrust, burying his thick shaft so far she felt it in her belly.

"Yes!" she screamed, uncaring who heard, who watched. This is what she'd wanted, what she'd needed from the minute she'd run away from him last night. No, she hadn't been nearly finished with wanting him then, and she wouldn't be after today, either. Whatever hold he possessed on her was magical, like nothing she'd ever known before. Right now she didn't care who or what he was, as long as he kept his hard cock inside her.

Such sweet torment, his thick shaft filling her with each thrust of his hips. She rocked against him, pushing her swollen clit into his questing fingers, urging him to stroke the nub faster as she moved like lightning against him.

"Yes, baby. Fuck my cock," he groaned.

She lifted up and then dropped down over his shaft, harder each time. He kept his thumb on her clit, massaging gently. She reached behind her and cupped his balls in her hands, lightly tugging until he groaned long and loud.

The faster she moved against him, the faster he strummed her clit. The dual sensations of his cock stroking her inside and his fingers plucking at the sensitive bud outside had her reaching the pinnacle in an enormous burst.

She heard the screams but didn't know if they were hers or another woman on the beach. Dax's fingers dug painfully into her hips as he lifted up and released inside her, his groans loud and guttural. She rocked against him and squeezed her pussy, milking the last drop of come from his straining body.

He pulled her alongside him, both of them drenched in sweat and fighting for breath.

Her heart pounded against his chest in time to his own rapid beat. She smiled thinking about how they lay right where they fell together, in the way of anyone wanting to walk up the path, and more than certainly in prime view of every person on the beach.

She should care that they were so visible, but she didn't. She should care that the man she made love with wasn't even human. But she didn't. Completely satiated and enjoying the afterglow of spectacular lovemaking, she'd do a naked table dance in the middle of the hotel lounge right now and it wouldn't faze her a bit.

Dax's origins could plague her later. Right now she wanted to shut off the logical part of her mind and simply enjoy the moment.

"How about a swim to get the sand, sweat and other stuff off?" Dax murmured, kissing the top of her head.

The tiny gesture warmed her and she nodded. "Yes, definitely."

"Then a long, cool drink, and then I promise you we'll talk."

Talk. As in finding out about him. He stood and she admired his body. So perfect, so lean and muscular. He must be some sort of athlete judging from his build. He held out his hand and pulled her up, taking her into his arms for a blistering kiss. When he pulled away, his ocean blue gaze held hers, his expression dark and unfathomable.

What was he thinking? About her, about them, about what they'd just shared? She'd love to know his thoughts. Hell, at this point, she'd be satisfied knowing anything about the mysterious Dax.

Isabelle pondered what would happen next. What secrets did Dax hold? And how much would he reveal to her?

The biologist in her wanted, needed to know. The woman in her feared the revelation, wondering how it would change things between them.

Chapter Eight

"Okay, talk," Isabelle said, leaning back in her chair at the poolside bar. She crossed her arms, giving her the appearance of a detective interrogating a prisoner.

"Did you enjoy what we did earlier, Isabelle?" Dax knew he was stalling, but couldn't help it. Not only did he want to avoid any and all discussions about who he really was, he also wanted to focus on Isabelle, on her reactions to the wild sex they'd just shared.

It had been hot, that much was certain. Hotter than he'd ever imagined sex between two people could be.

"Yes. I enjoyed it very much. Now start talking."

"You're very beautiful." At least on that subject he wouldn't have to lie. Her face glowed with the aftereffects of her orgasm and her eyes glittered like amber jewels in the afternoon light.

"You're trying to distract me."

"Is it working?"

"Not this time. Now spill."

"I just did," he said, winking at her.

Her lips twitched, curving into a sensual smile that shot straight between his legs.

"I'm serious, Dax," she said, the smile leaving her face. "I need to know about you."

He reached for her hand. "Why?"

"Why? Because I'm a biologist. Because there aren't supposed to be people who can do what you do."

"Does the unknown frighten you?"

She paused, then shook her head. "Actually, no. Just makes me curious. And the things I've seen you do defy human biology."

His first thought was to blurt out that he wasn't human and therefore not tied to the rules of human biology. But he didn't. Wouldn't. Some things she was better off not knowing. Which meant he'd have to dream up a pack of lies about who he was and how he could do what he did. This would require some careful thought.

"Not here," he said, once more stalling for time.

"What do you mean, not here?"

"We're in a public place, Isabelle, and there are other people nearby. While I trust you with what I'm going to tell you, I don't want anyone else to hear."

She turned her head to one side, then the other. Apparently she just now noticed they weren't alone. The poolside bar was filled with people, many of them couples they'd watched during this morning's beach sexfest. She blushed, her skin coloring a crimson gold. "Sorry. I hadn't noticed."

He beamed, for some reason pleased that he had her full attention.

"Then let's go back to my bungalow," she suggested.

They stood and headed for Isabelle's golf cart. Dax stayed silent during the drive, trying to manufacture the lies he was about to spout.

"I need a shower first," she said as soon as they arrived at the bungalows.

Dax nodded. "Me too. I'll be back after I've cleaned some of the sand off."

Among other things. Remnants of Isabelle still clung to him, her sweet and musky scent lingering on his skin. Although loath to wash her off, he went to his bungalow and quickly showered, his body relaxing under the warm spray.

After he dried off and donned a pair of swim shorts, his first thought was to head to the beach and dive down to his sanctuary, altogether avoiding having to invent bogus explanations for his existence. Hiding out seemed like a very attractive option.

Coward. This was his doing in the first place. He'd made himself visible to her, then did a dive without an oxygen tank. Had he thought she wouldn't notice?

Heaving a disgusted sigh, he walked across the sand and rapped on the door to Isabelle's bungalow. She yelled out for him to come in, but when he entered she was nowhere to be found.

"I'm just finishing up with my shower, Dax. I'll be right out."

Intrigued, he walked toward the sound of her voice. He smiled and leaned against the open doorway to her bedroom. Isabelle stepped out of the bathroom and stopped in front of the mirror on her dresser. She was clad only in a towel tucked around her body, her dark hair streaming in long, wet strands down her back.

His cock leaped to life at the vision before him. She still hadn't spotted him. She was focused on her reflection in the mirror, busily brushing out her wet hair. The white towel was a stark contrast to her golden skin, which was still damp from her shower. He longed to kiss the lingering droplets on her shoulders and arms, then move down her body and lick every inch of her until his mouth settled on the sweet spot between her legs.

He dragged a ragged breath out of his lungs, his shaft rigid and pulsing with an ache that seemed a constant presence whenever Isabelle was around.

Finally, she caught sight of him in the mirror and turned. He expected her to yell for him to get out, but she merely smiled. A seductive, sensuous smile that tripped down his nerve endings and exacerbated his already pounding erection.

Now that she faced him, his gaze caught the knot of the towel tucked between her breasts. Without a word he stepped toward her, noting how she placed the brush on the dresser and stood there, waiting for him. Anticipating maybe? He hoped so. Their minds were connected in some way. Perhaps their desires were the same, too.

He stopped an inch or so in front of her, breathing in the fresh scent of peaches, watching her breasts swell above the towel with every deep breath. Her eyes darkened, her pupils dilated rapidly and he knew she felt the same vibrations of desire that swept through his body like a lightning storm.

Would she ask him to leave her bedroom, remind him that they needed to talk? She'd seemed adamant about nothing getting in the way of their discussion.

What coursed through his mind right now would definitely interrupt their discussion about him.

She stepped into that inch of space he'd left open between them, threaded her fingers through his hair and pulled his mouth down to hers.

Shock electrified his heart as her tongue dipped inside his mouth, sliding against his teeth and curling alongside his tongue. This he hadn't expected. She'd wanted answers to her questions, not more sex. At least that's what he'd thought.

Quit questioning the why of things. Put your arms around her and take what she's offering. He pulled her fully against him, his cock nestling against her mound. Blood roared through his ears like a crashing surf as she yielded to him, her body pliant and inviting. Her whimpers and moans led him to believe she was as eager as he, that she wanted him as much as he wanted her.

At this rate they'd never have that conversation he was dreading. It seemed as if they couldn't occupy a room or location together for more than a few minutes without passion erupting between them and taking over completely.

Not that he minded. In fact, he preferred it this way. If they didn't talk about it, they could simply enjoy each other until...until what? Until he got called away and had to leave her? Or even worse, until he told her about himself and she ran, unable to face who and what he was?

Right now he refused to think about that possibility. He'd waited too long for her and they'd just begun to learn about each other. He wished he could tell her everything, but he couldn't.

For now, he'd simply enjoy having her in his arms. She tasted like the ocean—full of magic and wonder. Her mouth moved slowly over his, her tongue teasing and tasting. Dragging his lips away from hers, he pressed light kisses down her neck and across her shoulders, then reached for the knot holding her towel together.

With a quick movement, her hand clasped his wrist and she pulled away. Instantly he dropped his arm to his side, thinking she'd decided to stop. Instead, her lips curled in a seductive smile.

"Go sit over there," she said, motioning with her head towards the king-sized bed centering the room.

At least she hadn't thrown him out. He settled on the edge of the mattress, his cock clamoring for release.

"Watch me." Her eyes glittered with unspoken words.

Like his gaze could focus on anything but her lush body. He was mesmerized and she was the seductress, the siren who hypnotized him.

She seemed hesitant, uncertain, as if she didn't realize how seductive she really was. Yet just standing there, she oozed more sexuality than any woman he'd ever known. She reached for the knot on the towel and slowly pulled it from between her breasts. The towel slid to the floor as if in slow motion, revealing her bronzed body inch by glorious inch. Dax swallowed past the lump in his throat and fought to keep from reaching between his legs and stroking his cock.

"Slip off your shorts," she commanded.

She didn't have to ask him twice. He stood, his gaze never leaving her heated eyes, and reached for the waistband of his shorts, sliding them down and off.

Her eyes gleamed with passion as she looked her fill of him from head to toe.

"You have a gorgeous body, Dax," she said, approaching him slowly. "Tanned a golden color, your skin soft, your muscles lean and defined, your—"

She'd stopped her visual assessment, focusing on his straining cock. "Yes, quite a hard body."

He willed her to touch him, his thoughts urging her soft hand to palm his shaft and stroke it. But she didn't, instead raised her head and met his eyes, stepping close enough that he could see the gold flecks dancing around the green. "You know, the other day you did something wonderful for me."

"What's that?" he rasped, barely able to find his voice.

With the tips of her fingers she traced lazy circles over his shoulders and chest. "You licked me and made me come."

His throat went completely dry. "Yes. I enjoyed it. You taste sweet, Isabelle."

When he would have reached for her she placed her palms on his chest, stopping him. "No. I want to do something. Sit down."

He sat quickly, his balls tightening when she dropped to her knees between his legs, her mouth at perfect eye level to his engorged shaft. As if it recognized Isabelle's mouth, it leaped toward her. Her eyes widened and she threw her head back and laughed.

"I take it this is okay with you?" she asked, leaning forward and resting her arms on his thighs.

"Hell yeah. Get to it, woman," he teased.

She giggled and leaned up to capture his mouth in a kiss, her tongue darting in and out. Her breasts brushed his chest, teasing and tantalizing him with their beaded tips. But when he tried to touch her, she wriggled away and settled back down between his legs.

Her fingers pressed deeply into his thighs, massaging his muscles, bringing that part of his body to raging life. Her hands were magic, inching closer and closer to his erection and yet not touching him there. His first impulse was to grab her wrists and force her fingers around his shaft, but this was her game and he'd let her play it out in her own way.

After all, right now they should be talking about who he was and where he was from. This wasn't at all what he'd envisioned and he wasn't going to do anything to take her focus away from what she wanted to do to him.

He just hoped he had the patience to sit still while she touched him. He dug his fingers into the mattress and held on tight.

"You have a beautiful cock, Dax," she said in a husky voice that made him shudder with the need to bury his shaft inside her. "Not too big, *definitely* not too small." She rested her palms at the juncture of his thighs, mere inches away from his pounding hard-on.

Touch it, he willed silently. The burgeoning ache consumed him. Every ounce of blood in his body was centered between his legs. If she didn't touch him, and soon, he might have to resort to begging.

Isabelle didn't touch him, at least not with her hands. She leaned forward and licked the head of his shaft, then slowly slid his cock into her mouth. He sucked in a breath at the heat of her mouth surrounding him, at the visual of her sweet lips closing over his shaft. Pleasure arced through him when her gaze caught and held his.

Her mouth was magic, creating hot explosions of electricity as she took him deep inside her mouth. When she released his shaft, it glistened with her saliva. Drops of pre-come trickled from the head and she captured them with her tongue. He shuddered at the erotic vision.

"You taste salty, like the sea," she whispered, then grasped his shaft and stroked upward. He lifted his hips to give her easier access to his raging hard-on.

He lost it when she bent forward and traced her tongue around his balls. They tightened against his body, urging a release he knew he couldn't hold off for long.

"Damn that's good, baby," he moaned.

Her hands and mouth were heaven and hell, tormenting him with sweet pleasure and sins of damnation. She took the twin sacs gently in her mouth, the warm wetness of her tongue firing his blood and nearly taking him over the edge. Her hands moved rapidly over his shaft and he pumped his hips in time to her rhythm.

Her long hair tickled his thighs, adding more fuel to his already scorching fire. When she lifted up and coaxed his cock deep into her throat, he reached for the silken tresses and threaded his fingers through her hair, matching his thrusting hips to the rhythm of her movements.

"Ah, God, Isabelle, I'm gonna come."

She leaned up and covered his cock with her lips, sucking him deep as the first spasms of his climax shot hot come into her throat. She drained him, milking his balls, swallowing every drop of fluid until he had nothing left to give. Still, he pulsed within her heated mouth.

Dax fell back on the bed, exhausted and thoroughly sated. Isabelle climbed up and lay beside him, fitting her body against his. He wrapped his arms around her and pulled her close, inhaling her sweet fragrance. Her hair and skin held the peach scent he now associated with all things Isabelle. He pressed a kiss to the top of her head and ran his hands over her back.

She'd surprised him. More than surprised him—shocked the hell out of him, actually. Expecting an inquisition and getting a seduction instead was only part of what attracted him to Isabelle. Her wit, her thirst for knowledge and her acceptance and curiosity about him and his life totaled into one attractive package.

The fact they matched so incredibly well sexually only added to her allure.

"Did you like that?" she asked.

He had to laugh at her question. "What do you think? I must have pumped gallons of come down your throat."

She leaned up and over his chest, licking her lips in a way that had his cock stirring to life again. "You tasted good. I loved feeling your movements against me, hearing your heavy breathing and your moans. It really excited me."

He arched a brow. "Is that right?"

"Yes. It made me wet."

Her eyes widened as he brushed his cock against her thigh. "You're ready again?" she asked, the surprise in her voice making him laugh.

"I can't help it. You excite me."

"You excite me too, Dax. So much that I..."

Her words trailed off. He tipped her chin and forced her gaze to meet his. "Tell me what you want, Isabelle."

She sucked in her bottom lip and tilted her head to the side, hesitating for a few seconds before she said, "I think I'd like you to fuck me from behind."

The blush she wore on her cheeks was adorable. Clearly she wasn't used to talking about sex in such a graphic way. He, on the other hand, found her willingness to tell him what she desired exciting as hell. A quick glance around the room failed to give him the location or props he wanted. He leaped from the bed and pulled Isabelle up with him.

"Where are we going?" she asked.

"You'll see." He led her out of the bedroom and into the living room. Hmm, yes. The chair in there was perfect.

He placed her in front of the chair, pushing her forward until her body draped over the cushion of the low-backed chair. He stepped back and sucked in a breath, mesmerized by Isabelle's long legs stretched wide, her beautiful ass and pussy so clearly visible in this position.

"Hurry, Dax," she pleaded.

Reluctant to leave the vision she presented, he stepped forward, nestling his hard-on between the cheeks of her delectable ass. He patted her rear, then gave it a light tap.

Isabelle jumped and giggled. "That didn't hurt."

"Does this?" He smacked her right cheek, a little harder this time, feeling her muscles clench.

"A little."

He bent and kissed the slightly reddening spot left by his hand. "I'm sorry."

She half turned to look at him and grinned. "I wasn't complaining. I liked it."

Holy hell. Isabelle was a constant surprise to him. He reached around and grasped her breasts, her nipples hardening into the palm of his hands. He gave them a squeeze and she whimpered her pleasure.

"Are you going to fuck me soon or not?" she asked, passion-tinged impatience evident in her voice.

"Oh yeah, I'm gonna fuck you. Right now."

He pulled back and guided the tip of his shaft between the moist folds of her pussy. She spread her legs further apart and wriggled her ass, trying to get him into position. Her impatience made his hard-on more rigid, his anticipation more intense.

When he slid inside her, she gasped and shifted back, grinding against him. He pulled back and thrust harder, her pussy squeezing him. She was hot and tight and he nearly came again from the pressure of her clenching muscles.

She gripped the arms of the chair, her nails digging into the fabric as he plunged repeatedly inside her, each time deeper and harder. Dax could sense from her encouraging pants and moans and her drenched pussy that she wanted it rough and primal.

He reached for her hair, winding the long, dark strands around his fist and pulling her head back. She moaned and he pulled harder.

"Yes," she hissed. "Like that."

Grabbing one shoulder with his free hand, he pumped hard and fast, meeting her rearward thrusts with as much heat and fervor than she gave.

"Harder, Dax," she whimpered, her vaginal muscles quivering and squeezing him. He fought for control but her wild response to their lovemaking made it difficult.

"You like it rough, don't you, Isabelle?" he managed through clenched teeth.

"Yes. Spank me, Dax. Make it hurt."

Maintaining hold of her hair with one hand, he smacked one round cheek. Giving in to her request, he used a little more force this time, and her pussy flooded with moisture. "Like that?"

She bucked wildly against him. "Harder."

Aware of how strong he was, he hesitated, afraid he might hurt her.

"Harder, dammit!" she growled.

His mind was in a whirlwind, his body nearly out of control. Her voracious desire spurred him on. She was a wildcat, bucking against him and screaming out her demands that he take her roughly. He smacked her with much more effort and thrust faster. His balls drew up like hard knots against his ass and he knew he couldn't hold back any longer.

"Dax, I'm coming!" she cried, giving him all the impetus he needed to let go. Her pussy tightened around his cock and he shot another load of come deep inside her, pumping furiously until their juices mingled, drenching them both.

His legs trembled and he leaned against her back, his heart pounding out a rapid rhythm. Fighting to catch his breath, he held onto her, finally righting her to a standing position and turning her around to give her a scorching kiss. She returned the kiss with fervor, winding her arms around his neck and holding him close.

When he pulled away, he smiled at her satisfied expression. "I hope you enjoyed that."

She nodded. "More than I can ever tell you."

"I didn't know you liked it…shall we say, a little rough?"

Her cheeks reddened. "There are a lot of things I like that I'm just discovering now."

Dax wanted to think it was because of him. Or maybe she'd just never felt free enough to explore her sexual desires until she reached the island.

She might have a lot of questions about him, but he had quite a few to ask her, too. A sudden interest to know everything about Isabelle fixated in his mind.

"Location bringing out the wild woman in you?"

She snorted. "Hardly. I've been to many tropical islands before, Dax, and I've never behaved like this. Actually, I've never made love to a man while on a research trip."

Which of course begat questions in his mind about other men she'd been with. Questions he had no business asking. But damn if he could stop himself.

"No other guy has explored the rough side of sex with you?"

She sucked in her lower lip and shook her head. "No."

"Why not?"

"I guess I was never really interested in sex before…"

"Before what?"

"Never mind. Maybe I'm just a late bloomer."

She obviously didn't want to talk about her sexuality any further and he didn't want to press her. But she sure as hell made him feel like king of the world right now. If she'd let go with him like she'd never let go with another man, then there had to be something between them.

"Did you want to have that talk now?" he asked, knowing he should have let it lie, but also aware that Isabelle wouldn't forget.

She surprised him again when she shook her head. "I've got some phone calls to make and a little work to do on the laptop. Then I need to take a dive. Maybe later?"

"Of course."

"Why don't you come dive with me about six tonight?" she asked.

"Great. I'll meet you at the beach."

Isabelle kissed him lightly and left for the bedroom. Dax gathered up his shorts and went back to his bungalow, thoroughly confused by her demeanor. First she'd been dying to get answers to her questions about him. Now it seemed as if she didn't want to know.

Could he get lucky enough that he'd never have to reveal his secrets to her?

He hoped so. Once she found out who and what he was, any hopes for him and Isabelle would be lost in the depths of the ocean he called home.

Chapter Nine

Isabelle stared at her laptop screen, trying desperately to concentrate.

Impossible. All she saw, all she thought about was the way Dax made love to her, the way his body seemed to fit hers perfectly, the way he seemed to instinctively know exactly what pleasured her the most.

But she still didn't have answers about Dax, only this time she had herself to blame for delaying the inquisition. After her shower she'd stood in front of the bedroom mirror combing her hair and mentally compiling the list of questions she was going to ask him. Then he'd walked in her room and she'd spotted him, his gorgeous body reclined against her doorway, his perfectly chiseled face smiling at her. In an instant her mind had gone to mush and her libido had taken over.

Her skin burned at the thought of how she'd responded to him this afternoon, the way she'd shouted out her need for him to fuck her harder, spank her, pull her hair. Who knew she had latent masochistic tendencies? She sure as hell didn't know that about herself. Before Dax, the sexcapades she'd had were of the bland vanilla variety. Plain, routine, maybe a change in positions now and then, but nothing like the wild, no-holds-barred-beat-me-hurt-me-fuck-me-make-me-like-it saga she'd asked for. She chuckled at the phrase. Dax had certainly given her everything she'd wanted.

And more.

She picked up the document on her desk and fanned her heated face, forcing thoughts of Dax aside. Plugging in her laptop phone line, she checked her email, pulling the message from the Institute on free diving without oxygen tanks. She printed and scanned the report, not surprised at all to find that the world record for free diving didn't come anywhere close to matching the length of time Dax had been submerged.

Dammit! With an angry flick of her wrist she tossed the document to the floor. She knew it, and yet she didn't want it to be true. She'd hoped that perhaps Dax was some free diving world record holder, which would logically explain his ability to remain submerged for ten minutes or more. She knew enough about human biology to realize it wasn't possible.

Not with a human, anyway. So, how did *he* manage it? What was he, an alien or something?

Back to the questions. Questions she'd not-so-subtly avoided by sucking his cock and fucking him this afternoon. She couldn't do that forever. The marine biologist in her begged for answers to the mystery of Dax Seagrove. The woman in her was already emotionally involved with him.

Which spelled disaster no matter how many different ways she looked at it. He was a stranger, and at that she wasn't even certain he was human. She knew nothing about him other than what she'd found out during the past few days, which wasn't too damn much.

Just like her mother, she'd fallen for a man she shouldn't have fallen for. But unlike her mother, she wouldn't spend her life wishing for something that wasn't going to happen. She refused to live her life with an aching heart.

The laptop screen blurred, her concentration shot. She heaved a sigh and turned it off, knowing she'd get no work done. At least not paperwork.

She craved the ocean, the freeing expanse of water as far as her eyes could see, the weightlessness of floating through the depths with the creatures she'd come to know and love.

After getting into her swimsuit, she grabbed her dive gear. She glanced at the clock, then walked next door and rapped on Dax's door. He opened it and graced her with a wide grin that set her heart kickboxing against her ribs.

"You ready?" she asked, trying to still the emotions boiling within her. She had to keep emotional distance from Dax for so many reasons it made her head spin.

"You bet."

She was aware of his eyes on her body as he followed her. How could one make oneself walk ramrod straight? The last thing she wanted or needed was to give Dax any thoughts about sex. God knows she had enough of those kinds of thoughts for both of them.

She stopped at the water's edge to put on her tank and fins, inhaling a breath of fresh sea air. The ocean had always calmed her. She could pull up a chair and do nothing but sit and stare at the waves for hours and be perfectly content.

"It is beautiful, isn't it?" Dax asked, holding her tank up for her to slip her arms in the straps.

"Yes, it is. I've always loved the water."

"I know."

She turned and looked at him. "What do you mean, you know?"

"I just meant that you're a marine biologist. Clearly you wouldn't have gone into that field if you didn't like the water."

His innocent expression was ridiculous. There was much more to his statement than he'd let on. She mentally added it to her already too-long list of questions.

"So, what are we diving for today?"

She frowned. "Don't you have a turtle to find?"

"Yeah. But I figure I can help you with whatever you're doing, too."

"As it turns out I'm on a turtle expedition myself. "

"That works out well, then. We're both after the same thing." He stepped a foot or so into the water, stopping when she didn't follow. "What?"

"No tank again?" *Please put on a tank. Show me you're normal, human, don't make me ask the questions I don't want to ask.*

He seemed to ponder the idea for a few seconds, then shook his head. "Nah. Too confining."

She sighed and followed him into the surf, wishing she had answers but at the same time not wanting to find out the truth. She knew it would change things between them.

Maybe the dive and search would take her mind off Dax. Although having him swim beside her wasn't helping. She couldn't even look over at him as they swam out and began the dive, knowing he was somehow holding his breath and not understanding why or how he had the ability to do so.

Shaking off the plaguing uncertainties that bombarded her mind, she took the welcome plunge into the depths of the sea. Turtles may be nesting near the shore so she didn't want to go too far out today. Dax seemed content to follow along her chosen path, so she took the lead.

It didn't take long to reach the shallow ocean floor. Coral sprung up like the skyscrapers in a large city, some taller than others, their colors vibrant. As always, the sight took her breath away. The water undulated around the brightly painted creatures, making them appear as if they waved to her in greeting.

A relaxing calm settled over her. Every dive seemed like a return home to Isabelle. She'd long ago stopped questioning why she felt more comfortable under the water than she ever had on land.

Colorful Angel Fish swarmed around them, so thick she could barely see in front of her. They swam along with her, surrounding her like a cloak of protection. She giggled at their back and forth antics. Sometimes she could swear that the sea life spoke to her, but she knew it was only her overactive imagination. Or maybe wishful thinking.

She was so enthralled watching the waving coral that when Dax grasped her wrist she nearly jumped out of her skin. When she turned to him, he pointed to a rock ledge several meters away. Several Leatherback sea turtles nestled under the ledge, sound asleep. Not wanting to disturb the sleeping creatures, she barely took a breath.

They were huge, their barrel-shaped bodies more than six feet long. She wondered how much Dax knew about the Leatherbacks, and suddenly found herself wanting to share her knowledge and love of the creatures with him. She mentally cursed the disadvantages of diving—no conversation.

You forget who you're underwater with.

Dax's voice penetrated her thoughts. He'd spoken to her again! Or thought to her. Or something. God, how did he do that? How did he get into her head and talk to her?

Stop that. Or don't stop. Explain. Dammit, Dax, I have questions!

I know you're frustrated, Isabelle. I'm sorry. We'll talk soon, I promise. Tell me about your turtles.

Even in her thoughts his voice was hypnotic...husky and warm like a blanket in the coldest winter.

She looked at her watch. They'd been down for fifteen minutes. No human could withstand lack of oxygen for that long. Instead of shock or resignation that her guess was right—it was now a certainty that Dax wasn't human—curiosity took hold. What was he? Was he even from earth? The old childhood excitement at the mysteries of the sea came rushing back to her.

All in due time, Isabelle.

I have so many questions, Dax. So much I want to know about you. She wished she wasn't wearing the tank or the mask, which obstructed her view of him. A part of her was filled with jealousy that she couldn't swim the same way he was...without a tank, without a mask, just her body and the sea.

You can. I'll help you. Take off your mask.

She heard him, but couldn't quite believe he'd even suggest such a thing. *I can't.*

Yes, you can. Take off your tank and mask. Trust me.

Trust him? She barely even knew him. And still he hadn't answered a single question. Okay, maybe she hadn't really asked him many questions yet, but it wasn't like he was jumping up to volunteer information.

And yet a curious excitement welled up within her. The opportunity to do what no other human had done. Was she actually considering the idea of taking off her mask and tank? Surely he wouldn't let her drown, would he? Indecision weighed her down more than the dive weights on her belt.

Trust me, Isabelle. Nothing bad will happen to you. I'll protect you.

But how? Oh, God, this was all so confusing! And yet deep down she knew instinctively that she could trust him. Even more, she *wanted* to do this.

Talk about a leap of faith. A giant leap that could cost her life if she was wrong. She unbuckled the belt holding the tank on her body. Dax swam behind her and lifted it off, but she was loath to let go of the regulator providing her oxygen.

Trust me.

She nodded and pulled off her mask, shutting her eyes against the briny water that she knew would sting and blind her. At the same time she felt his hand on her mouthpiece and pulled it away, he grabbed hold of her hand.

A sudden vibration shot through her palm and up her arm. Warmth soared through her, intensifying as if she drew closer and closer to a burning inferno. Fear sent her into a panic and she reached for the regulator, her arms flailing wildly. She couldn't see, couldn't hear, had lost her bearings completely. She was going to drown!

Relax, Isabelle. You can breathe.

No, she couldn't! Her lungs tightened painfully with her efforts to hold on to the last oxygen she'd inhaled.

Open your mouth. Breathe.

I'll die. I'll drown! She was on fire, the burning in her lungs equal to the flames licking at her skin. *Help me!*

Dax pulled her against him. *Open your eyes, Isabelle. Look at me. Trust me. You can breathe down here.*

She didn't want to trust him, shouldn't trust him. Her ability to hold her breath dwindled with every second that passed. She opened her eyes, wanting him to see her damning look right before she sucked in an ocean full of water, wanting him to know that he'd done this to her. With a shudder of resignation, she gave herself over to her soon-to-be watery grave and opened her mouth.

The water rushed down her throat and she waited for the choking sensation that she knew happened when one drowned. Expecting the clawing, gasping for air, she was shocked when it didn't happen. She could breathe, although she was breathing in water, not oxygen!

Confusion took over where panic had been. How could this be? How could she breathe ocean water? Her eyes weren't blurred by the water. She could see — more clearly, in fact, than she'd ever been able to with her mask on. Every color was more vibrant, the water pristine and transparent.

And she wasn't floating to the surface! She'd forgotten all about dropping her weight belt, and yet she hadn't drifted up. In fact, she realized as she tentatively began to swim about, she had more control under the water without the belt and dive gear than she'd ever had before. Slipping out of her flippers, she swam about like a fish, undulating through the water, rolling and swirling like a child enjoying a lawn sprinkler on a hot summer day.

She turned to Dax, who had perched on a ledge.

He grinned. "Enjoying yourself?"

His lips moved, and she could actually hear what he said. Could she do that, too?

"Can I talk down here?" She heard her own voice as she moved her lips. "Yes, I can! Oh my God, Dax, I can speak down here!"

He laughed and swam off the ledge, stopping in front of her and gathering her into his arms. "You can do anything you want down here, my golden mermaid."

Her heart flipped over at the endearment, but that's exactly how she felt. Like she had a long tail and a fin. She *was* a fish. An overwhelmed, ecstatic fish. "How is this possible? Tell me. I have so many questions I don't know where to start."

"I know you do. Come with me and I'll try to explain some of it to you." They pulled apart and he held out his hand. She grasped it willingly, wonder filling her with every deep breath of ocean water.

With one inhalation, Dax had changed her life. What lie ahead she didn't know. Where he was taking her she couldn't even hazard a guess. But he'd asked her to trust him once, and opened up a new world for her. A world she hadn't imagined existed. She didn't know what kind of world it was, or even what would happen to her now that her very biology had changed.

But one thing she did know for certain. At this moment, she'd follow Dax to the ends of the earth and beyond.

Chapter Ten

Isabelle let the tears flow, the salty drops mixing invisibly with the water surrounding her. She was swimming along like a fish—like the golden mermaid Dax had called her. He held her hand, periodically turning his head and smiling that boyish grin that never failed to make her insides churn with need.

But her tears hadn't come from the awe-inspiring events she'd already witnessed. When a dolphin swam up beside her, and she swore it smiled at her, she'd lost it completely, breaking down into a weeping puddle of joy.

The grey creature still moved along beside her, keeping pace with them. It looked over at her the same way Dax did, as if studying her.

"That's Zeus," Dax said, nodding toward the bottlenose.

"I see. And you know his name, how?"

"Because I told him."

Isabelle stopped and pulled her hand from Dax's. Okay, now that dolphin had *not* just spoken to her. She turned to Dax. "Did he do what I think he just did?"

"Yeah. He talks. Everything has a voice down here, Isabelle. Most people just can't hear them."

"I don't talk to just anybody, either, but Dax tells me you're okay for a land creature," Zeus said, his smiling mouth moving open and closed with his words.

She knew her eyes must be bugging out of her head as she stared open mouthed at the dolphin. Her mind spun. This wasn't happening. This world could not be real. "I'm dreaming this, right? We actually completed the dive earlier and I'm dreaming this entire thing. Or maybe I died when I took off my mask and tanks and this is heaven?"

Dax's lips curled in a smile. "If that's what you want to believe, then sure. You're dreaming, my golden mermaid." He held out his hand again and she tentatively slipped her palm in his, allowing him to propel them rapidly through the water. Zeus followed along, whistling. Isabelle shook her head, completely awed by this new world.

They reached a ledge in the ocean's floor that seemed to stretch for miles in either direction. Dax moved forward but Isabelle stopped, tugging at his hand. Below the shelf appeared a crevice that fell into complete darkness below. "I can't."

He turned and frowned. "Why not?"

"The depth...I'll be crushed."

"No, you won't. Come on."

She chewed her bottom lip and shook her head, refusing to budge. "I'm not going, Dax. I know the maximum depth a human can travel and survive. We're practically at that depth now."

He tilted his head and said, "Can a human breathe water and live, like you're doing right now?"

"Well, no."

"Then trust me. I haven't killed you yet, have I?" He winked and held out his hand.

He did have a point. She'd survived all the miraculous changes so far. Chances were he knew what she was capable of withstanding. She reached for his hand and let him lead her down into the darkness. Each meter they descended propelled them further into the black depths, much further than any known or documented exploration.

Isabelle tried not to let fear overtake her, yet she couldn't help the trepidation shivering along her spine. This murky trek was the unknown. The dark, blind, unknown. More so than anything she'd ever experienced. Before, she could at least see. Now she was forced to trust that Dax knew where he was going. She felt him alongside her, and clung to his hand like a lifeline, surely hurting his fingers in her squeezing grip. But he didn't complain once, just held on tight, his firm grasp reassuring her.

With every meter their speed seemed to increase. Before long they were bulleting downward at such a fast pace the water pressed in against her skin.

After descending for nearly ten minutes, she expected to feel the pressure. But she didn't. Dax had told her she wouldn't, and yet she still had a hard time believing she could defy physics.

The darkness began to close in around her, a suffocating squeezing of her body as if invisible walls were crushing her. Further and further they traveled down at lightning speed. Nothing physical affected her, merely the claustrophobic sensation of not being able to see. The only sound she heard was the fast rush of water flowing past her ears. Adrenaline kicked in and she tugged at Dax's hand. She wanted to stop, to go back up. But he wouldn't let her go.

And he wasn't speaking to her, either. At least not to her mind as he had before. She couldn't even look over at him to gauge his expression since she couldn't see. The silence unnerved her.

No. She couldn't do this. Fear coursed through her. She wanted to go back up. Back to the surface, where there was light. Where was he taking her? She didn't want to be in this blackness, this complete void of sensation.

When she would have told him so, a flicker of light appeared below them. Faint at first, then growing as they drew closer. It was almost a glow now, spreading out before them, a golden light shooting out rays of colors.

Her anxiety forgotten, she propelled herself forward with renewed enthusiasm, wanting to reach the light, needing to know what was down here when nothing was supposed to live at this depth. Hell, *she* wasn't supposed to live at this depth.

They were almost there, the light revealing a building of sorts. A structure? Like a house? But how?

Dax led her to some kind of glass enclosure. Intricate carvings of mermaids and sea creatures were etched on the outside of the glass, architecture like she'd never seen before. She looked over to him, intent on questioning him, but he looked straight ahead, leading her to an archway with no door. But where she would have swum through it thinking it was an opening, Dax stopped, waved his hand across the center of the archway and a nearly invisible door slid open. He pulled her inside, the door closing with a swoosh behind her, and suddenly they weren't swimming any longer.

The water she'd been breathing completely disappeared and she sucked in a lungful of oxygen. Fresh, clean oxygen.

Despite the pressure of the ocean surrounding them, there was no water inside the structure. The place was a house of sorts. Although everything was glass, or at least appeared to be transparent. She walked over to what looked like a sofa, surprised to feel the give of its cushioned softness when she pressed on it.

"I don't understand," she said, turning to Dax.

"Ask your questions." He had his back turned to her, fiddling with some kind of console against the wall. Oddly enough, with everything nearly transparent she could still make out objects. There was a dimension to everything, almost as if it were varying colors of transparency, from the brightest white to a near black, and yet no color at all. How confusing—stark, and yet utterly beautiful.

"What is this place?"

"My laboratory. My sanctuary. And occasionally, my home."

"You live here?"

"Sometimes."

"Where do you live at other times?"

He was touching invisible buttons and dials when suddenly a color image appeared on the wall in front of him, almost as if projected onto television screens. She peered around him, startled to see their beach and bungalow on one screen. Three other images captured the ocean, although she couldn't pinpoint exactly where.

"How?" she asked.

"Advanced imagery. I couldn't explain it to you because the technology as you know it doesn't exist."

"Try me. I'm fairly intelligent."

He looked over his shoulder at her and smiled. "I know. One of the things I...like about you."

She frowned, not sure what he originally started to say before he stumbled over his words.

"It's a mental imagery," he continued. "I can think of a specific area and it'll show up here."

"Any place you want?"

"Yes. For example, the hotel." Without turning to look at the screen, Paradise Resort appeared.

"Is it a real time image?"

"Yes."

"How are you able to do that?"

"I can't explain it."

"Like I said before, Dax, I'm smart enough to—"

"There are some things I can't explain to you right now, Isabelle. Trust me."

She supposed, given what he'd already revealed to her, that she'd have to be satisfied with that answer. At least for now.

"Look around, if you'd like. I have a little work to do here."

She nodded, grateful for the opportunity to get her mind around all that had happened in such a short time.

The place appeared to be like a regular house, with a living area complete with sofa and chairs, a kitchen and even a bedroom. She walked down a hallway, still giddy over traversing through a nearly transparent house, and entered a bedroom which contained a king-sized bed and a cover that felt like jelly. Yet it wasn't sticky, just warm. It contained a regular looking bathroom that she couldn't see through to the outside. She guessed even sea people like Dax wanted their privacy. Isabelle chuckled at the thought of taking a shower or a bath while surrounded by the ocean. How odd.

Everything was strange and different and yet in so many ways exactly the same as her house above the surface of the water. Her head pounded with the thoughts jackhammering her mind. She headed back towards Dax and found him still standing at the monitor screens. She heard his voice and looked around, expecting to find someone, but he was alone.

"Who are you talking to?" she asked.

Dax turned and smiled at her. "No one."

She crossed her arms and fixed him with a stare. "I heard you talking."

"I talk to myself sometimes. Make mental notes of things I need to do."

"Uh huh. And what are those things you need to do?"

"Work things."

"What kind of work is that, Dax?" But before he could answer, she hit him with another question, the one that had been burning inside her for days. "Wait. Don't answer that. First, who or what are you?"

He opened his mouth to speak, then closed it. Opened it again, closed it again. Jammed his fingers through his hair. Finally he sighed and asked, "Are you hungry?"

That wasn't the answer she was looking for. But now that he'd mentioned it, her stomach growled. "As a matter of fact, I am."

He motioned her into the kitchen and pulled the lid on a box, setting out plates and filling them with shrimp and what she could only assume was vegetables.

"What do you eat?" she asked.

"Well, we don't have cows down here so there's no red meat," he said with a half-smile. "But we eat small shrimp and other fish, along with sea vegetables that won't be familiar to you."

He set a plate in front of her and joined her, watching as she took a bite of a long, green crispy substance. A tangy flavor burst into her mouth and she turned to him in surprise. "It's delicious! What is it?"

"It's like plankton. Loaded with vitamins."

Vegetables of varying colors, from purple to green to red, lined her plate. Some were round, some star-shaped, some flat like a piece of bread. All the flavors were different from sweet to salty. The shrimp, of course, tasted just like it did above the water. By the time she emptied her plate she was stuffed.

"That was fabulous. Thank you."

"You're welcome." He cleaned the plates at the sink and handed her a glass of blue liquid.

"What's this stuff?" she asked, swirling the liquid in the glass.

"Think of it as sea tea."

She sipped it, grinning at its sweet taste. "Yummy."

"Thought you might like that."

Satiated, at least as far as her hunger, she knew it was time. "Dax, about those questions I had…"

He lifted his shoulders and nodded. "Come with me and we'll talk."

She followed him to the sofa. It felt just like the one in her apartment back home in Texas. Dax turned to her and grabbed her hands.

"Okay, let's start with your first question, who or what am I. I can tell you I'm as human as you are."

"Not possible. You can breathe underwater."

His lips curled in a smile that took her breath away. "So can you."

"That's different. You did…something to me. How did you do that, anyway?"

Dax laughed. "One question at a time. I'm human, with an added capability for underwater survival."

"How?"

"Biology." He picked up a strand of her hair and let it slide slowly between his fingers. "You know about biology, right?"

Oh no. This time she wasn't going to let him distract her with sex, despite her body's response to the quickly heating look in his eyes. She gently slapped his hand away from her hair, rewarded with his soft chuckle. "Yes, I know plenty about biology. Now tell me about you. Are you a subspecies of humans? How long have you lived under the water? Are there more like you, and if so, where are they? And what is your purpose down here?"

He blinked, then smiled. "Damn, you're smart."

"Don't compliment me. Answer my questions."

"Kiss me first."

"Huh?"

"You heard me. Kiss me first and I'll answer a question."

"That's not fair."

His eyes widened. "I had no idea you thought my kisses were that bad."

"That's not what I meant at all and you know it. You...distract me."

The heat in his gaze melted and moistened her. Her body thrummed to life in anticipation of his mouth, his touch. Dax leaned in and ran his hand over her hair, his touch igniting the fire he'd started with just one look. "Distract you, do I? I like that. Now do I get that kiss?"

"No." Though she really wanted to. Her body was near demanding she lean forward and press her mouth against his. But she remained firm.

"Aw, c'mon, Isabelle. Just one little kiss?"

Oh, hell. "Fine," she said, intending to brush her lips against his and then hit him with more questions. But when she leaned toward him, he reached out and pulled her tight against him, fitting his mouth over hers in a kiss that surely raised the temperature of the water outside the glass enclosure.

His breath, tasting sweet from the blue tea they'd had, enticed her mouth. He swept his tongue inside and claimed hers, teasing with sensuous strokes until her heart pounded against her chest and her insides turned to complete liquid.

She was falling, spiraling down in the sensations of his mouth, his touch on her body. Her pussy moistened in anticipation, her breasts tingling as they brushed against the fine hairs of his chest.

The warning bells clanged. She had to stop or she'd never get her questions answered, and she wasn't going to let it happen. Not this time. She placed her palms on his chest and broke contact before she fell under his spell again.

"No, Dax. We have to talk."

"I *was* talking." He leaned forward and kissed her neck, sending shivers throughout her body. "Didn't you hear what I was telling you?"

Isabelle tried not to groan, but a whimper escaped as his lips seared her skin. "Umm, yes, but it wasn't in answer to any of my questions about your origin."

Oh, that felt nice. His lips moved down over her collarbone, his tongue leaving a moist trail of sizzling fire.

They shouldn't be doing this. But, frankly, right now she didn't care. All she knew was his mouth was heaven and she'd rather die than have him stop. Then she remembered, again, those burning questions that filled her mind, and realized Dax was once again stalling.

Isabelle pushed him away and stood, needing some distance between them to clear her head and calm the sensory overload caused by his kisses.

Dax arched a brow. Did he feel the same way that she did? Was his mind filled with passion and lovemaking rather than thoughts of explanations and revelations? Or was he purposely doing this to avoid answering her questions?

Chancing a glance at his shorts, she saw the evidence of his erection straining against the material. Desire flooded between her legs and she wanted nothing more than to jerk his shorts down, stroke his hot, hard cock and suck him until he erupted.

Her desire must have shown on her face, because he stepped forward, grabbed the straps of her swimsuit and yanked them down to her waist. He leaned down, capturing one nipple in his mouth.

She cried out with the searing ecstasy of his mouth on her aching bud, forgetting her questions, forgetting her desire for any knowledge other than knowing what it felt like to have his hard shaft plunging between her legs in these indefinable depths.

She needed his possession of her. Like a ravenous shark she dropped to her knees, tearing at his shorts until they pooled at his feet. With a greedy hunger that shocked her, she took his length into her mouth, cupping his balls and feeling his life force pulsing against her throat. He threw his head back and groaned, threading his fingers into her hair and holding her still while he pumped his cock once, twice, three times in succession against the back of her mouth.

She looked up at him and experienced a sense of feminine power that thrilled her. His head was tilted slightly back, his eyes closed, his body coiled tight with tension, jerking slightly each time she took him in her mouth.

Isabelle dug her nails into the flesh of his naked buttocks. She pulled back slowly, licking the tip of his shaft, loving the salty taste of his fluid.

"Damn, Isabelle," he choked, then looked down and watched her suck him. The juices of her arousal coated her pussy as their eyes met and held. She took him deep, then quickly, using her mouth and her hands to pleasure him.

"Enough," he said.

Dax pulled her up and kissed her, his body quaking with tense passion. "I want to see your body, all of it." He quickly discarded her swimsuit and scooped her up in his arms, then effortlessly swam through the archway of his home and into the open sea. Water rushed into her lungs again and yet her breathing never missed a beat. If she hadn't been filled with the desire to make love with him, she'd have questioned how that could happen.

Where was he taking her? Why outside? Why not in his house where it was dry?

Oh, screw the questions. Isabelle had only one question on her mind right now. How long would it take before she could get Dax inside her?

Chapter Eleven

Isabelle's heart beat swiftly against Dax's chest as he carried her outside his lab. Her arms were wrapped tight around his neck, her body tense with anticipation and an equal amount of the raging desire coursing through his body.

While he swam, he captured her lips in a heated kiss, plunging his tongue inside her mouth. His sonar made it easy to determine location so he could concentrate his gaze on the golden mermaid in his arms.

Damn, she was hot. Hot and full of passionate urgency. He'd been prepared to talk, to tell her as much as he dared, when her eyes had darkened, her pupils dilating, her gaze focusing on his growing hard-on. Then she'd attacked his cock with her sweet, hot mouth and he'd lost all capability for rational thought.

He pulled his lips away from hers, settling her on a soft embankment. Her eyes were closed, her dark lashes resting against her cheeks.

"Open your eyes, Isabelle," he said softly, wanting her to see where he'd brought her.

She did, then smiled at him, her half-hooded eyes sexy as hell.

"Look around you."

"I only want to look at *you*."

She reached for him and he was caught in her spell. But he stopped himself before his need for her took him over completely. "I want you to see this."

With a huge sigh she sat up, her eyes widening as she caught a glimpse of what he'd brought her here to see. "Oh my God!"

Exactly the response he'd hoped for. The grotto was his favorite place to relax, think and enjoy his life. He'd never shared it with anyone before now. And now, he saw it anew in Isabelle's eyes.

"Dax, this is...it's amazing!"

He followed her gaze to the waving underwater ferns and the rainbow of coral in every shape and size. Some were as small as a few inches in height, others tall as an oak tree. He'd always loved swimming among his sea-life friends. The Angel Fish were out in force today, their yellows and blues, stripes and solid colors a near blur as they swam quickly by. He let out a contented sigh. This was his wonderland and always had been.

"It's like a playground of color."

What he enjoyed the most right now was watching Isabelle's awestruck expression. His heart swelled with the love he could no longer deny. He'd hoped she'd fit into his world, and she'd exceeded his expectations. Where most land humans would be paralyzed with fear over the unknown, Isabelle embraced the beauty and wonder of his life in the same way he always had.

He reached for her hair, stroking the silken tendrils until she turned her head, her amber eyes bright and glittering with tears that no normal human would be able to see under the water. But he saw them. They sparkled like diamonds falling from the corner of her eyes and touched him in ways he couldn't begin to fathom.

"It's beautiful, Dax. I don't understand how this can all be. I have so many questions my head is spinning. But thank you for sharing your world with me."

"You're welcome." He leaned in for a kiss, lightly brushing her lips with his. She slipped off the embankment and reached for him, drawing herself against his body. When she wrapped her legs around his waist, his cock came to life, pulsing and hardening.

Isabelle kissed him back, her tongue dancing against his until sparks of arousal shot between his legs. His heart pumped madly as she explored his body with her feather-like touch, brushing his shoulders with caresses and moving her hands ever so slowly downward.

His cock rubbed against her soft mound and she whimpered, then leaned back, exposing her breasts to his touch. Wrapping her legs firmly around his hips, she tilted backward in the water. Dax petted the rosy nipples with his thumbs until they stood like hard peaks. His hands caressed her breasts and she tightened her legs around him, rocking her pussy against his cock.

With little maneuvering he slid fully inside her. She grabbed his arms and held on, grinding herself against him. He reached between them and stroked her swollen clit, rewarded with her cries of pleasure.

"Yes, touch me there, Dax." Isabelle leaned up and grasped his shoulders, her heated gaze meeting his.

Utilizing as much control as he could gather, he extricated himself from her vise-like grip, then pulled her body fully against his until they were entwined, legs tangled together, their hearts beating in rhythm against each other's chest.

He rolled them around the water together in positions they'd never be able to get into on land. When he turned them upside down, her hair stood on end and she laughed. When they stood upright but didn't touch their feet to the ocean floor, his cock pumped hard, buried to the hilt in her hot pussy. But side-by-side and undulating through the water was the position he enjoyed the most. Their lips touched, their bodies became one and he felt every part of her against him.

Especially the part of her that was soft, feminine and made for him. That part of her drove him to the brink of distraction and beyond. He couldn't think straight when he was inside her, could only bask in the pleasures of her sweet body and inhale her peach and musky woman scent that even under water remained a part of her essence. When she tightened around him, he knew her orgasm was close.

He wanted this to be special for her, this first time making love fully under the sea. He learned her body so quickly it stunned him, but every gasp, every small contraction of her pussy around his cock told him when he'd touched the right part.

"Dax," she breathed his name in a throaty whisper. Her voice was barely a whisper as she worked feverishly against him. She ground her pussy against his pelvis, pulling him ever deeper inside her until she cried with her climax. Dax held on tight and rode out the storm with her, never wanting to let go. Finally, he crested with her, his orgasm so powerful it rocked him to his toes.

They sailed through the water as their orgasms rushed through them. Dax finally slowed their pace, coming to rest against the soft embankment where he'd set her earlier.

After catching his breath, he sat up on the ledge and pulled Isabelle into a seated position in front of him. They sat together with fingers entwined, content to watch the colorful wonderland. Dax grinned at the sea creatures swimming playfully around them. He felt at ease when Isabelle laughed contentedly.

"Thank you," she said, brushing her back against his chest.

"No, thank you. I can't seem to think straight whenever you look at me the way you did."

She tilted her head back and met his gaze. "I look at you a certain way?"

"Yeah. Your eyes darken like molten gold and I lose myself in you."

"I like that. I can't help it. You do something to me."

He knew the feeling. She was certainly doing something to him. Making him forget who he was, who she was. Falling in love with Isabelle wasn't something he should have done, and now that he had, he knew he'd end up hurting her.

A school of dolphins approached, hovering no more than an arm's length away from them. Isabelle raised her hands to them, giggling when they swam just beyond reach of her fingertips. When they drew close enough for her to pet them, she squealed with delight, pushing away from Dax and swimming along with them. They swarmed around her as she hovered in the water, and Dax caught his breath, wishing he could paint a portrait of her just like she was at that moment.

She was beautiful, her hair billowing out in all directions, at least a dozen dolphins surrounding her. Her bronzed body glimmered like a golden statue, giving her the appearance of a sea siren calling the creatures of the oceans to do her bidding.

Apparently word had gotten out about her arrival, because the neon blue Parrotfish made their appearance shortly thereafter, along with yellowtail and blue tangs, all rushing in to catch a glimpse of the human water nymph who had joined their world.

Dax sat back and fed on Isabelle's delight, still in awe that she'd adapted so well to undersea life. A glimmer of hope ignited inside him, and he wondered if —

"Don't even think about it."

Isabelle's playland of fish stopped their circling and swarmed immediately around Ronan.

Damn. Just what Dax didn't need or want right now.

* * * * *

Isabelle froze at the imposing figure who'd magically appeared next to Dax.

Imposing was an understatement in describing the tall man. Dark hair flowed behind him, nearly long enough to capture in a ponytail. His cerulean eyes glowed against his tanned face as he frowned in her direction. He had the body of a god, beautifully sculpted muscles that rippled against the water. Clothing similar to a long loincloth covered the lower half of his body, but his gorgeous chest was bare.

Older than Dax, the man appeared to be in his forties, if age were even a factor with the mysterious undersea people here. And there had to be *people*, many of them. Instinctively she knew that more than just Dax and this stranger lived down here.

The stranger was gorgeous. Not like Dax, who possessed looks and a body that made every cell inside her tingle with awareness. No, this man was so incredibly handsome it was almost painful to look upon him. And yet something about his imposing countenance frightened her. She longed to swim to the safety of Dax's arms, but was afraid to even twitch. The stranger carried a trident in his hands, a long pitchfork that she didn't want to get any closer to than she already was.

"Isabelle, come here," the stranger commanded in a voice that reverberated deeply through the water.

Shocked that he knew her name, she looked to Dax, who shrugged nonchalantly and nodded. Surely he wouldn't send her to someone who would hurt her. With great trepidation, she slowly approached the giant, stopping in front of him, trying not to notice the tan cloth that rode low on his hips, barely concealing his genitals.

Then it struck her. Oh God, she was naked! How could she have forgotten that? She quickly moved to cover her breasts and crossed her legs as tight as she could.

The stranger lifted a brow and said, "Many are naked or nearly so down here, Isabelle. We think nothing of our natural state unlike you land people."

Easy for him to say, he had clothes on. Damn. This was mortifying.

"You're scaring her to death, Neptune. Knock it off." Dax swam over to her and put his arms around her.

The name hit her instantly. "Neptune? You're Neptune? *The* Neptune?" She looked at Dax then back at the striking man. "I thought the gods were mythological, a fictional fantasy that didn't exist."

Ronan smiled benignly at her. "I never use that name and Dax knows that. I am Ronan and that's what you can call me." He glared at Dax, who shrugged. "And this legend of Neptune it *is* mythology. At least what you land humans have read. A bunch of nonsense written by people like you who could only guess at our lives down here. Believe me, I'm nothing like what you've read about."

Oh yeah, that made her feel so much better. She'd just met Ronan, sometimes called Neptune, or Poseidon. He was the god of the Sea.

"Not god of the Sea. Not even close. I'm just a guardian here."

Ronan read her mind just like Dax could. Was there no end to the magic she'd discovered down here? "A guardian?"

"And you give *me* a hard time for revealing too much," Dax said, folding his arms and casting a smug look in the man's direction.

Ronan glared at Dax. "Mind your manners, boy, or I'll turn you into a sea slug."

Isabelle gasped, but Dax just snorted. "No you won't. And quit scaring her."

This whole scenario was surreal. She had to be dreaming it all. She finally exhaled when it became apparent she wasn't going to be run through by Ronan's trident. Then the inevitable curiosities came bursting forth from her mind. "Would someone mind answering the, oh, let's say about a thousand questions I have?"

Ronan's eyes narrowed as he looked at Dax. "I warned you this could happen. You'll have to take care of this, you know."

"I'm aware of that."

Ronan sighed and turned to Isabelle. "Ask your questions. Some I'll answer, some I won't."

She started to object, but knew it would get her nowhere. "Who are you?"

"I'm Ronan. I think we already established that."

"Okay, then *what* are you?"

He arched a dark brow. "I'm a man."

Isabelle rolled her eyes. "Yes, clearly you are. I mean what do you do down here?"

"We're guardians," Ronan replied.

"Of?"

"The oceans."

"What exactly does that mean?" Ronan certainly had an uncanny way of answering questions but not giving her any information.

"Our job is to protect the sea and its inhabitants."

"How do you do that?"

"I can't say."

Lord, this was frustrating.

"Give it up, Isabelle," Dax said, turning angry eyes to Ronan. "He's toying with you. He's not going to tell you anything."

Trying to keep her irritation at a minimum, she said, "Look, Ronan. I'm already down here. I know much more than any other human does, so it's pointless to keep things from me."

Ronan regarded her with a sly smile that made her very uncomfortable.

"It's time to end this, Dax," Ronan said, his gaze never leaving Isabelle's face. She shifted uncomfortably, not liking the smug look he gave her.

"No," Dax replied, his voice tinged with irritation. "It's not time yet."

Why did she feel as if they were talking about her? A shiver of dread tingled along her spine.

The ground shook as Ronan's fingers tightened around the trident. "Yes, it is time. You have work to do. You're needed elsewhere."

Dax paused, and then nodded. "Fine. I'll take care of it."

"When?" Ronan asked.

"Soon."

"Not good enough. It has to be now."

What had to be now? What were they talking about? Before she could open her mouth to ask, Ronan reached out and touched her cheek. Instantly, warmth spread throughout her body and she fought the sudden drowsiness that overcame her.

"Sleep, Isabelle. When you wake you won't remember," Ronan whispered to her, his voice softening to a lazy drawl.

Dizziness made her lightheaded and unable to concentrate, but she still heard Dax say, "Stop it, Ronan. I mean it."

"She doesn't belong here."

"Yes, she does. She belongs with me."

Dax's voice sounded so far away. She fought to stay alert, but her limbs were like cement, heavy and pulling her down. She couldn't even lift her hands any longer, and her eyes fluttered closed. A sweet voice sang to her, calling her toward something pleasant. Her mind drifted toward the lilting music, darkness closing in around her.

She wanted to stay, but the lure was too great. She was losing the battle to remain conscious, the strains of a song beckoning her ever closer to the all-encompassing shadows of sleep.

The last thing she heard was Dax's voice saying, "I'm in love with her."

Then her world went black.

Chapter Twelve

Isabelle blinked at the sunlight streaming through the open blinds in her bedroom. Based on the location of the light, it was way past dawn already.

She jumped out of bed, disoriented and groggy. What time was it? For that matter, what day was it? Rubbing her temples as she walked toward the bathroom, she couldn't grasp what had happened before she went to sleep. Her hair and skin smelled tangy and salty like the ocean, so she must have been diving.

That's it. She turned on the shower as it all came back to her. She and Dax had gone diving yesterday afternoon. And then…and then…

And then what? Why couldn't she remember?

She stepped into the shower, hoping the warm spray would clear the cobwebs from her head. But by the time she'd showered and dressed, she still couldn't recall anything past diving with Dax. She'd remembered finding the sea turtles, and then after that…nothing.

Had she even catalogued the turtles? And where was her dive gear? Hurrying into the living room, she spotted the gear on the entryway tile, along with her camera and waterproof notepad.

She picked up the pad hoping her notes would shed some light on what she'd done. Blank. Not a single notation on there. The camera was empty, too. What the hell had she done down there? Looked at the turtles and then surfaced and gone to bed?

Dax would know. She went next door and rapped on his door, but he wasn't there. She even peeked in his half-open window but saw no sign of him.

None of this made sense and trying to recall yesterday's events only made her head pound. Maybe coffee and some food would help. She drove over to the hotel, relieved to find the place nearly deserted. Looking at her watch, it was clear that she'd slept through the better part of the morning. By now, most of the resort guests would be busy with their sexual adventures of the day.

She ate in the restaurant alone, sipping her coffee and wracking her brain for clues as to the missing hours. Bits and pieces of memory assailed her, but it was more a jumbled mess than anything. Besides, all the little scenarios sailing through her head were bizarre as hell — it was more like a dream sequence than reality.

Diving into the darkness without an oxygen tank. Swarms of dolphins surrounding her. She and Dax making love under the water, and some glass enclosure reminiscent of Superman's Fortress of Solitude.

Oh yeah, that smacked of reality, didn't it? Isabelle heaved a frustrated sigh and added more cream to her coffee. Clearly the only thing she was able to remember from last night were her dreams. And they were weird ones at that.

Maybe she wasn't sleeping well.

"You look a little lost today."

Isabelle looked up and smiled at Morgan, then motioned for her to sit at the table. She needed company and some rational conversation.

"I'm feeling a little lost and confused," she admitted.

"Why?"

"I don't know. I think I had some kind of weird memory lapse last night."

Morgan raised a brow. "Really?"

"Yeah. I remember diving with Dax yesterday afternoon, and then the next thing I knew I woke up this morning in my bed."

Morgan pursed her lips. "Hmm, that's odd. Were you drinking at all yesterday?"

Oh, great. Now Morgan thought she was a lush with frequent alcohol-related memory loss. "No, at least not that I can recall."

She rubbed her forehead, flashes of memory coming back to her despite the sharp pain in her temples. She and Dax, naked at the bottom of the ocean. Then a tall man, dark-haired, piercing blue eyes, gorgeous, in fact. He spoke to her, but she couldn't make out what he said.

"Headache?"

Isabelle looked up and met Morgan's concerned gaze, then laughed. "Sort of. You probably think I'm a walking medical problem. It seems like every time I run into you I'm having either physical or mental issues. I really am a normal person."

Morgan laughed. "Of course you are! I didn't think otherwise. But I'm also a little worried that maybe you've been drugged."

"Drugged? What do you mean?"

Tapping a long fingernail on the lacquered table, Morgan said, "You know, those drugs they give women sometimes to make them forget."

"You mean date rape drugs?"

"Yes."

Isabelle laughed at that. "I didn't even have anything to drink before the dive yesterday. And I was alone in the bungalow. So that's just not possible."

"What about after the dive?"

"I don't remember anything after the dive. I don't remember anything past finding some sleeping sea turtles on the bottom of the ocean floor." Hell, for all she knew Morgan could be right. She could have come to the resort and had cocktails after the dive and just didn't remember it.

"Well, it's doubtful you were around here last night. Tony and I had dinner here and I'd have remembered seeing you."

So much for that theory. "I think it's more stress and fatigue than anything out of the ordinary, Morgan. But I do appreciate your concern."

Morgan reached out and squeezed Isabelle's hand. "I like to take care of my guests. And with you being almost completely alone on the other side of the island, I can't help but worry."

"That's because you're a mother at heart, gorgeous."

Isabelle looked up to see Morgan's husband, Tony, standing at the table and smiling warmly at his wife.

"I am not," Morgan replied with a blush.

"Well, soon you will be."

Isabelle looked to Morgan. "A baby?"

She nodded and grinned. "Yes. Hadn't planned on it happening so soon, but we're very happy."

Tony leaned over and brushed his lips over his wife's, then squeezed her hand. "So soon? I wanted to get you pregnant from the first moment I saw you."

"Well it was damn close to that," Morgan said.

Tony shrugged and grinned. "What can I say? I'm a stud."

Isabelle laughed. "Congratulations to both of you. You must be thrilled."

"Thank you, we are," Morgan replied, wrapping her fingers around Tony's. "Hard to keep my Italian Stallion here from wanting to use me as a brood mare. He's made up some ludicrous number of children he'd like to have. How many kids were we suppose to have?"

Tony arched a brow. "Six, I think."

Morgan snorted and caressed Tony's cheek. "Only if you're going to birth at least three of them yourself."

The love and affection between the two of them was obvious. They hung out with her for awhile, then Morgan excused herself to attend to some resort details and Tony followed, saying he had a writing deadline to meet. She watched them walk away, hand in hand. Tony stopped in the lobby and pulled his wife into a passionate embrace that even had Isabelle's heart pounding.

So that was love. Real love. The kind she'd never witnessed growing up, the kind she'd never experienced herself.

Funny, she'd never thought that love, a husband and family were things she wanted. In fact, she'd purposely lived her life with her career coming first and no intention of ever wanting or needing that elusive thing called love.

Then why, after watching the way Morgan and Tony were together did her heart ache so badly? Why did she feel a craving so strong it made her entire body tremble and tears well in her eyes? Why did she suddenly think she wanted to be loved by someone? Why did the thought of children running about fill her with a longing she'd never felt before?

Why? Why? Why? The whys of her life were driving her crazy lately.

Probably lack of sleep and the weird dreams she'd had. Plus the loss of a part of yesterday that frustrated her beyond belief. Stress like that would make anyone act irrationally. And wanting love and marriage was about as irrational as she could get.

Her life had been happy before she'd arrived at Paradise Resort. But the past few days she'd begun to question her so-called-satisfying life, had begun to feel that maybe something integral was missing, but she couldn't put her finger on what that missing piece was.

It sure as hell wasn't love. Love was for the foolish, for people who didn't know the disastrous consequences of giving your heart blindly to someone. She wasn't like that. She knew better.

This was all Dax's fault. His mysterious ways, her inability to get her questions answered, all of it had led to her infatuation with him. He was a mystery and she loved mysteries. Which didn't mean she loved Dax.

And she still had no answers, but at this point she wasn't sure she even cared. She'd gotten too wrapped up with him too quickly and it was beginning to affect her reasoning. Paradise Resort was like a fairytale wonderland and she'd allowed herself to get caught up in the fantasy and romance of the place. Clearly it was distorting her vision and her goals. She needed to get her head on straight and focus on her job.

Starting right now. She waved the waiter off, signed the check for her meal and headed back to the bungalow, determined to keep her distance from Dax and concentrate only on work for the remainder of her time at the resort.

Isabelle's resolve lasted as long as it took to drive back to the other side of the island, where she found Dax waiting on the beach for her. His blue shorts matched the turquoise of his eyes, his tanned body glittering with sweat as he stood out in the open sun.

He smiled and her heart skipped a beat. She ignored the pulsing awareness of him and calmly exited the golf cart and swept past him to her bungalow to change for a dive.

Dax followed her inside. "Hey, beautiful. I've been looking for you."

"I was at the resort having lunch." She busied herself gathering her gear, camera and notebook, then went into her bathroom to change in to her swimsuit, making sure she closed and locked the door. The last thing she needed was Dax coming in and making her forget her new resolve. Taking a few minutes to catch her breath and calm her emotions, she came out, smiled politely at Dax then walked toward the beach. Dax walked with her, as silent as she was.

She couldn't look at him, afraid she'd melt if she glanced into his eyes. Her body was completely in tune to him—his clean, crisp scent, the husky tone to his voice, the way he smiled at her, touched her, kissed her—no! Not this time, not ever again.

Quickly fastening her dive gear, she headed toward the water. Dax grabbed her arm but she looked straight ahead, focusing on the sun glinting off the ocean's waves.

"Hey, what's wrong?" he asked.

"Nothing. I'm just behind schedule."

"You going for a dive?"

"Yes."

"Still cataloguing turtles and coral?"

"Yes."

"I'll go with you."

"No!" She chanced a look in his direction, only to catch his confused frown. She quickly averted her gaze and stared out over the water. "I mean, I'm really busy here, Dax. I need to get down there and finish notating the sea life in this area. My time is almost up and if you don't mind I'd like to finish this alone."

"Why alone? I can help you and you'll get it finished faster."

She had to do it, despite the fact she knew it was going to cause pain, both to herself and to him. "I appreciate the offer, Dax, but no. Having you along is really a distraction that I can't afford right now."

Dax clenched his jaw, but she saw the pain on his face. An ache like she'd never felt before enveloped her heart. She knew she'd hurt him, but couldn't help it. It was either that or she'd lose herself in him completely, and she couldn't, wouldn't allow herself to become like her mother. Because Dax *would* leave her eventually, that much she already knew. Better now than later when she wasn't certain she'd survive it.

"I see," he said, his voice softening to a near whisper.

She bent down to grab her flippers, thankful for menial tasks that prevented her from looking at him. "Good. I'll catch you later, then?"

"Maybe. Maybe not. I've got some work of my own to do and I need to be leaving soon."

A sharp pain stabbed her stomach and spread out, nearly paralyzing her. "Okay. When are you leaving?"

"Now, I guess. There's really nothing to keep me here anymore, is there?"

His enigmatic question gave her pause. Was that meant to lead her into confessing her feelings for him? She refused, knowing the disastrous road love would lead her down. "I guess not."

241

Isabelle turned away from Dax and closed her eyes, forcing the deep breaths she knew would calm her rattled nerves. Her first instinct was to whirl around and beg him not to leave. But then what? They'd have one more night together and he'd be gone? No, it was better this way. End it clean, with no entanglements.

She dug the knife in as far as she could, wincing at the self-inflicted pain. "I guess if I see you before you leave, great. If not, good luck to you."

Before he could say anything else she stepped into the water, the waves carrying her out while she slipped on her fins. She swam as far out as she could, refusing to look back, knowing Dax stood on the beach watching her. Fighting back the tears that threatened to fog her mask, she dove down, hoping the job she had to do was enough to keep her mind from wandering to the man she'd just treated so carelessly.

Damn him for making her fall in love with him. And damn herself for not remembering what a disaster love could be.

Chapter Thirteen

By the time Isabelle returned to shore it was nearly dark. She half expected to see Dax still waiting there for her, but the beach was empty. Ignoring the surge of disappointment, she dropped her dive gear on the inside tile of her bungalow and stripped, heading straight for the shower.

Her muscles ached from the effort of holding the camera for so long. But she'd found the turtles and taken shot after shot of them nestled together, their huge bodies all lumped together like one, big rock. She'd guess they were ready to nest given the time of year and location, and she made a mental note to do a little searching tonight to see if she could find their nesting ground.

After that she'd catalogued their numbers, species, state of maturity, then moved on to the patch of coral and did the same thing, following up with photographs.

She put on her night vision goggles and went in search of the turtles' nesting area, rewarded with a find not too far into the forested area of the beach. With very little sand and lots of trees for cover, the turtles were busy brushing back the sandy loam and nestling inside the holes to bury their eggs. Isabelle shivered excitedly at the find, making a mental note to come back to the island and check on the hatchlings around the time they'd be breaking free of their eggs.

She'd also have to notify Morgan to string up a barrier around this area to keep tourists from damaging the incubating eggs.

By the time she crawled away from the now exhausted turtles, she was fairly wiped out herself. But thrilled that she'd managed to view the nesting process.

And besides, watching the turtles dig their nests had at least helped the time pass.

Might as well keep herself busy, since it seemed as if Dax had taken her words to heart and disappeared. She refused to go next door and see if he'd left the bungalow yet. If she saw him, fine, if not, then more the better.

Yeah, right. And there really were flying turtles named Pegasus.

How could one man have wiggled his way inside her heart in such a few short days? A mysterious man at that, if he were even a man at all. She wished she'd had the time to get answers to the questions that had plagued her since the moment they met.

After she cleaned up she dragged a lawn chair down to the beach to watch the moonlight rise. Its glow cast a silver beacon over the calm sea. She dug her toes into the cooling sand, wishing she could blanket herself with the gritty substance and forget she'd ever met Dax.

The night quiet unnerved her, whereas it never had before. She'd always enjoyed this part of the day, the peaceful feeling of being completely alone with nature. Now, she wanted to hear dark, husky laughter, feel a certain man's warm hands around her waist, touch her mouth against a living, breathing man who desired her as much as she desired him.

No sense in missing him. She'd told him to leave, brushed him off as if he'd meant nothing to her.

The problem was, he did mean something to her. She loved him. Yes, she'd admitted it before, but part of her held back. Acknowledging that she loved him didn't mean she wanted a future with him.

Now it was different. No matter what her mother had gone through, no matter the pain she'd known as a child watching her mother suffer because of the man she loved, none of that mattered to her.

Her heart opened and swelled with joy and a bittersweet agony brought about by the fact she'd lost the man she loved. And had no earthly idea how to find him.

Looking to the sea, it hit her like a punch to her middle, nearly toppling her over. Her heart beat frantically against her ribs and she broke out in a sweat.

She remembered! Everything. From that first night until yesterday.

When she'd had the stomach pain in the water the first night, it had been Dax who'd rescued her and brought her to shore. She even remembered the conversation he'd had with Ronan.

She remembered Ronan, the gorgeous god-like guardian of the sea people. Dax's laboratory, even Zeus, the talking dolphin.

Most importantly, she remembered what Dax had said before she'd lost consciousness last night. He'd told Ronan that he loved her!

None of it had been a dream, it had all been real. Hadn't it? Or was she so wrapped up in hope that she was manufacturing reality where it didn't exist? Maybe it had been a dream, after all.

The only person who could verify that for her was Dax.

She jumped out of the chair, searching the ocean's surface, hoping against hope he'd show up if she willed it hard enough.

Back and forth she paced along the shoreline. A half hour, an hour, sending mental signals to Dax to come out of the water and talk to her. A week ago she'd have thought herself insane for even thinking someone lived in the sea. Now, she believed it to be true, hoped for it to be true.

There! She saw a spot in the water. A dolphin, probably. She refused to get her hopes up until she was certain.

Dax, please, I need you.

Over and over and over again she repeated the mantra. The tide was rising, water rushing over her feet, then her ankles, higher and higher each length of beach she paced.

There it was again! This time, she was certain it had to be him. She ran inside and threw on a swimsuit, nearly stumbling in the sand in her haste to get to the water. She dove in and swam quickly, keeping her eyes focused on the spot where she'd seen him. She had to talk to him, had to know if what she remembered had really happened.

By the time she'd reached the spot she thought she'd seen him, he was nowhere to be found. And she was exhausted. Stupidly, she'd gone too far out and further lung power was nearly nonexistent. She'd never make it back to shore. Taking a chance, she fought for breath and dove down, knowing somehow he'd see her and make contact.

The sea was dark, nothing like what she remembered. Tears filled her eyes at the effort she expended to hold her breath, and still she kept diving, spurred on by faith that he was close, that he wouldn't let anything happen to her.

It wasn't a dream, she was convinced of it. Everything she'd remembered had been real. It *had* happened.

But she was running out of air, and still she dove further, knowing she'd never be able to hold her breath long enough to get back to the surface. Would she die for him? Would she die here because she was as foolish as her mother?

She squeezed her eyes shut, fighting the panic, the feeling that she'd just made a fatal error in judgment. And now she was going to drown.

Just as she was about to let go, a hand snaked out and pulled her against a warm, living, human body. Water rushed into her lungs, but instead of a clawing panic she could breathe. Relief soared through her.

Light flickered against her tightly shut lids and she opened her eyes. Dax smiled at her.

With a whoop of joy she threw her arms around his neck and kissed him long and hard.

He returned the kiss with fervor, his mouth devouring hers, his tongue plunging inside her the same way she wanted his cock to do. His erection bobbed between her legs. She shifted, wrapping her legs around his waist. Not wanting to take time to remove her swimsuit, she yanked it to the side and guided his shaft inside her.

"God, you feel good," he whispered as he entered her, lightly biting the tender flesh of her neck.

He moved quickly against her, their bodies rising and falling together, an electricity surrounding them as they clashed like a fierce storm. Isabelle clawed at Dax's back, unable to assuage the fierce hunger that made her desperate for each thrust of his shaft.

She panted in his ear, he licked her neck, his heart pounding against her breast. It was fast and furious and heart rendering. This could very well be the last time she felt this connection to Dax, and she wanted it to last an eternity.

Unfortunately, her body had other ideas. Intense pleasure rose up to meet her and she threw her head back, screaming out an orgasm so filled with emotion it made her cry.

Dax clutched her to him and groaned his release, spilling his seed deep into her core.

Breathless, she clung to him, not wanting to let go, not yet ready for reality to intrude on this ultimate fantasy she'd created with him. For it was a fantasy, and she finally realized it. Unless...

She kissed him lightly and smiled. "It's all true. I wasn't dreaming."

He nodded. "You remembered it all. You even fought through the memory spell Ronan gave you. No one has ever done that before. That makes you one strong woman, Isabelle."

She didn't feel strong. She felt weak, helpless and thoroughly overjoyed to find him. She didn't care if he didn't want to be with her past this week, she only knew she couldn't leave things the way she'd left them with him earlier.

"I'm sorry about today," she said. "I didn't know how to handle my feelings for you."

"And what are your feelings for me?"

"I..." She started to tell him she loved him, but something in his face, some hesitation tensing his body, stopped her. "I care about you, Dax. I didn't want to leave without letting you know that. Without telling you that I remembered everything. I wanted to thank you for showing me your world, even though there's so much of it I don't understand."

"Come with me."

They swam together into the ocean's depths, each meter they descended reminding Isabelle of the same trek she'd made with Dax before. This time she didn't shut her eyes to the darkness, knowing she'd find the light at the bottom of the ocean.

When she spotted his lab, she smiled, an idea forming. She just hoped he'd go for it.

She sat down on the transparent sofa, watching Dax as he worked the scanners. He seemed lost in thought, and very quiet.

"What's on your mind?" she asked.

"Gimme a second here," he said without turning around, his gaze still focused on the screens in front of him.

Isabelle waited patiently, growing more excited as her idea began to take shape. It made perfect sense to her and was definitely workable for both of them. And if Dax agreed to it, she could tell him how she felt about him. Was it possible for her happily ever after to be looming around the corner? She didn't want to hope, but couldn't stop the joy that swelled within her.

When he finished, he sat next to her on the sofa and took her hands in his. She smiled at him, more nervous than she'd ever been before.

"I have to leave soon," he said, his gaze focused on her hands.

She frowned. "What? Leave?"

He nodded and looked up at her. She could get lost in his turquoise eyes, so achingly blue like the ocean she loved.

"I have work to do in another part of the world."

"I see." Disappointment stabbed at her. Maybe her hopes had been unfounded after all.

"But I think I have a solution to our problem."

"Our problem?"

One corner of his mouth lifted. "Yeah. That problem we have of wanting to be together."

Hope swelled again. He did feel the same way she did! "Oh good, because I have a solution, too. I'll bet it's the same one."

"Really? Go ahead, then."

She wiggled, unable to contain her enthusiasm. "I do want to be with you, Dax. More than anything. And I thought you might want to come with me when I leave the island."

His brows knit together. "Come with you? Where?"

"To Texas. Where I live."

He shook his head, his tense grasp on her hands lessening. "I can't."

"But I thought you said—"

"I can't go with you, Isabelle, but I thought you might want to come with me."

Her first reaction was to object, but before she spoke she thought about it. She could travel with him. She had autonomy in her work, and there were oceans all over the world. She could certainly make it work. "Where are you going? Don't you live here?"

"Sometimes. We really don't have one spot that we call home."

"Do all of you live like that? However many of you there are? By the way, how many of you are there?"

Threading his fingers through her billowing hair, Dax pressed a soft kiss to her lips. "I can't tell you any more until you decide."

Confusion reigned within her. "I don't understand. You can't come with me to Texas, and you don't really have a place you call home. So, why can't you just live with me, and when you have to work you can go do your...thing?" Whatever the hell his thing was.

Again, he shook his head. "It's much more complicated than that, Isabelle. I can't just leave the ocean and live on land with you."

"Why not? Are you physically prevented from doing so?"

"No."

"Then what's stopping you?" Dread formed a knot in her stomach. She didn't like the direction this conversation was headed.

"I have commitments. Promises to keep. My life is under the sea, not on land."

"Are you some kind of alien species? Like from another planet or something?" She'd seen so much in the past few days nothing would surprise her any longer. But she wanted to, desperately needed to understand who Dax was and what prevented him from coming with her.

His soft chuckle unnerved her. "No, we're not aliens. We're humans, just a little different than the ones like you who live on the land."

"Tell me more," she pleaded. *Tell me everything, Dax. Make me understand*. But she already knew he wouldn't.

"I can tell you everything, as soon as you commit."

"Commit to what?" Now he'd really lost her.

"Commit to me, and to spending the rest of your life under the sea. Only then can I tell you everything."

Chapter Fourteen

Dax knew he wasn't going to get the answer he'd hoped for. At his mention of committing to living under the sea with him she'd paled, her confusion replaced by something akin to fear.

It had been a gamble to even suggest it, but he couldn't help but hope she'd surprise him.

"I don't understand, Dax. What do you mean commit to living under the sea? I'd have to vow to live in the ocean forever?"

"Yes."

"Why?"

"Because it's the only way we can be together. The only way I can explain everything to you. Without your oath of commitment, I can't tell you any more than what you already know. And at that, you're lucky they've allowed you to return here after you fought past the memory block."

"Lucky to be allowed to return? Surely you don't mean to suggest they'd have tried to stop me?"

He refused to tell her what could have happened to her had he not interceded. But her joyful face as he watched her on the beach, the way she had jumped into the ocean and come looking for him, had given him enough hope to stall Ronan from placing a deeper memory loss on her. He'd explained he was certain she'd commit, so there was no reason for his concern.

Besides, he knew Isabelle. Even if she didn't commit, she'd never tell the world about their existence. Convincing the League of that fact was a different matter entirely. But convince them he would. He couldn't live with himself if something happened to Isabelle because of his stupidity.

Isabelle's hand on top of his brought him back to reality. "Dax, you're scaring me. Please explain."

"I'm sorry. There's nothing to be afraid about. If you decide not to commit I'll put a deeper memory block on you. I guarantee you won't remember anything about me or what you've seen the past few days. You'll be safe."

"I don't like the idea of not remembering you. Oh, this is all so complex!" She stood and paced the laboratory. Her arms crossed like a protective shield, she worried her bottom lip in the way he found so amazingly sexy it never failed to harden him. His cock rose and twitched. He wanted her again.

And again and again and again. Like he always would. Today, tomorrow and forever, no matter what choices she made. If she walked away today, his heart would still be hers, just like it had been from the first moment he saw her.

Her breasts rose and fell with every breath, her nervousness apparent in her wringing hands and near hyperventilating state. Dax wanted to offer comfort, but the decision rested with her. He couldn't help her.

"Tell me again how this works?" she asked, turning her bleak amber gaze toward him.

Dax read the defeat in her eyes, and felt it deep within himself. "You have to make a commitment to live the rest of your life as an ocean dweller. Once that's done, you're transformed."

"Physically?"

"Yes."

"You mean I become like you are."

"Yes."

"But I could still survive out of the water."

"Of course."

"Forever, or just temporarily?"

"Forever."

"So I can change my mind if I wanted to, after the transformation is made."

"Not really. I mean, yeah, it's happened before, but only once. They don't want it to happen again."

"Who are *they*, Dax?"

Frustrated at his inability to adequately explain, he said, "I can't tell you."

"In other words, you just expect me to accept this at face value, commit to changing my life, my very biological makeup and live under the sea with you."

"Basically, yes." If she loved him, she'd do it.

Tell her you love her. Tell her she means everything to you. Beg her if you have to.

No, he wouldn't do that. Isabelle had to decide for herself if a life with him was what she wanted, and not because of love, but because of choice. Her choice, not his.

She turned and stared out at the ocean, then nearly whispered her response. "No, Dax. I can't do it. I *won't* do it. You're not giving me enough information to base my decision on."

He knew that would be her decision. "I've given you all I can, Isabelle. I know it's a lot to ask."

Still, a part of him hoped *he'd* be enough for her. Her hesitation dashed his hope.

"I've loved the ocean since I was a child," she said, the sadness in her voice tearing him apart. "This is my element and I've always thought it was the place I was meant to be."

"Then why not stay here with me?"

She turned to him. "Because I also love my life on the surface. A life I've worked very hard to build. I have family, Dax. Am I supposed to tell my mother I'm disappearing for the rest of my life, see you later? What about my career? People might notice if I disappeared."

"You can quit your job. People do it all the time. You don't need money down here, or any of the superficial trappings that land humans need. Here, food is plentiful and everyone works. As far as your mother, your job, your friends...I don't know what to tell you. I know it would be difficult to leave them behind."

She shook her head. "It's impossible to just disappear. And it's not only the money and family. I love my job, Dax. 'I love what I do."

"What better place to do it than down here?" Dax grabbed her hands, feeling their icy chill. "Isabelle, the things I could show you...there's magic down here."

Her eyes widened, that old familiar sparkle of enthusiasm appearing for a flickering second, then gone. "I can't. It's just too much change for me. Too much risk."

Her words were all too real, making the concept nearly impossible to fathom. "It's difficult, I know."

"No, it's beyond difficult. It's impossible. I love my job. I'm a marine biologist and a damn good one, if I say so myself. And I'm a teacher, too. Children's eyes light up when I tell them stories of the sea and the wonderful life that can be found below the ocean's surface."

"You can teach down here."

She shrugged. "I don't know what I can or can't do down here. I mean, I love it in the ocean, Dax."

"But?" He knew there was more, something that she wasn't telling him.

"But nothing. I can't give up my life to follow you. If I did that I'd be no better than my…"

Her eyes widened and she sank into a nearby chair.

Dax followed her, crouching down to peer up into her dejected face. "No better than who, Isabelle?"

She waved him off. "Nothing. Forget I said that. I can't do this, that's all, I just can't. I want to go back to the surface, Dax. Take me back home, where I belong."

The finality in her voice pained him. Her rejection couldn't have hurt him more if she'd physically stuck a knife in his heart. She didn't care enough about him to make her life down here, and he refused to abandon his promise to protect the seas in order to live with her.

"You're right, Isabelle." He stood and pulled her up.

Without so much as a glance in her direction, he grasped her hand and led her out of the laboratory, starting the swim to the surface. "Neither of us is willing to give up the life we have to be together. Some things just aren't meant to be."

* * * * *

When they surfaced, Isabelle breathed in the humid air, no longer able to take in the seawater that had been her breath just seconds before. She and Dax swam to shore in silence.

She'd never hurt so much, had never suffered a pain so deep. How could she have known what it would be like? She'd never loved anyone before. No wonder her father's abandonment had nearly killed her mother. She had no idea the ache of loss was this severe.

Dax followed behind her onto shore. She stopped and turned to him, not knowing what to say, and yet knowing this was their final goodbye.

The thought of never running her fingers through his sun-tipped hair, never feeling his heart beat against hers again, caused an anguish so deep she wanted to curl up and die.

"Stay with me tonight," she pleaded. Yes, she knew it was postponing the inevitable, but she wanted one last night in Dax's arms. A memory to hold onto forever. If he'd even let her keep her memories.

She waited, breath held, while he stared at her, the unspoken pain they both felt alive and burning in his sea blue eyes.

"Of course I'll stay with you."

Letting out her breath, she held out her hand and offered as much of a smile as she could.

She couldn't give him forever, but she could give him tonight.

"Would you like something to eat or drink?" she asked, fumbling for what to do next.

He shook his head and stepped toward her, gathering her in his arms. Without a word he crushed his lips against hers.

She met his assault eagerly, desperation tinged with her growing passion. Their bodies melded together, wet and glistening with the drops of the sea. Had she noticed before how perfectly they fit together? How every part of her connected with every part of him?

He really was her destiny. And she was about to defy the love she'd been fated to have.

"Let's take a shower," he murmured against her lips, not waiting for her response. He picked her up and carried her past the bedroom and into the bathroom, setting her down only long enough to reach in and turn on the shower.

The warm water heated the room, providing respite from the chill that had nothing to do with the air conditioning inside the bungalow. Dax's eyes never left her face as he stripped off her swimsuit and then his. They stood naked together and Dax turned her around to face the long mirror in the bathroom.

"You're so beautiful," he said, his tongue licking at her neck. She watched as his hands cupped her breasts, letting them rest in his hands as he shifted behind her. His cock, already hard, brushed between the cleft in her ass. She shivered, wanting him so badly she feared she'd resort to begging if he didn't make love to her soon.

When he stepped around and stood next to her, Isabelle's gaze roamed appreciatively over the body she'd come to know so well over the past several days, wanting to memorize every part of him so she'd never forget.

Dax opened the shower door and pulled her inside, drenching them both with spray. He gathered her in his arms and kissed her deeply. She met each thrust of his tongue with her own, pouring out the longing and regret she couldn't speak. But she felt it, so deeply it was like an illness, sucking the life and joy from her.

Desperation born of the sense of aching loss spurred on her passion, and she reached for his buttocks, pulling his hard shaft against her mound.

He cupped her breasts, searching and finding her distended nipples, plucking at them relentlessly until she captured his cock between her legs. She rocked against his erection, her desire spilling over his turgid flesh.

"You're so wet, Isabelle," he ground out between panting gasps.

"I want you, Dax. I need you inside me. Now."

He pulled back, searching her face, his eyes dark like an impending storm. "Not yet."

Frustration caused the moan to escape her throat. Dax pushed her back against the cool tile wall of the shower, then dropped to his knees and spread her legs apart.

"Oh, God," she murmured, watching his head bend toward her throbbing pussy. His tongue snaked out and sipped her nectar and her legs trembled.

"I'll miss the taste of peaches," he said, and tears welled in her eyes. She threaded her hands through his hair and pressed her back against the shower wall as he licked her outer lips, then plunged his tongue deep inside her.

She couldn't hold back the shrieks of pleasure at the magic his mouth and tongue performed on her sensitive flesh. The shower spray rained over her, pouring off her body but not cooling her desperate passion.

Instead, it built, like a rising wave, ever higher and higher. When he took her clit in his mouth and sucked, she cried out in agonizing bliss. He pulled and nibbled the aching bud until she was mindless with the quest for completion.

When he inserted two fingers into her pussy, she bucked against him, the dual sensation of his mouth on her clit and his fingers fucking her driving her over the edge. She held on to his head and screamed as her orgasm washed through her, a wave so intense her legs nearly buckled.

Panting so hard she could barely catch her breath, she looked down at Dax. The water pummeled them both, but still he looked up at her and smiled. She caressed his cheek and he stood, covering her lips with his.

She tasted her juices on his mouth and tongue. The intoxicating sensuality of licking her own essence from his lips had her pussy aching for his cock.

But not yet. She pulled away and pressed him against the shower wall, then kissed his neck, slowly trailing her tongue over his collarbone and finding his nipples. She flicked her tongue over one, then the other, smiling when they hardened. Dax sucked in a breath as she leisurely moved down his body, palming his flat stomach and feeling it quiver under her hands. Where her hands explored, her lips and tongue followed.

Finally she dropped into a crouch, his hard-on at eye level. She looked up at him, his eyes like a wicked hurricane, dark and violently hungry. Never taking her gaze from his, she enveloped his shaft between her lips.

"Christ, Isabelle!" he shouted, his body tensing.

His salty flavor spilled onto her tongue and she lapped it up greedily, sucking him deep, the tip of his shaft bumping against the back of her throat. She took him in deeper. When she began to move, taking him from tip to base in rapid rhythm, he groaned and cursed, wrapping his hands around her head and setting the pace.

"Do you like that?" he asked, his gaze meeting hers as he fucked her mouth. "God, Isabelle, I love to watch my cock disappear between your lips. It's so fucking hot I can hardly stand it."

She cupped his balls in response, tugging lightly until he groaned out loud.

If she were any more aroused she'd pass out. His cock was hot and twitching against her tongue. When she moaned, he did too, then pulled his shaft from her mouth and lifted her up.

Quickly he turned off the shower and gathered Isabelle in his arms, kicking the shower door open and marching into her bedroom. Water dripped along the floor as he moved through the room. He laid her on the bed, then climbed on top of her.

"You drive me crazy, do you know that?" he asked, settling between her legs.

She raised her hips to stroke his cock with her damp mound. "No more than you do me," she replied, holding out her arms for him, desperate for this last union with him. She realized with a start that she wanted to crawl inside him and make him hers for the rest of her life. How was she ever going to let him go?

Dax leaned into her, his cock searching between her parted legs. She reached between them and guided him to the entrance. He plunged inside with a single, hard stroke and she cried out, wrapping her legs around him. This was completion, fulfillment, all those things people spoke about sex. Only it wasn't the physical pleasure she felt the most— it was the joining of their souls and it tore her apart.

Her pussy throbbed, tiny quakes squeezing his shaft until he was deeply embedded inside her.

Passion took over and no more words were necessary. Dax reached underneath her and grabbed her buttocks, pulling her snug against him. Her clit brushed against his shaft as he moved in and out of her with rapid strokes. The wave began to build inside her again and she clutched his back, her nails scraping his flesh until he growled and buried his face in her neck.

When he sank his teeth into her tender skin, she shivered and screamed, the pain and pleasure mingling to drive her to the brink of sanity. And still he drove inside her without pause until she couldn't think, couldn't breathe, couldn't do anything but feel the sensations soaring through every part of her body.

You're mine, Dax. You always will be. Maybe he heard her, maybe he didn't. At this point she didn't care. Tears rolled down her face as the depth of her love for him mixed with her desire.

He tensed against her and thrust deeply, so hard she felt it in her womb, so deliciously intense it toppled her into a climax that shattered her into pieces. He came along with her, their cries of ecstasy mingling until she didn't know where she ended and he began.

They'd no more recovered their breath when he made love to her again, this time more slowly. The entire time they were joined Dax watched her, his gaze focused on hers, their lips and tongues mingling in kisses so tender she couldn't hold back the tears. He kissed away every drop that fell, taking her over and over again to the pinnacle and beyond, until she fell into exhausted slumber, their bodies tangled together.

It was still dark in the room when she woke again, and yet Isabelle knew it was dawn. She turned over but Dax wasn't in bed with her. The pillow where he'd laid his head was cold, no warmth from his body left on the pillowcase. Quickly, she threw off the sheet and stepped into the living room, but he wasn't there, either.

She searched the bungalow and couldn't find him. Her heart beat frantically as she dressed and opened the front door to step onto the beach.

Gray clouds sailed overhead, signaling a coming storm. No wonder her bedroom had been so dark. Daylight fought to break through the gathering clouds. The wind whipped her hair against her cheeks, the stinging bite of salt spray blinding her progress to the water's edge.

He was gone, had left her sometime early this morning while she slept. She'd known it the minute she woke, had felt the emptiness inside her but didn't want to acknowledge it yet. She'd needed a few more minutes of denial.

And she remembered. Dax was gone, but he'd left her memories intact. He trusted her not to reveal his secrets. His faith in her was humbling and overwhelming.

A loss unlike anything she'd ever experienced crushed her heart. Her father's abandonment didn't compare. Rage and pain and frustration mixed inside her, a rumble as fierce as the thunder in the distance.

Rain began to fall in huge droplets, soaking her. The downpour mixed with her tears, falling quickly into the sand at her feet.

She knelt in the wet sand, covered her face and sobbed.

Chapter Fifteen

Isabelle sat numbly in the chair at the ocean's edge, staring at the cresting waves of the sea.

The storm had rushed through quickly, leaving a steamy, sunny day in its wake. Sweat poured off her body, traveling in rivulets to the sand below.

And still, she didn't move. Paralyzed by grief, she couldn't bring herself to do what needed to be done. The thought of packing, of gathering up her things and leaving the island, brought a fresh bout of tears that she couldn't seem to stem.

For someone who had rarely cried in her lifetime, she'd sure pulled forth the water works lately.

Maybe because this time her heart was involved. The last time she remembered this aching pain was when her father had abandoned them. Even then it was different. Even despair over her mother's pain had been nothing like what she felt now.

This was her first love, her first heartache, and she wasn't certain she'd survive it.

Now, staring out at the ocean that had always filled her with life, she felt empty. The ocean held nothing that appealed to her any longer. The thought of diving without Dax at her side stabbed her with nearly unbearable pain.

She turned her gaze sharply toward the path in the rain forest as the sound of a motorized golf cart caught her attention. For the briefest of seconds she envisioned Dax riding out of the jungle, his typically wicked grin plastered on his gorgeous face.

But it wasn't Dax. Pushing aside the disappointment that dropped her heart to her feet, Isabelle smiled at Morgan. Morgan waved and stopped the cart in front of her bungalow, then walked down to the water's edge. Isabelle motioned to the other chair next to hers and Morgan sat.

"Checking out today?" she asked.

Isabelle nodded, trying not to think about it. "Yes. Did you need me to get a move on?"

"No, not at all. I just stopped by to ask you how you enjoyed your stay."

She looked at the ocean. "It was heaven. I don't want to go."

Morgan laid a hand on her arm. "You can stay awhile longer, if you'd like. The bungalow isn't booked for the next week."

Isabelle turned her head and tried her best to smile. "No, thank you. I need to get back to work anyway."

"Dax checked out early this morning," Morgan said.

At the mention of his name, a rolling knot formed in the pit of her stomach. "I know."

"I thought maybe you two would end up together."

Isabelle managed a weak laugh. "Not quite."

"Hmm."

"What?"

Morgan shrugged. "It's just that you and Dax seemed to be more than just an island fling."

Island fling? Morgan didn't know the half of it. But it was still interesting to hear her observation. "It *was* more than an island fling. Unfortunately, we live in two different worlds."

And that was the understatement of the year.

"So? How do you feel about him?"

"I love him," she said before she could stop the words from spilling out of her mouth.

Morgan raised a brow. "Then make it work."

"I can't."

Morgan inhaled deeply and offered a patient smile. "Honey, I've been where you are. In love with a man and thinking no way in hell was it going to work."

"What did you do?"

"I married him and am having his baby," she said with a contented grin.

"You and Tony."

She nodded.

"How did you make it work?"

"We both had to give. I wasn't willing to give up my life, and neither was he, but we both finally realized that neither of us was complete without the other. It's funny how we can decide our career and our current lives are so important. Until you're faced with losing the person you love. So we made it work."

"And has it?"

Morgan laughed. "I'm not saying it hasn't been difficult at times, but our love keeps us strong, keeps us bonded together. Whatever the obstacles, we've overcome them together."

Isabelle trembled at Morgan's words, tears welling anew. She fought them back, refusing to give in to the melancholy of loss threatening to overwhelm her.

Morgan seemed to sense her tenuous hold and patted her arm before standing. "Just think about it. I'll be at the hotel if you need to talk to someone."

"Thank you," she said, grateful that at least one person knew of her struggle.

After Morgan left, Isabelle went inside the bungalow and packed, her thoughts occupied with Dax and her inability to commit to him and his life under the sea.

Was she wrong? Would she be able to live with the regret of not going with him?

No. He lived in the ocean, for God's sake. She wasn't like him, could never be like him, and damned if she'd follow a man like her mother had, giving up everything she knew for love.

Oh sure. It would be great to start, then as the years went by Dax would grow more and more disillusioned with her. Just like her father had with her mother.

Love didn't last. At least not in her limited experience.

So, she'd just go back to Texas and continue her work and her teaching. She'd have to be satisfied with her career as the number one love in her life.

Right?

She looked over at the pillow where Dax had laid his head last night. At first she hesitated, then finally reached out for it and pulled it toward her face.

His scent still lingered. Crisp and fresh like the sea. She closed her eyes and willed back the soaring pain of regret, then sat on the bed, clutching the pillow to her middle.

Dax loved her. No, he'd never said it outright to her, but she'd heard him tell Ronan that night before she passed out. And he was probably just as hesitant to utter the words as she had been.

Maybe he was as afraid as she was. Or maybe he'd given her the opportunity to make her own decision about living with him without his declaration of love to cloud her judgment.

Oh God, why wasn't this easy?

She already knew the answer. Because she was terrified. Never had she been faced with declaring her love for a man. A man she'd opened her heart to, a man she adored with all her being.

Cowardice wasn't a word she'd use to describe herself.

In her work, she was fearless, but have her heart involved and she'd cower in a corner like a frightened child. Is that really what she wanted for herself? To live her life so anxious about being hurt that she was reluctant to love?

With an angry toss the pillow went sailing across the bed.

No, this wasn't what she wanted. But it was the life she'd chosen. Dax was long gone and she wouldn't go after him again. She'd hurt him already, told him without words that she didn't care enough about him to stay. If she changed her mind now, he'd just think she was flighty, like she really didn't know what she wanted. And honestly, she didn't know.

There just weren't enough guarantees.

With a resigned sigh she finished her packing and placed her luggage in the golf cart. Knowing she shouldn't but unable to resist, she took one last walk to the ocean's edge, digging her toes into the surf.

The wind whipped around her legs. She glanced up at the gray clouds marching quickly along the sky.

Another storm was coming in.

She took one long, last look at the turquoise water, wishing for sunlight, wishing for that glint off the surface, wishing for…

For what? For Dax to magically appear, tell her he loved her and that he'd live in her world? That he'd make all her dreams come true by sacrificing his way of life for hers?

Yeah, right.

"I'm sorry, Dax," she whispered to the water. "Sorry I don't have enough faith in love to make the choice to live in your world. But I *do* love you. I have since the moment I met you, and I always will."

On a shaky sigh, she blew a kiss out onto the water, feeling silly and yet loath to turn away and leave.

For a brief moment the sun peeked through the thickening clouds, casting its rays across the ocean's surface. Something crossed her line of vision.

Isabelle blinked, then closed her eyes, refusing to believe she'd seen a spot on the water.

No. You did not see anything. Wishful thinking. Stupid, stupid, stupid. Turn away, don't look back.

She looked again, and saw an object bobbing out on the water, too far away to make out what it was. Her heart stopped beating and her fingers curled into tight balls of tension at her side.

It couldn't be.

The object moved toward the shore. Toward her. Blond hair glinted in the sunlight, strong arms sweeping in and out of the water.

She clutched her chest, her heart pounding so hard she could hear the roar of her blood in her ears.

Frozen to the sand, she couldn't move, unable to believe what she saw.

Move, damn you. Go to him. Tell him how you feel. You've been given a second chance, don't screw this up.

Fear held her in place and she fought against it. Her life turned before her eyes. What did she want?

Dax. Dammit to hell, she wanted Dax. And screw anything that would get in her way. She wasn't her mother. She was stronger, much stronger, and she loved. By God, she loved this man and she'd fight to be with him. Fight herself and her own doubts, if she had to.

The fear anchoring her in place dissolved in the water lapping at her feet. She jumped into the surf, heedless of the dress now soaked and clinging to her body.

Propelled as if by motor she soared through the water, closing the distance between them.

This wasn't happening fast enough. Her body ached for his touch and she couldn't wait to get her hands on him, her mouth on him. She had so much to tell him, so many things to declare, the first thing being her love for him.

The clouds hovered overhead, obliterating the sun. Rain fell in sheets, the sudden storm whipping at her, preventing her from making any progress in the churning water.

But Dax could. She finally stopped and treaded, gulping in mouthfuls of salty sea as she struggled to stay afloat.

Her eyes widened as she watched him sail through the water as if he had a motor attached to his feet. No one could swim that fast! In seconds he was by her side, his arms snaking around her waist and pulling her underneath.

She opened her mouth and took the ocean into her lungs. In seconds, she could breathe again.

Before she could utter a word Dax's lips closed over hers in a searing kiss that finally cracked the shell she'd constructed around her heart. She pulled away to tell him everything she'd been dying to tell him, but before she could utter the words, he spoke first.

"I love you, Isabelle. I need you. My life isn't complete without you."

Then came the tears again. "I love you too, Dax. I want to—"

"Wait. Let me," he interrupted.

She nodded, near to bursting with the words she'd longed to say to him.

"I'm leaving the ocean," he said.

His words at first not registering, she blurted, "I need to tell you …what? What did you just say?"

He drew her hand in his, kissing her knuckles, then turned his gaze to hers. "I'm leaving the ocean. I don't want to be separated again."

"You can't leave the ocean, Dax."

"Sure I can," he replied with a grin. "I do it all the time."

"Not permanently. What about your work, what you do down here?"

"Doesn't matter. I love you too much to lose you."

Could it be possible? Could she have found a man willing to give up *his* life to be with her? She heard his words and believed them to be true, and yet couldn't fathom he could love her enough to leave his world for hers.

She thought this was what she wanted. To have Dax living in her world. But now that he'd made the offer, she realized it wasn't what she wanted at all.

Yes, she wanted to be with him, but not like this.

"No, Dax."

His brows knitted in confusion. "No? What do you mean no?"

"You can't live on land with me."

"Why not?"

She smiled at his wary expression. Her heart soared as she made the decision she knew in her heart was the right one. The one *she* wanted. "Because I want to live in the sea with you."

His jaw dropped. "You do?"

"Yes, I do. I love you, I want to be with you and the ocean has always been my home. I can't think of a better place to spend the rest of my life."

He caressed her shoulders and her body responded to his touch by warming, opening like a flower on a spring morning.

"What about your family? Your work?"

She shrugged. "My mother and I don't even connect on the same level. We rarely even speak to each other, let alone visit."

"I'm sorry. I didn't know."

"It's okay. I can't live my life the way she did, anyway. She's been frozen in time, living in the past for over twenty years, wanting something she couldn't have. But maybe I can visit her now and then?"

Dax frowned. "I told you that's not possible. You can't go from living your life in the ocean to popping up on land. We don't allow it. Too much risk...too much opportunity for you to tell someone about your life down here. I know it's too much to ask of you, but maybe we can find a way to work it out so you can visit."

They'd work out the details on that later, she knew. If she wanted something badly enough, she'd fight for it no matter who this League was and how determined they were to tell her what to do. "And as far as my work, I'll quit my job. I've always wanted to be closer to the sea to do my research. How much closer can I get than right in the middle of it?" She finished with a hopeful smile.

He cupped her neck with his palm, his thumb grazing her jaw line. Isabelle shivered at his touch.

"I first saw you when you were a young girl."

Her heart skidded to a halt. "What?"

"You were on the beach in Puerto Rico, standing there with your mother. I'd guess you were maybe thirteen or fourteen, just beginning to grow into young womanhood."

Propelled back in time by the memories, she couldn't believe the destiny she'd caught a glimpse of back then. "That was you."

He nodded. "Yes."

"I remember. I saw you, and smiled at you. When I told my mother about it she said it was a figment of my imagination, but I never forgot about it. You were the reason I fell in love with the magic of the sea."

"I've loved you since that first moment, Isabelle."

She realized suddenly that she had, too. She'd waited her entire life for the mystery of the ocean to unfold before her, and now it had. Not only had the sea given her the career she loved, it had also given her the man she was destined to love.

"I really want you to think long and hard about this. It's a lot to ask of you to give your life up for me."

She shook her head, the realization making her giddy. "It's not too much to ask at all. It's what I want, Dax."

"But what about—"

"Would you just shut up and kiss me?"

He did. A long, emotion-packed kiss, filled with all the love she had ever hoped for. Joy soared within her and she gave back all that she'd received, knowing how lucky she was to have someone like Dax.

In an instant her dress had been swept away by his expert hands. Where he touched her, she burned, her desire for him melting her like molten lava.

Would she ever get enough of him? Or would each time be like the first? Hot, passionate, filled with powerful emotions she'd never thought possible.

She reached for his shaft, eager to possess him, desperate to have him inside her, filling her, making her a part of him.

"Hurry Dax," she whispered, pulling him toward her.

He tilted her sideways in the water and she felt as if she were floating on a cloud. Weightless, he slid his cock effortlessly inside her, the shock of him filling her making her gasp.

"I don't ever want to be separated from you again," he murmured, tracing his tongue along her bottom lip. He slid his tongue inside her, mimicking the rhythmic thrusts of his cock.

This was heaven, where she'd always been destined to be. Safe, secure and satisfied in Dax's embrace.

Suddenly his cock wiggled. Her eyes widened and Dax grinned wickedly.

"Oh, I have a few tricks I haven't tried on you yet."

No kidding. He did more than just stroke inside her. His cock undulated like a moving wave, sending her into spasms of ecstatic delight.

"Oh my God!" she exclaimed when it seemed to turn over inside her. He hit her hot spots, over and over and over again, driving in and around until she was nothing but a puddle of damp, aroused flesh. Her juices poured over his cock and balls and he groaned when she squeezed his shaft with her spasms.

"I want children with you," he said, kissing her so tenderly she thought she might dissolve into a sea of tears. "Lots and lots of them. With your dark hair and amber eyes and skin like a bronzed mermaid."

"No," she gasped, panting through the contractions threatening to take her over. "Like you. Tanned and athletic with eyes the color of our ocean."

"Mmm maybe a couple of each," he murmured, capturing her mouth in a kiss that sizzled the water around them.

They rolled in the water, over and over again until she was dizzy and laughing out loud.

Then he got serious, clutching her buttocks and raising her hips to drive in deeper. Isabelle cried out with the climax that hit her suddenly, crashing over her and drowning her in its intensity.

Dax roared out her name and held her close as he spilled inside her.

They stayed together, floating along near the surface of the water, when suddenly something brushed against her. Dax pointed and she turned her head, her mouth gaping open at the sight of a turtle with wings making a run toward the surface before disappearing.

Excitement coursed through her and she focused her gaze on the flying turtle until it leaped through the water into the sky above. She turned to Dax. "Pegasus?"

He nodded. "Pegasus. Welcome to my world, Isabelle."

Overcome by emotion, she could only smile at him through the tears that nearly blinded her.

Dax kissed her brow and held her tenderly. Then he smiled and said, "Let's go home."

Home. She held his hand and sailed through the water with him, for the first time feeling like she really belonged down here.

"Now are you going to answer all my questions?" she asked.

He turned to her and smiled. "Sure."

"Good. So tell me who you are, who is Ronan, how many of you are there? What is your purpose? Where are you from? And what about..."

"Geez you ask a lot of questions, woman," he teased, pulling her next to his side and wrapping his arm around her as they swam toward the lab.

"Get used to it. My curiosity must be appeased."

Dax arched a brow. "Well, you have been patient. But I have to warn you. It's a very long story."

She looked at the approaching glass house and knew it as home. Well, not home exactly. Home was by Dax's side, where she'd stay the rest of her life. They swam inside and Dax pulled her into his arms.

"Then get started," she said, unable to believe her happiness. Where her mother had failed, she would succeed. She'd found a man she instinctively knew would love her until the day she died. And she'd love him the same. With every breath she took, every move she made, every sunrise and every sunset, she'd give him all of her heart.

"We are the League of The Seven Seas," he started.

Isabelle smiled and listened, knowing the real story had only just begun.

Enjoy this excerpt from

A STORM FOR ALL SEASONS: SUMMER HEAT

© Copyright Jaci Burton 2003

Preview

Aidan led Melissa to his office, watching as she unloaded her laptop, presentation folders and notepad, lining them up neatly on his conference table.

He resisted the urge to laugh. He'd be lucky to find a pencil somewhere in his office. Having a near photographic memory helped, considering he rarely wrote things down. He had a secretary to enter important dates and information on his computer, not that he'd ever look at it.

When it was time to design a marketing plan he'd drag out the laptop and printer and go at it, pulling forth all the vital information he'd stored in his brain. Other than that, he kept it all within handy reach of his memory.

Apparently Melissa did things differently. She slid a neatly designed binder in front of him. "Now, if you look at the presentation folder in front of you, I've developed a initial marketing plan as a starting point. Open to your suggestions, of course."

"Of course." He quickly scanned the contents, impressed with her expertise. Then he closed it and looked at her, enjoying the way her green eyes flashed whenever they made eye contact.

Melissa Cross might insist she was all about business, but Aidan had a sixth sense about these things. And his sense told him underneath her cool Bostonian exterior beat the heart of a wildcat. The sudden urge to peel her frosty layers away piece by delectable piece had him hardening painfully.

"That's it? You're not going to look at it any further?"

The play of emotions in her expression was priceless. Shock, then indignation soared across her face. Her pert little nose wrinkled and she crossed her arms.

"I read it. It's good. I'll have more to add. There are a few changes I'd like to make, specifically on page four, paragraph three of the marketing plan. I think we need to play up the background of the two companies more, as well as identify the strategic marketing concepts in a bullet point presentation to make it clear what our primary goals are."

Her eyes widened. "How did you do that?"

"Do what?"

"You know what. You barely glanced at the binder, which has over 100 pages. And yet you pointed out an exact page and paragraph and knew precisely what it contained."

"I read lightning fast and have a photographic memory. No magic involved."

At her arched brow he nearly cringed. Why did he have to say that? Magic was an intrinsic part of his life, but he rarely mentioned it outside the family. Although the thought of using some magic to heat up Melissa Cross had already crossed his mind more than a few times. In fact, right now might be a good time. Maybe a little play and that was all. Just to see how she'd react—gauge if his intuition about her was right.

He rubbed his index and middle finger together, the warmth beginning deep inside. The singe of heat lightning was never painful, only a tingling excitement that never failed to arouse him. The air swirled, charged with electricity, centering in his middle like a gathering storm.

He opened his hand and let the magic sail across the table.

Oh, yeah. An invisible breeze wafted Melissa's hair and her eyes widened. Her creamy cheeks blushed pink, and she opened the top button of her blouse, shuddering when the warm air crept inside.

He leaned back in his chair and felt her, the heat buried deep inside her, and knew right then there was something different about this woman. No one had ever reacted instantly to the slightest bit of magic from him. No one had ever fired the heat waves back toward him, letting him experience exactly what he'd sent out.

Hot damn, that was exciting.

"Something wrong?" he asked, trying to sound innocent.

"Don't you feel it?"

"Feel what?"

Blowing out a quick breath, she said, "It just got really hot in here."

"No kidding. I didn't feel a thing."

She fanned herself with her hand. "I don't know what's wrong with me. I guess I must be more unaccustomed to the New Orleans heat and humidity than I thought. Mind if I take off my jacket?"

"Go right ahead." *Take anything off you like, darlin'. Jacket, skirt, panties and bra, anything.* He shifted to accommodate his burgeoning erection, welcoming the heady ache that came with arousal.

About the author:

Jaci Burton has been a dreamer and lover of romance her entire life. Consumed with stories of passion, love and happily ever afters, she finally pulled her fantasy characters out of her head and put them on paper. Writing allows her to showcase the rainbow of emotions that result from falling in love.

Jaci lives in Oklahoma with her husband (her fiercest writing critic and sexy inspiration), stepdaughter and three wild and crazy dogs. Her sons are grown and live on opposite coasts and don't bother her nearly as often as she'd like them to. When she isn't writing stories of passion and romance, she can usually be found at the gym, reading a great book, or working on her computer, trying to figure out how she can pull more than twenty-four hours out of a single day.

Jaci Burton welcomes mail from readers. You can write to her c/o Ellora's Cave Publishing at 1337 Commerce Drive, Suite 13, Stow OH 44224.

Why an electronic book?

We live in the Information Age—an exciting time in the history of human civilization in which technology rules supreme and continues to progress in leaps and bounds every minute of every hour of every day. For a multitude of reasons, more and more avid literary fans are opting to purchase e-books instead of paperbacks. The question to those not yet initiated to the world of electronic reading is simply: *why?*

1. *Price.* An electronic title at Ellora's Cave Publishing runs anywhere from 40-75% less than the cover price of the <u>exact same title</u> in paperback format. Why? Cold mathematics. It is less expensive to publish an e-book than it is to publish a paperback, so the savings are passed along to the consumer.

2. *Space.* Running out of room to house your paperback books? That is one worry you will never have with electronic novels. For a low one-time cost, you can purchase a handheld computer designed specifically for e-reading purposes. Many e-readers are larger than the average handheld, giving you plenty of screen room. Better yet, hundreds of titles can be stored within your new library—a single microchip. (Please note that Ellora's Cave does not endorse any specific brands. You can check our website at www.ellorascave.com for customer recommendations we make available to new consumers.)

3. *Mobility.* Because your new library now consists of only a microchip, your entire cache of books can be taken with you wherever you go.

4. *Personal preferences are accounted for.* Are the words you are currently reading too small? Too large? Too...**ANNOYING**? Paperback books cannot be modified according to personal preferences, but e-books can.

5. *Innovation.* The way you read a book is not the only advancement the Information Age has gifted the literary community with. There is also the factor of what you can read. Ellora's Cave Publishing will be introducing a new line of interactive titles that are available in e-book format only.

6. *Instant gratification.* Is it the middle of the night and all the bookstores are closed? Are you tired of waiting days—sometimes weeks—for online and offline bookstores to ship the novels you bought? Ellora's Cave Publishing sells instantaneous downloads 24 hours a day, 7 days a week, 365 days a year. Our e-book delivery system is 100% automated, meaning your order is filled as soon as you pay for it.

Those are a few of the top reasons why electronic novels are displacing paperbacks for many an avid reader. As always, Ellora's Cave Publishing welcomes your questions and comments. We invite you to email us at service@ellorascave.com or write to us directly at: 1337 Commerce Drive, Suite 13, Stow OH 44224.

Discover for yourself why readers can't get enough of the multiple award-winning publisher Ellora's Cave. Whether you prefer e-books or paperbacks, be sure to visit EC on the web at www.ellorascave.com for an erotic reading experience that will leave you breathless.

WWW.ELLORASCAVE.COM